Past Perfect

Summer watched as Brand undressed. His time-less perfection crossed every century there had ever been, and ever would be. Desire keened through her like a wild hunt as he swept her up in his arms and carried her to the bed.

"You are a woman to die for, my sweet Olivia," he whispered, slowly lowering himself upon her. Then he looked into her eyes and said, "We are one now, Olivia, joined in the most exquisite way of all."

"Brand," Summer breathed. Her entire body felt as if it were floating. This felt so very right, and she wanted it to last forever, wanted to be with him forever, as she arched beneath him, her fin-gernails digging into his back. She clung to him, tasting the salt of her own tears on his lips, trea-suring the firm warmth of his body. As his ten-der lips brushed hers again, she prayed the dawn would be a long time coming.

But time was out of Summer's control, just as her heart was lured by this man, this love, back through time . . . no matter what the price . . . no matter what the peril. . . .

SIGNET REGENCY ROMANCE
Coming in August 1997

Sheila Walsh
Kate and the Marquess

Patricia Oliver
Double Deception

Evelyn Richardson
My Wayward Lady

SIGNET
Published by the Penguin Group
Penguin Books USA Inc., 375 Hudson Street,
New York, New York 10014, U.S.A.
Penguin Books Ltd, 27 Wrights Lane,
London W8 5TZ, England
Penguin Books Australia Ltd,
Ringwood, Victoria, Australia
Penguin Books Canada Ltd, 10 Alcorn Avenue,
Toronto, Ontario, Canada M4V 3B2
Penguin Books (N.Z.) Ltd, 182–190 Wairau Road,
Auckland 10, New Zealand

Penguin Books Ltd, Registered Offices:
Harmondsworth, Middlesex, England

First published by Signet, an imprint of Dutton Signet,
a division of Penguin Books USA Inc.

First Printing, July, 1997
10 9 8 7 6 5 4 3 2 1

Summer's Secret

by

Sandra Heath

A SIGNET BOOK

Chapter One

"How do you feel, Summer?"

"Mm?" Her eyes were closed, and she was drifting pleasantly.

"How do you feel?" Her English brother-in-law's voice sounded distant, even though he was holding her hand as she lay on the sofa.

No longer able to feel his touch, she hesitated. How did she feel? Well, wonderfully drowsy and warm for one thing, but revitalized too, filled once more with the get-up-and-go she thought had gone forever. It was a heady mixture, as if all the recent grief and ill health hadn't taken its toll, but although she was full of energy again, at the same time the drowsiness was as relaxed and sensuous as she used to feel after making love with Jack. But she wasn't with Jack now; she was slipping into a hypnotic trance.

"I feel out of this world," she murmured lazily, her eyes still closed.

"Don't you dare go to sleep on me!"

She gave a start as his sharp tone penetrated. "I'm sorry, Andrew. I feel good, fighting fit actually, which makes a very welcome change."

"Where are you?"

She opened her eyes and was unnerved to find she'd come from the sunshine of a modern September morning into the icy darkness of a long gone winter night. "It . . . it's a bit bewildering; I need a moment or so to get my bearings."

"Are you all right?"

"Yes, I'm fine." She began to recover from the initial shock, and gave a quick laugh. "It's really weird. A few seconds ago I was in the beach apartment with you; now I'm somewhere that probably doesn't even exist anymore."

"Let's get this straight once and for all. Your body is still here with me, it's your memory that's gone walkabout in the past. So tell me, where are you, exactly? England? The States? Outer Mongolia?"

"England. The courtyard of a coaching inn called the Black Lion, in the market square of Tetbury in Gloucestershire, and I've just gotten out of a carriage." She shivered. "It's dusk on Twelfth Night, 1807, there's a freezing fog, and I'm chilled to the bone after traveling since first light."

"Go on," Andrew prompted.

"Well, the inn is four stories high, and the courtyard has wooden galleries all around it. The weather has been really bad for days now—snow, then this fog, so there are icicles hanging from every conceivable thing, and all the snow has been cleared into piles around the sides of the yard. The cobbles are strewn with straw, and the whole place is very busy." Her nose wrinkled. "It reeks of horses, I mean, *really* reeks!"

Andrew laughed.

She went on. "There are several other private carriages like mine, and a stagecoach has just arrived. The main entrance is through an archway from the square, and there's another archway at the rear leading into the stable yard. There are quite a few people around, passengers, ostlers, stable boys, and so on, and a bell is ringing inside the inn to warn other travelers that the stagecoach is about to leave again. Anyone too slow off the mark will be left behind."

She glanced around a little more, especially through the brightly lit window of the nearby dining room. "There's a real Twelfth Night get-together going on inside, with dancing, eating, and general merrymaking. Christmas greenery is everywhere, although I suppose it will be thrown out after tonight." She smiled. "They're all having a great time," she murmured, watching the happy faces.

Andrew breathed out with immense satisfaction. *"Well,*

from the sound of it we've succeeded. You've regressed to a previous existence!"

His words sank in, and suddenly she felt a surge of almost childish excitement. "Yes, I have! Oh, Andrew, I've traveled back in time!"

He corrected her again. *"No, Summer, it's only a subconscious memory; the real you is in a hypnotic trance here in the future."*

Plain facts didn't meet with her approval at a moment like this. "You're not going to spoil it all with all that stuff about the collective conscious, are you?" she demanded.

"All that stuff, as you call it so disparagingly, happens to be part of a hypnotherapist's bread and butter. So let's be clear about it: Your mind has regressed to a previous life, but no matter how real it may all seem, what you're seeing is only a deeply buried memory. So relax, enjoy it, and I'll see nothing bad happens to you. You trust me, don't you?"

She smiled. "I guess every girl trusts her therapist."

"Especially if he also happens to be married to her big sister."

"Right." Summer smiled. Andrew Marchant was probably the last guy on earth she would have expected her sister to marry. Chrissie had always gone for the bronzed, muscular, sportsman type, and Andrew was slightly built, with thinning brown hair and owlish glasses, but he had one of the kindest natures anyone could wish for, and if Chrissie's smiles every morning were anything to go by, he had quite a talent between the sheets.

There was a pause, then Andrew spoke again. *"Chrissie wants to know what it's like to become someone else."* He laughed. *"As if that's the sort of question that can be answered in a single sentence!"*

"Chrissie just spoke?" Summer was puzzled that she couldn't hear what her sister said, even though she was only a few feet away, but she smiled again. "Tell her it gives 'learned by heart' a whole new meaning. She'll understand."

"She's nodding." He pressed on then. *"Okay, so it's*

Twelfth Night, 1807. Let's start with who you are. Are you male or female?"

"Female, thank goodness, for I don't think I could handle being a guy! My name is Olivia Courtenay, I'm a widow, comfortably off, and I'm freezing to death out here in this yard!"

"Never mind the weather; I want to know more about Olivia. How old are you?"

"Twenty-seven."

"Exactly the same as you are here in the future."

Summer nodded. "Give or take a few months."

"You say you're a widow. How long has your husband been dead?"

"Two years, so I'm just out of mourning. His name was Roderick Courtenay, Major Roderick Courtenay, and he died in a shipwreck returning from Gibraltar."

"Did you love him?"

She paused. "No, not love exactly, but I was very fond of him. It was an arranged match, you see. Hearts and flowers didn't enter into it."

"Have you any children?"

"No."

"What do you look like?"

Summer didn't need a mirror to describe herself, for she knew exactly what she looked like. "Well, I'm about five feet four, shorter than the future me, with a good figure, really hour-glass, if you know what I mean. My hair is a mass of long black curls that I have difficulty pinning into the dainty, Grecian-statue styles that are all the rage, and my eyes are a clear gray. I'm rather proud of my eyes, actually, for they're large and long-lashed, and are said to be very beautiful." She smiled, for this nineteenth-century self bore no physical resemblance to her at all. Summer Stanway was tall, willowy, fair-haired, and blue-eyed.

"What are you wearing?"

"A hooded dark green cloak lined with black fur, over a high-necked empire-style damson velvet gown. You know what I mean; the waistline's just under the bust, and the skirt is soft and clinging, with a slight train that I've had to loop up slightly to protect it from the snow and everything else one finds in inn yards. There are warm overshoes on my feet, and my hands are in a large muff that matches the cloak. Quite stylish, I suppose."

"You said you'd been traveling all day. Where have you come from, and where are you going to?"

"I'm on my way from my house in Kensington to visit relations at their new residence near the town of Berkeley, which is farther west from here but still in Gloucestershire. I mean to spend the night here at the Black Lion, then complete the remaining twenty miles or so tomorrow."

"Who are these relations?"

"My widowed uncle, Henry Merriam, and his daughter, my cousin Caroline. I call her Caro, and she is more like a sister to me than a cousin. I'm going there because on her birthday in two weeks she is to be betrothed to the son of Lord Lytherby, a local landowner. She only met Francis when she and Uncle Merriam moved to Oakhill House six months ago, and from all accounts it's a real love match. I'm so happy for her, because she is the sweetest person imaginable, and after my aunt's sudden death three years ago, followed by poor Uncle Merriam's recent financial setbacks, it's wonderful that something good should happen at last. Actually, it's quite astonishing that Lord Lytherby should have consented at all, for Caro can no longer be described as a catch, whereas Francis definitely is."

"So this is set to be a happy visit?"

"Yes, the visit itself is, but . . ."

"But what?"

"Well, I'm being foolish by coming here."

"Here? Oh, you mean the Black Lion. Why? Isn't it respectable?"

"Oh, perfectly respectable, but I've agreed to meet an old friend of my husband's, Major Jeremy Fenwick. He and Roderick were in the same regiment, and he was very good to me when Roderick died. In fact, I don't know what I would have done without him, but he's what you'd call a charming rogue, and if it gets out that I've met him at a country inn, it won't do my reputation any good at all. I wouldn't normally have agreed to it, but he has to travel from his home in Bath to re-join the regiment prior to its departure for Ireland, and when he learned from one of my letters that I would be coming this way at the same time, he suggested dining here at the Black Lion, as it will be over a year before we see each other again. His letter arrived around the anniversary of Roderick's death, and I kept thinking how good Jeremy had been to me—you know how it is. Anyway, I agreed, and now I wish I hadn't. You see, if it should get out, it won't just be my reputation that could suffer; it might also cause trouble for Caro's betrothal."

"Why?"

"Because in the past month or so Lord Lytherby's attitude has apparently changed, and Caro is now convinced he wants to call the match off. In her letters she's told me she suspects he's looking for *any* excuse, no matter how small. If she's right, shocking misconduct at an inn by one of the bride's closest female relatives might be just the thing he needs."

"What shocking misconduct? You're only going to dine with this Jeremy person, aren't you? Or are you?"

"Yes, of course, but I'll also be staying overnight, and so will Jeremy. A night under the same inn roof? Can't you imagine how the tongues would clack if it were to be discovered? I'll be deemed disreputable, and Lord Lytherby will view me as manna from Heaven."

"Then forget dinner with Jeremy and drive on to the next inn."

"I'm tired after traveling all day in such bad weather, and before you suggest another inn here in Tetbury, the ones I've seen *are* disreputable. It's the Black Lion or nothing at all, so the moment I alighted, I asked an ostler to go see if Jeremy had arrived. I'm praying he's been delayed somewhere en route from Bath, so I can stay here safely and finish my jour-ney tomorrow without a blemish on my character." Hearing steps approaching, she turned quickly and saw the ostler re-turning. "Hush, Andrew, the ostler's coming now," she whis-pered.

The inn servant was a squat man, with a wide-brimmed flat

hat and a dirty coat. He was unshaven and unkempt, and smelled more like a horse than a horse. There was a sly, knowing look in his eyes as he removed the wisp of straw he was chewing. "There ent no one 'ere by the name of Major Fenwick, ma'am," he said in a broad Gloucesterhire accent. "But that's not to say 'e won't get 'ere by and by." He grinned, showing blackened teeth.

She colored, knowing exactly what he was thinking. Oh, *why* had she been so stupid as to agree to meet Jeremy like this? "Thank you for your trouble," she said, startled to hear herself suddenly speaking with a very English voice, low, modulated, and—to her American ears—rather reserved.

He almost snatched the coin she held out to him. "That's right gracious of you, ma'am," he said, touching his hat and then hurrying away again.

She waited until he had gone, then spoke to Andrew again, and when she did, her voice was her native American again. "Did you hear that, Andrew?"

"No."

She was taken aback. "No? But—"

"I can only hear you when you speak directly to me; in between there's just a long silence as far as I'm concerned. It's like someone speaking on two phones, picking up to speak to one person, then using the other to speak to someone else. That's why you couldn't hear Chrissie a few minutes ago either. Do you follow what I mean?"

"Yes, I think so."

"So what happened? Is Jeremy there?"

"No, thank goodness. I've got my fingers crossed he doesn't make it, then my conscience will be clear. By the way, the weirdest thing . . . When I speak to you like this, I have my usual voice, but when I spoke to that ostler, I was really English." Her breath caught suddenly. "Oh, no, there's another carriage arriving. It might be Jeremy after all!"

She drew back into the shadows by her own vehicle, watching as the other coachman deftly maneuvered through the archway from the market square, but as the new arrival drew to a standstill, she breathed out with immediate relief. "No, it can't be Jeremy; he couldn't possibly own anything as grand at that! Oh, Andrew, it's the most splendid carriage, green-lacquered, with gleaming brasswork, a perfectly matched team of four bright chestnuts, a liveried coachman, and a *very* impressive coat-of-arms on the door."

As she watched, a gentleman alighted. He was tall, athletically built, and fashionable without being in the least foppish or dandified, but she couldn't see his face because his top hat was pulled low over his forehead, casting his features in shadow. He wore an ankle-length charcoal greatcoat trimmed with Russian lambskin, and his Hessian boots sported gilt spurs that rang as he stepped down onto the straw-strewn cobbles.

He exuded that air of authority that always comes with wealth and breeding. Here was a man who was used to issuing orders, and who expected them to be obeyed without question. His movements were supple and graceful, and his whole demeanor was arrestingly confident. Very little would faze him, Summer thought, wondering who he was.

He turned, his face still in shadow as he flicked a coin to the ostler she had spoken to a few minutes before. "I require a room for the night," he said. His voice was softly English, clear-spoken and precise.

"Yes, sir."

"And it had better be the best you have here."

"Of course, sir."

"No bugs."

"There ent no bugs at the Black Lion, sir."

"Well, if there are and they have my hide, I'll have yours come the morning."

"Sir!" The ostler hurried away, his heavy boots clumping on the cobbles.

At last the gentleman removed his hat, and by the light of one of the carriage lamps she saw he had unruly blond hair that he had to push back into place with gloved fingers. His face was memorably handsome, with finely sculpted but strong features, and a complexion that even in this poor light she could see was that of a man who liked the open air. His mouth was straight and firm, with lips that were neither too thin nor too thick, and his eyes were quick and intelligent as he glanced around the yard.

Shrinking back by her carriage in order not to be seen, Summer stared at him as if at a ghost. She felt rigid with shock, and the character of Olivia Courtenay fell away, leaving Summer Stanway in all her raw pain. "Jack?" she whispered.

Her fingers must have tightened over Andrew's, for suddenly his voice broke in. *"Is something wrong, Summer?"*

"Andrew, it's Jack!" she cried.

"It can't be," he replied, his voice taking on a disturbed note.

"It *is*, I tell you! Jack Windham just got out of that carriage. He may be dressed like something from Jane Austen, but he's still my Jack!"

Andrew was now very uneasy. *"I think I'd better bring you out of this . . ."*

"No! I have to speak to him!"

"Be sensible, Summer! Jack's dead!"

But she ignored him as she stepped into view beside her carriage. The gentleman saw her, and for a heart-stopping moment their eyes met. An avalanche of feelings tumbled chaotically through her, and her heart seemed to turn over as he held her gaze.

A faint smile played upon his lips, and she felt as if her very soul were exposed to him, but then the inn and the long gone winter night disappeared, and she was staring up at Chrissie and Andrew as they leaned anxiously over her in the sunlit modern apartment overlooking the English Channel.

Chapter Two

For a few minutes Summer was so disoriented that she almost felt faint, but then she started to get up agitatedly.

Andrew pushed her gently but firmly back. "Oh, no, you just lie there quietly for a moment." He glanced at Chrissie. "Bring a glass of water, there's a love."

Chrissie nodded and hurried through to the kitchen. She was Summer's elder by two years, and very like her to look at, with the same willowy figure, bobbed fair hair, and blue eyes. She wore a simple blue-striped cotton dress, and her flip-flop sandals pattered on the parquet floor as she went to get a glass from the cupboard.

Reality was pressing around Summer now, and she lay back. The vitality she'd regained so briefly during her visit to the past had vanished, and in its place was the familiar tiredness she hated so much. Her thoughts were in turmoil. The atmosphere of the inn yard was still almost tangible, but she knew she was here in the future again.

The morning sun was shining dazzlingly through the open French windows of the second-floor apartment, and only yards away outside she could hear the gentle lap of waves on the Sussex shore. There was a light breeze that moved the curtains, and seagulls wheeled against the cloudless sky. She turned her head slightly and gazed southwest through the balcony railings toward the undulating green patchwork of Isle of Wight. Ferries and yachts dotted the blue-green water, just as they always did. It was all so normal, and yet normal was the last thing she felt right now.

Chrissie returned with the water. "Here you are, honey," she said, and Summer leaned up on one elbow to take the glass. Chrissie looked down at her. "You have to accept that Jack was killed in an automobile accident six months ago; he's buried in Boston, and we all went to the funeral."

Summer nodded. "Don't look so worried. I know it wasn't Jack," she said quietly, remembering the mysterious gentleman's eyes, so deep and blue, like the sea outside . . . Jack's eyes had been a shade of greenish hazel.

Andrew sat back in his chair beside the sofa, absently toying with the little piece of cracked medieval pottery he used like someone else might use worry beads. He'd found it in a plowed field during his student days and kept it as a memento. It was part of an ancient spell someone had cast on an enemy. *I, Gerald of Salisbury, do curse Thomas of Winchester. May he never profit from that which he stole from me, may he* . . . That was all, the rest of the inscription was lost forever.

Summer watched him turning it over and over in his hands. "You'll wear that thing out one day," she murmured, sipping the water.

He set it aside. "Look, Summer, if I'd suspected something like this might happen, I'd never have agreed to it. It was a damned fool thing to do anyway," he added.

"Nothing *happened,* so don't blame yourself, Andrew. Besides, *I* was the one who kept pestering after seeing that TV program about the woman who believed she was Marie Antoinette reincarnated. It really freaked me when she said all those things under a trance, and I just couldn't *wait* for you to do the same to me."

"I know all that, Summer, but after all you've been through recently, I still should have known better. It's one thing to try regression for therapeutic reasons, quite another to do it out of idle interest when the subject is in poor health and as stressed out as you."

She stretched across to put a reassuring hand on his knee. "Olivia Courtenay hasn't got my health problems, so I felt great. Don't worry so, I'm quite okay, truly."

"It's hardly okay to think you saw Jack again," he pointed out quietly.

"I've already said I know it wasn't him, but whoever it was sure as hell *looked* like him. If it weren't for his eyes . . ." She shrugged and didn't finish.

Chrissie sat on the floor beside her. "As long as you're quite clear about that, it's okay," she said, then leaned her head right back to look up at Summer. "So it put a whole new meaning on the phrase 'learned by heart,' did it?" she said.

The words sent Summer's thoughts winging back to childhood. Their mother had died at Summer's birth, and because their air force father moved constantly from base to base around the world, he didn't think it fair to inflict such a nomadic life on his motherless daughters, so they'd always lived with an aunt. He came home every chance he could though, and whenever he was going somewhere new, he gave them a different phone number to call. "Learn it by heart, honeys," he'd say. He was dead now too, lost somewhere over the Pacific when his plane just disappeared, but the phrase remained special to them. It was their phrase.

She nodded at Chrissie. "That's all I could think of to describe it. You see, although Andrew kept telling me it was all a deep-seated memory and so on, it still felt really weird to just instantly *know* everything about this new self. It was all there inside me, no having to make an effort to learn. In my heart already, if you follow my meaning."

"Yes, I guess I do."

Andrew had relaxed a little now and looked at Summer. "So you used to be a classy Olivia Courtenay, eh?"

"It seems so. You know, I was almost afraid to go back in case I used to be Lizzie Borden, or maybe some awful old trapper who smelled as high as his pelts!" A little of the excitement began to stir through her again, and her eyes lit up hopefully. "You *will* let me do it again, won't you?" she begged.

He avoided her gaze. "I'm not sure I should, Summer . . ."

"Don't be a spoilsport. I'm here on vacation, so humor me. After all, I'm the only sister-in-law you have."

"Thank God," he muttered.

"I heard that."

He shuffled awkwardly. "Look, Summer, I'd like to, truly I would, I just don't think it would be a good idea. In the last six months you haven't just lost Jack, you had pneumonia, and then became diabetic as well."

"Gee, thanks for reminding me what a little bundle of fun and energy I am," Summer replied wistfully, recalling how animated she'd felt as Olivia. It had felt good. Very good indeed.

Andrew sighed. "All right, so I'm putting a damper on it, but you *must* face facts about your health. It takes a while to get over a bad bout of pneumonia; that's why you're here on vacation. And as for the diabetes, well, you know what a job they had getting your insulin and so on balanced properly. The last thing you need right now is a lot of stress."

She sighed and put her glass down. "The pneumonia's over and done with, and I'm coming to terms with losing Jack. As for the diabetes, well, it's hardly the end of the world, is it? I do my insulin on time, I eat on time, I do my tests when I should, and I don't rush around. In fact, I'm such a nauseatingly good girl, my doctor all but patted me on the head the last time I saw him."

Chrissie looked reproachfully at her. "It's all very well to be flippant, Summer, but in spite of what you say, you've far from regained your strength after the pneumonia, and stress can definitely upset the diabetic status quo."

Summer sighed again. "Look, I'm getting all the darned sea air I can, and since they got the insulin right, I haven't had a trace of hypoglycemia."

"Okay, maybe you haven't actually gone into a coma, but you've gotten all shaky, hot, and bothered from time to time, and don't try telling me it was the weather!"

Summer's jaw set obstinately.

Andrew leaned forward quickly. "Don't let's fall out over this, for it really isn't worth it."

Summer caught his unwilling eyes. "I really enjoyed being Olivia. It was the first real fun I've had in ages, and you're going to stop me doing it again," she said plaintively.

He gave her a long-suffering look. "You fight dirty," he complained.

"Yes, because I want my own way," she admitted frankly.

A wry grin played on his lips, and Chrissie looked at him in dismay. "Don't give in to her wheedling, Andrew Marchant, or I'll never forgive you."

Summer prodded her between the shoulder blades. "You keep out of this. You're just jealous because when you tried regression, you didn't get any further than your first birthday in *this* life!"

Chrissie was forced to laugh. "Oh, go to hell," she muttered.

"I'd rather go to 1807." Summer raised hopeful eyebrows in Andrew's direction.

He looked at his wife, who shrugged resignedly, so he nodded at Summer. "All right, but on one condition."

"Anything!" Summer promised triumphantly.

"At the first sign of anything untoward, it's to be understood that I'll bring you straight back here to the present."

"That's fair enough. When can we do it? Tonight?"

"God, you're a pushy woman." He sighed.

"I don't believe in hanging around."

"Don't I know it. Okay, tonight, but it will have to be late."

"Late? Oh, yes, I forgot, you're both going out to eat."

Chrissie eyed her. "You're still invited, you know. We can fit in with your times."

"Have you any idea what it's like looking at the dessert trolley and having to settle for fruit salad? No, thanks, I'm not into that kind of torture, so you guys go out and enjoy yourselves." Summer got up and glanced outside. "I think I'll walk on the beach," she said.

Chrissie looked at the clock on the TV. "You'll be sure to remember the time, won't you? You mustn't eat late."

"I'll be back on the dot to eat my regulation crust," Summer promised.

As the door closed behind her, Chrissie got up from the floor and went to sit on the arm of Andrew's chair. "I wish I could stop worrying about her, but she's still my kid sister."

He caught her hand and pulled her down on to his lap. "I know, but your kid sister is a big girl now," he said, hugging her close.

* * *

The tide was going out, and gulls screamed overhead as Summer strolled along the wet sand. There were only a few people around, some sailboarders, a woman walking her dog, and two lovers dawdling hand in hand. Bracklesham wasn't a large resort; indeed it was very small, little more than a shore-line of assorted residences—houses, bungalows, apartments, and trailer parks—directly facing the beach. Pebbles were heaped against the sea wall, and low wooden breakwaters jut-ted unevenly across the sand that was only exposed at low tide. It wasn't the British coast at its most beautiful, but it was pleasantly intimate, and there was enough sea for everyone.

Something made her glance back toward Chrissie and An-drew's apartment. Chrissie was watching from the balcony and waved. Summer returned the wave, then walked on. She could almost feel her sister diligently counting the minutes until the next obligatory snack that was needed to keep the dreaded dia-betes at bay. It was as if she feared that even the tiniest lapse of vigilance would bring the walls of Jericho tumbling down.

After a while, Summer leaned against one of the barnacle-encrusted breakwaters to watch the lovers, who'd paused right by the water's edge to embrace. They were so rapt in each other they didn't notice the waves creaming around their feet. Summer smiled. This time a year ago, she and Jack had kissed like that right here on this same English beach, except it had been at night, and they'd done much more than just kiss and hold hands!

She remembered it had been an unusually still warm night for the time of year, and they'd gone for a swim, then watched the moonlight on the water. Jack had quoted Byron. *When the moon is on the wave, And the glow-worm in the grass, And the meteor on the grave, And the wisp on the morass; When the falling stars are shooting, And the answered owls are hooting, And the silent leaves are still, In the shadow of the hill* . . . Every word came back to her now, as clearly as if he stood with her again.

She lowered her eyes for a moment, and then allowed the memories to flow again. She'd teased him for waxing so poetic, so he'd chased her along the shore to an isolated spot where they'd rolled over and over in each other's arms in the waves. Not quite like the famous old movie, but close enough, and right now from here to that sweet moment seemed like an eternity.

The images flooded through her mind. Jack's lips were on hers again, and his hands roamed her skin in that way that made her come alive to everything about him. Her breasts tightened with need, and it seemed the coldness of the sea rippled over her again now. She could almost feel the heat of Jack's body piercing her as he made love to her amid the waves. Oh, God, how she missed him; how every empty day and night ached with desperate longing for what had gone forever.

Her hands tightened into helpless fists as she brought them down on the breakwater. "Damn you, Jack, why did you have to go out that day? Why didn't you walk, instead of taking the car? Why didn't you stay in bed and make love to me again . . ." The whispered words were lost in the noise of the gulls overhead.

She made herself walk on, climbing over the breakwater and then setting off along the next expanse of shining sand. Her thoughts were still of Jack. They'd gotten to know each other in one of the most romantic settings in the world, a ruined Inca temple. She was a researcher for a travel company, and had been sent on an assignment into unusual working vacations in exotic places. Jack was the leader of an archeological team offering just such opportunities to those with sufficient interest and stamina. Sleeping uncomfortably under canvas and spending hours scratching in the earth in the hope of finding artifacts hadn't made any difference to the effect Jack had on her. Within days she'd fallen hook, line, and sinker for his golden California looks and wry sense of humor. Soon they were lovers, and when the dig was over, he'd come to live with her at her Boston apartment.

Their happiness had been complete until March this year, when he died in that stupid, stupid car accident she'd actually witnessed from the apartment window. He hadn't seen the truck coming the other way, and the police report showed that the truck driver wasn't paying attention because he was too busy lighting a cigarette. It was true what they say, things like that seemed to happen in slow motion, but for her those few seconds had now lasted six long, wretched, heartbroken months.

She glanced up at the clear blue September sky, her fair hair blowing in the salt breeze. "I miss you, Jack Windham," she said softly.

But there was no answer. There never was.

Chapter Three

It was dark and the tide was just in as Summer looked out of one of the rear windows of the apartment. Chrissie and Andrew were getting out of the car after returning from their dinner in nearby Chichester, but as they began to walk from the parking lot toward the door, a thought struck her.

She dashed to her bedroom and rooted through the chest of drawers for the little portable cassette recorder she knew was there somewhere among the photograph albums she'd brought with her. At last she found it, but to her dismay there wasn't a cassette inside. She hurried down the passage to Andrew's study to get one of the many he kept in readiness for his work. As she then ran into the living room, she heard Chrissie and Andrew exchanging greetings with the people who lived in the apartment across the landing. She slid the loaded recorder under the sofa and was seated watching TV when they came in a few seconds later.

Half an hour after that, as Andrew prepared to regress her for a second time, she fussed around with the sofa cushions and allowed one to fall to the floor. Under cover of picking it up, she surreptitiously turned the recorder on, then lay back and closed her eyes as Andrew began. His voice was soothing, caressing almost, and the music he used began to beguile her senses. It was almost like being seduced, she thought, as she sank into the trance that opened her mind to the otherwise forgotten past.

Andrew waited until her breathing was steady. *"Right, Summer, if I've got this right, you should now be Olivia Courtenay."*

The vitality had returned, and she glanced excitedly around. "Yes, I am!"

"Tell me what's happening this time."

"It's the evening of Twelfth Night, I'm inside the Black Lion now, and have just come down the main staircase with a lighted candle. Guests have to light their own way to and from their rooms because the upper stories are always dark, and I'm returning my candle to the special candle table right next to me. The hall is brightly lit, though, with wall candles and a big log fire."

She continued describing what she could see. The long oak-paneled hall before her was almost deserted, but there was still a great deal of music and merriment emanating from beyond the closed door of the crowded dining room to her right. From time to time the kitchen door to her left would open, and waiters and maids would dash to and from the dining room with trays and plates of food. At the far end of the hall was the door into the inn yard, and next to it were four fully laden coat stands. Several dozen pairs of wet overboots had been left on the floor, and numerous walking sticks were propped against a great longcase clock. There were sprigs of holly tucked behind sporting prints on the walls, and a garland of ivy hung around the large stone fireplace in the alcove opposite the dining room. The fireplace was flanked by high-backed settles, where two clergymen dozed while waiting for the London stagecoach, their valises at their feet.

She could see her reflection in a faded mirror opposite. Her raven hair had been painstakingly but flatteringly pinned up in a knot on top of her head, with a frame of little curls around her face. The eyes she had earlier described as large and gray, were indeed very beautiful, and her lips were generous without being too full. Her figure could definitely be described as curvaceous, and was outlined to perfection by the soft folds of the same damson velvet gown she had worn before. The trained skirt wasn't looped up at the back now, but fell to the floor to drag against the lowermost step of the staircase. A white cashmere shawl rested over her arms, a little black velvet reticule bag was looped over her wrist, and she wore gold earrings and her wedding ring. It was like looking at a stranger, except that the stranger was her. And I'm really quite lovely, she thought in wonderment, continuing to stare at the reflection. Those were *her* eyes looking back at her, and that was *her* figure!

She was about to speak to Andrew again when suddenly the door from the yard opened and a middle-aged lady and gentleman entered. They were dressed in evening attire, but were clearly very distressed about something, at least the lady was, for she was weeping copious tears, but her husband was as much angry as upset.

They were an odd couple, Summer thought, he very military and precise with pale eyes that were close-set above a hooked nose, she a plump person with girlish russet curls that looked suspiciously like a wig. There was a little too much rouge on the woman's cheeks and lips, and beneath her costly sable-trimmed cloak she wore a pink gown that had the sort of frills that would have been more appropriate for a young woman than for someone old enough to be a grandmother. She could so easily have appeared ridiculous, but there was something so touching about her sobs and the way her stern-looking husband fussed fondly around her, that Summer suddenly found herself hurrying concernedly over to them. "May I help, sir?" she inquired solicitously, her new voice once again as English as her real voice was Bostonian.

The gentleman turned sharply, expecting to see one of the inn maids, but then his glance took in her gown and earrings, and his expression softened gratefully. "Oh, madam, if you would be so kind as to take care of my poor wife while I endeavor to receive some manner of service in this so-called hostelry . . . ?"

"Of course."

Belatedly, he remembered his manners. "General Sir Oswald Harvey, retired. Your servant, madam," he declared, according her a stiff bow.

Summer curtsied. "Mrs. Courtenay, widow of Major Roderick Courtenay," she replied.

His eyes warmed approvingly at her military connection,

then he strode toward the nearest door, which happened to be that of the kitchens. The door swung to behind him, and a moment later there came the sound of his raised voice as he berated the landlord about lack of service.

Summer turned kindly toward Lady Harvey, who was struggling to compose herself. "Please come and sit down by the fire, my lady," she said gently, putting a tentative arm around the plump shoulders.

"You . . . you must forgive me for piping my eyes like this, Mrs. Courtenay, but it was so dreadful . . ." the distressed woman said as Summer helped with her cloak. The clergymen dozed on unawares.

"What happened?"

"A highwayman attempted to rob us." Lady Harvey's plump hand crept to the only item of her apparel that was undoubtedly tasteful—her necklace. It was a black velvet choker to which was attached a little sunburst of pink diamonds that flashed and sparkled in the light from the fire. The design was unusual, the workmanship of high quality, and the stones obviously very choice, for pink diamonds were as much sought after in the early nineteenth century as they would be in the future.

Summer put a comforting hand on the other's arm. "Oh, how dreadful for you."

"We were on our way to the ball at Chavenage, when this . . . this masked *demon* appeared before us. He set his wolf upon the poor horses . . ." Fresh tears filled Lady Harvey's eyes at the memory, and she pressed a handkerchief to her trembling lips.

"This wolf? Surely you mean his wolfhound?"

"Oh, no, I know what it was!" Lady Harvey breathed in deeply, and then swallowed. "You know what night it is tonight, don't you?" she whispered then.

"Yes, of course, it's Twelfth Night."

"Twelfth Night is when werewolves go abroad," Lady Harvey said softly.

Summer stared at her. *"Werewolves?"* she repeated incredulously.

"Oh, mock me if you will, just as Sir Oswald does, but if you had heard that dreadful howl and seen how very large a beast it was." Lady Harvey's lips trembled again.

"How . . . how did you escape?"

"Another carriage happened along, and the coachman was armed. The highwayman took to the woods, taking his wolf with him, but I couldn't go on to the Chavenage ball after that."

"I understand completely," Summer replied, thinking that she'd probably feel the same if it had happened to her.

"Then we came here, and there wasn't anyone in the yard to assist us. Oh, what a horrid, horrid night," Lady Harvey dissolved into fresh tears.

The kitchen door opened, and Sir Oswald reemerged accompanied by the landlord, whose red face was evidence of the blistering reprimand to which he had been rightly subjected. He was a burly man whose hair had retreated so much it lingered only as a monk's tonsure, and he bowed and scraped to his furious guest. "Yes, Sir Oswald, no, Sir Oswald. At once, Sir Oswald. A maid for her ladyship? Certainly, Sir Oswald . . ." He was all subservience, but the look in his eyes boded ill for the unfortunate ostlers who'd neglected to be in attendance in the yard.

Summer assisted Lady Harvey to her feet and blushed a little as Sir Oswald gallantly kissed her hand. "You have been most kind, Mrs. Courtenay. I trust my wife and I will enjoy the pleasure of your company some time before we leave tomorrow. We will remain in our room tonight, for my poor dear wife is far too distressed to contemplate dining in company, but I trust that by breakfast she will be herself again. Perhaps you will join us then?"

"It would please me greatly to take breakfast with you, Sir Oswald."

He smiled, and Lady Harvey gave her another tearful little smile, then they followed the landlord upstairs. Shadows leapt and swayed over the paneled walls as the trio disappeared along the passage at the top.

Andrew spoke suddenly. *"Is everything okay, Summer?"*

She gave a start, for she'd been so engrossed in Lady Harvey's story that she'd almost forgotten the truth about her presence at the inn. "Oh, Andrew, I've just heard the most incredible story. Did you know Twelfth Night was associated with werewolves?" She told him all she'd learned. "I'm sure the poor woman truly believed it was a werewolf," she finished, recalling Lady Harvey's earnest expression.

"She sounds a little strange, if you ask me."

"Maybe, but I quite liked her. I certainly liked her diamonds," Summer added. "God knows how much those pink diamonds would fetch in the present. They were absolutely wonderful." She described the necklace.

"I expect the general got them in India. Many items like the sunburst came here because of the Raj."

"Probably." Summer sat back on the settle and glanced at the two clergymen opposite. They'd slept all through Lady Harvey's horrific tale of highway robbery and the supernatural, and still they slept while she talked to someone who was really in a future century! It was unreal! "Andrew, I know you told me about the two phones and all that, but when you speak to me like now, and I answer you, it seems impossible that you haven't heard everything I have. And what about people here in this time? Can they hear me when I speak to you? I mean, the two clergymen are still sleeping opposite, and I guess a bomb would have to drop on them before they'd awaken, but what if they *were* to awaken? *Surely* they'd hear me?"

"No, because you're speaking to me on the other phone as Summer Stanway. Okay?"

"I . . . I guess so."

"So let's get on with things. When we started tonight, you said you'd come down from your room. Does that mean you're going in to dinner?"

"No, I dined earlier." She laughed then. "It was great, I had all the things Summer Stanway isn't allowed anymore!"

"One of the perks of hypnotic regression."

"Yes, and another one is that I feel full of beans whenever I'm Olivia. It happened the first time, and has again now. I'd

give anything to feel like this when I'm Summer Stanway."
She paused, then drew a long breath. "Anyway, after dinner I
was tired after being on the road all day, so I thought I'd have
an early night. Fat chance of that with all the racket going on
in the dining room directly below my bedroom. It soon became a case of 'if you can't beat them, join them,' so here I
am."

"Did the galloping major arrive?"

"Jeremy? No, thank goodness. I think he must have been
held up by the weather."

Andrew hesitated. *"What of the gentleman in the courtyard?"* he asked after a moment.

"I haven't seen him since he arrived. I didn't speak to him
then because I lost my nerve. I just hurried into the inn and left
it at that. He didn't come down to dinner, and I suppose he's
still in his room." At that moment she heard footsteps approaching the top of the staircase and looked up to see the
flicker of candlelight as someone walked along the passage. "I
think the landlord's returning from seeing Sir Oswald and
Lady Harvey to their room, so I won't say anything for a moment or so, just in case you're wrong about those darned
phones," she said, and a second or so later was rather startled
when it wasn't the landlord who descended the staircase, but
the gentleman who looked so like Jack.

He wore a sage green coat, frilled shirt, close-fitting corduroy breeches, and the tassels at the front of his high Hessian boots swung from side to side as he moved. The pearl pin
in his neckcloth shone softly as he paused to place his candle
on the table. He was still like Jack's ghost, with tousled
golden hair that might have been burnished by the California
sun, but this was a nineteenth-century Englishman, and the
piercing dark blue eyes that raked her again now weren't
Jack's.

She was very conscious of a powerful sense of physical at-
traction, just as she had been for those few seconds in the yard.
Everything about him drew her, from the golden sun-god
looks that had always been her downfall, to that exciting air of
masculine strength that could make her feel weak at the knees.

There was a pent-up energy about him that stirred desires she'd been struggling to suppress since losing Jack, and the thought of surrendering to him was—

Her rather shameless contemplations broke off abruptly because he suddenly came toward her, his gilt spurs ringing on the stone flags. For a moment she thought he intended to speak to her, but instead he leaned across to tap the shoulder of one of the clergymen, who immediately awoke with a start.

"Eh? What? What is it?"

"Have no fear, sir, it is just that I presume you are waiting for the London stage?" The gentleman nodded toward the man's valise, which clearly bore a Chelsea address.

"We are, sir." The clergyman sat up and straightened his wig.

"Well, it's approaching. I heard the horn in the distance a short while ago. If you wish to partake of a warming glass of something before you leave, I believe you may have a minute or so."

"A thousand thanks, sir," the clergyman replied gratefully, and then turned to awaken his companion.

"Not at all."

Gathering up their valises, the two men hastened to the dining room, and the noise from within swept out momentarily behind them until the door closed again.

The gentleman lingered by the settle for a moment, gazing down into Summer's eyes as if he would speak. The air was as if charged, and a current of electricity seemed to pass between them. Never had she been more conscious of her own desires, and never had she seen those same desires so clearly reflected in those of another. There was a sense of danger about him, a suggestion that if she were to fly too close to this man's fire, like Icarus, she'd burn her wings and tumble to the earth. The seconds seemed to hang unbearably, and she felt almost naked before him, yet they hadn't even spoken, let alone learned each other's name. The protective cocoon she'd striven to keep around herself since Jack's death was being unwound by an invisible hand, and there was nothing she could do—or wanted to do—to stop it.

But suddenly the stranger walked away, leaving her to stare longingly after him. She wanted to call out, but instead her silent voice spoke deep within her. *Come back, whoever you are, please come back . . .*

Chapter Four

As the unknown gentleman disappeared into the dining room, Summer lowered her eyes and drew a long breath to steady herself. The emotions stampeding through her now were even stronger than those she'd experienced on first meeting Jack. Being close to *this* man aroused craving on a scale she'd never known before. If he'd touched her, if he'd bent his lips toward hers, she'd have met his kiss!

Andrew's voice interrupted her. *"Have you forgotten me?"*

She managed a laugh. "No, of course not."

"Is everything okay?"

"Yes. I know I was quiet for a long time, but the landlord spoke to me, and then the two clergymen were awakened because their stagecoach was on the way." She felt uncomfortable telling a lie, but it seemed the wisest course. Any mention of the gentleman might result in Andrew whisking her out of the trance, and that was the very last thing she wished to happen.

"What next? Are you still going into the dining room?"

Wild horses wouldn't keep her from it! "Yes, I'd like to take part in the Twelfth Night festivities. Andrew, can I ask something of you?"

"Such as?"

"Can you leave me like this for an hour or so?"

"Leave you? What do you mean?"

"Well, don't keep asking me to tell you what's going on. I still feel a little unsure about this two phones business."

"Oh, Summer . . ." he began wearily.

"Come on, Andrew. You can't pretend you and Chrissie intend to go to bed early, because you never do, and I'm enjoying this so much that I want to go on a little longer."

There was a long silence during which she knew he was consulting with Chrissie, so she spoke again quickly. "And tell Chrissie not to start on about my diet. I've eaten my quota for the day, in fact I stuffed myself with lettuce and similar rabbit food at supper tonight to make absolutely sure I was okay."

At last he came back. *"All right, you can have an hour or so, but I want you to promise that if anything happens to alarm you, you're to let me know immediately."*

"I promise."

"Right, you're on your own."

"Thank you, Andrew." She gazed toward the dining room door. What would the coming minutes bring, she wondered excitedly? What did she *want* them to bring? An anticipatory smile touched her lips, for she knew full well what she wanted them to bring!

The scene in the dining room was one of unbridled merrymaking. Twelfth Night celebrations had all but disappeared in Summer's own time, but here in the past they were still very much the thing. There was a great deal of stamping and laughter as people whirled to a riotous country dance, and so much of the hot cider punch known as "lamb's wool" had been consumed that the mood was now very merry indeed. The music was provided by a scratchy fiddle and beyond the general noise came the clink of cutlery as late diners finished their meals. The traditional King and Queen of Misrule had been selected by the time-honored method of concealing a bean in the Twelfth Cake, an immensely rich confection that had been associated with this night since medieval times. Whoever found the bean became king or queen for the night, and chose his or her consort. Together they presided from makeshift thrones on a dais at the side of the low-beamed room, issuing ridiculous commands that had to be obeyed, whether it was that couples should dance together back-to-back, drink tankards of cider from the side furthest from their lips, or even pretend to dance with a broomstick for a partner.

Thanks to the lamb's wool, these capers were found hilarious beyond belief.

There was Christmas greenery everywhere, although it was very dry and tired now. Evergreens were garlanded around the windows and mantelpiece, along the partitions separating the tables, over the trestle bar, and even around the barrels standing behind it. A mistletoe kissing bunch was suspended from the center of the ceiling, and was much resorted to by everyone who passed beneath.

Mummers who'd performed earlier in the evening mingled with the rest of the gathering. They were easily distinguishable by their blackened faces and outlandish costumes, which ranged from devil masks to animal skins, and they were even more merry than everyone else because they'd already performed at other inns and taverns in the town and imbibed hot cider punch at every one.

A mobcapped maid stepped forward to give Summer a glass of the hot punch, which was served from a huge wooden bowl that was decorated with ribbons. "Good wassail, ma'am," she said, bobbing a neat curtsy.

"Good wassail," Summer replied, accepting the glass. She glanced down at the heady drink. It was made from cider, sugar, roasted apples, eggs, and thick cream, and the fluffy pieces of apple floating on top did indeed resemble the lamb's wool that gave it its name.

She retreated to a relatively quiet corner and glanced around for the gentleman. At last she saw him. He was leaning back against the far end of the trestle bar, a glass of the punch in his hand. He was already looking at her, and his penetrating eyes bore an amused expression. In an instant she realized he knew she'd been searching the room for him, and her face flamed so much that she had to turn away.

A bell rang out suddenly, but the merriment continued unabated as four men, including the clergymen, hastened out into the misty yard. Icy night air swept in, and Summer caught a glimpse of the newly arrived London stagecoach. Three of its passengers, a farmer and two young men, came in, their faces blue with cold, then the door closed. The newcomers pushed their way to the fireplace to hold their frozen hands to the warmth, and accepted gratefully as the maid gave them glasses of lamb's wool.

About five minutes passed, then the stagecoach departed again with fresh horses, and half an hour after that, at the stroke of midnight, the landlord, warmly wrapped in a huge greatcoat, with a knitted scarf tied around his head, appeared in the yard doorway to clap his hands loudly. "Ladies and gentlemen, 'tis time to go a-wassailing!" he cried.

There was a huge cheer, and suddenly the floor cleared. People hurried to get their outdoor clothes from the hall, a collection of metal trays, pans, and buckets was brought from the kitchens, and more glasses of the punch were hastily handed around before the wooden bowl was carried ceremoniously out into the night. Some of the men lit flambeaux at the fire and took them out as well, and it was then that Summer saw some rifles leaning against the wall beneath one of the windows. What on earth did they want rifles for, she wondered, watching as they too were borne out into the night. The king and queen had risen grandly from their thrones, and everyone remaining in the room formed a column behind them, Summer included, but as the procession began to file out into the freezing cold, she realized she only had her shawl.

Suddenly, the gentleman was at her side with a woman's cloak. "Allow me, madam."

Summer's heart tightened, and her eyes flew to meet his.

He smiled a little. "The lady over there insists that you take her cloak as she will not be going out." He nodded toward a woman, probably a farmer's wife, who was seated at one of the tables, still eating her dinner with her husband.

The woman beamed and nodded, and Summer smiled in return before glancing up at the gentleman again. "Th . . . thank you, sir," she stammered, for his closeness quickened her pulse.

"Not at all," he said softly and slipped the cloak gently around her shoulders.

His touch affected her, even though it was through several

layers of clothing. She was sure his hands rested on her shoulders for a fraction longer than was strictly necessary, but then he was gone again as everyone began to file out into the night.

The mist swirled and the lanterns in the yard were indistinct in the icy gloom as the procession wended its way into the stable yard behind the inn, then toward a little wicket gate beyond. It opened into an apple orchard across which a path had been cleared through the snow. The lights of Tetbury twinkled dimly through the vapor that stirred eerily between the trees, and once or twice Summer heard the distant crack of rifles and a clatter very suggestive of trays, pans, and buckets like the ones carried from the Black Lion. She glanced around, and as the mist parted for a moment, she thought she saw the faint flicker of a bonfire, like a will-o'-the-wisp in the darkness, but she wasn't sure. She turned to look for the gentleman and saw him bringing up the rear of the procession. As before, his eyes met hers, and as before, she looked quickly away again.

The snow path led to the oldest apple trees in the orchard, around which nearly all the snow had been cleared away into heaps. In the center of the clearing, safely away from overhanging branches, a bonfire had been built, and as the flambeaux were held to it, flames began to leap eagerly upward, sending smoke and sparks up beyond the mist to the starlit night.

All empty glasses were replenished, then the wooden punch bowl was carried to the first tree, and some of the lamb's wool was carefully poured over the roots. Everyone formed a circle around the fire and raised their glasses to recite an old verse. "Old apple tree, old apple tree, we wassail thee; May you bloom well, and bear well, So merry we'll be, When next year we toast thee, old apple tree!"

As the gathering gave a mighty cheer, the rifles were raised and fired into the branches. Summer gave a start, for the reports were earsplitting. Then every tray, pan, and bucket was hammered so mercilessly she had to put her hands to her ears.

The wooden bowl was carried to the next tree, and the ceremony was repeated, but this time, as the din of rifle fire and drumming died away, another sound—long, mournful, and frightening—echoed chillingly through the darkness. A large hound had begun to howl somewhere in the rolling Gloucestershire countryside near the town, and the wassailing in the orchard was brought to a very abrupt halt, for there was a truly unearthly quality to the dreadful cry.

An icy finger passed down Summer's spine, and Lady Harvey's words rang in her ears. *"Twelfth Night, when were-wolves go abroad . . ."* Suddenly Sir Oswald's overrouged wife didn't seem quite as foolish as she had earlier.

The horrid sound died away, and in the ensuing silence the bonfire spat and crackled. Flame light leapt over the faces of the uneasy wassailers, and the lacework of apple tree branches overhead suddenly seemed like a giant spiderweb looming frighteningly above them all. The women in the gathering shrank fearfully closer to their menfolk as a primitive fear descended almost tangibly over the orchard.

It was the men who recovered first, or at least made out they recovered first. With laughs of bravado they prepared to wassail another tree. Then someone began to recite the old verse, and gradually everyone joined in again until the former bonhomie was almost completely restored. The rifle reports rang out once more, and the chaotic drumming followed, rattling through the night as if every shelf in an ironmonger's store had collapsed at once. But as the clatter died away, the terrible howl rang out once more, only this time it was much closer. For some of the wassailers it proved too much, and they chose to return to the inn, but others were made of sterner stuff.

Summer hesitated. She didn't really believe in werewolves, but at the same time . . .

"Les loups-garous do not exist," said a soft male voice at her elbow.

She turned quickly and once again found herself looking into the stranger's amused dark blue eyes. "You . . . you seem very sure of that, sir," she said.

"Well, I'm as sure as I can be, although I wouldn't care to

stake my life on it." He gave a faint smile. "However, I'm sure I'm not the subject of some dread supernatural curse, so if I offer you my protection, you need not fear I will suddenly transform into a frenzied canine with an inordinate desire to bite you."

The gentle mockery lessened her fear a little, and she smiled too. "I'm relieved to hear it, sir." But then her breath caught with alarm as the howl was heard again, even closer than before. Whatever it was seemed to be approaching the orchard!

Most of the remaining wassailers took to their heels, riflemen and all, leaving only a few diehards whose courage probably owed more to a surfeit of lamb's wool than anything else.

The gentleman glanced at Summer again. "How is your nerve, madam?" he asked then.

"Surely *my* nerve isn't in question, sir, for since you've offered to protect me, I fancy it's *your* nerve that must be tested."

He laughed. "Well, I'm prepared to stand my ground."

"Then so am I," she replied, with more conviction than she actually felt. Right now she was torn between wanting to linger out here with him, and a huge desire to take to her heels for the safety of the Black Lion.

So they stayed where they were, with the light of the bonfire flickering over them. Those few seconds had a dreamlike quality for Summer. Here she was, in a long gone Gloucestershire orchard, with a nineteenth-century gentleman to whom she was so fiercely attracted it was an agony to be next to him without touching him, listening to a macabre sound that may or may not be the Twelfth Night howling of a werewolf!

The long silence, broken only by the crackling of the fire, was suddenly disturbed by another new sound, the rustling of a large animal in the hedge at the far end of the orchard. It was the final straw for the last few wassailers, who made off as one for the inn.

The gentleman put a swift arm around Summer's shoulders and turned her toward the inn as well. "Discretion is perhaps the better part of valor," he murmured, beginning to usher her out of the orchard.

They hurried toward the wicket gate, but then Summer heard something bounding through the snow behind them. She glanced fearfully over her shoulder, then screamed as she saw a huge black hound bearing down on them.

The gentleman whirled about, pushing her behind him so that he stood between her and the beast. Then he drew a pistol from his pocket and fired it into the air. The hound slithered to a standstill, then crouched low as if about to leap at Summer. The firelight shone red in its eyes, and its teeth were jagged. There was a movement beyond it at the end of the orchard, and both Summer and the gentleman saw a horseman rein in.

The gentleman shouted, "Call off your hound, or I'll shoot both it and you! And believe me, this pistol and my aim are equal to the feat!"

For a moment the horseman did nothing, but as the gentleman leveled the pistol toward him, he gave a quick whistle. The hound responded immediately, loping back through the snow toward its master. Then both disappeared through the hedge.

The gentleman pocketed the pistol and turned swiftly to Summer, who was almost faint with relief. He took her by the arms to steady her. "It's all right, it's over now," he said gently.

She struggled to regain her composure. "So . . . so it wasn't a werewolf," she said, trying to smile.

"Definitely not."

"I think the man must be the highwayman who attacked Sir Oswald and Lady Harvey earlier this evening." She told him briefly what Lady Harvey had told her.

He nodded. "It seems very likely. Are you quite sure you're all right now?"

"I . . . I think so," she said in a small voice.

"It *is* quite safe now, you know," he reassured her.

"I don't think I've ever been so frightened in my life," she confessed.

"With me as your champion? Fie, madam," he murmured.

She raised her eyes to his, and he put a hand to her chin to tilt it upward a little. "Is the champion to receive a favor from his lady?" he asked softly.

Now her heart was beating swiftly for a very different reason. There was no mistaking the dark warmth in his eyes or the seductive inflection in his voice. "Does he wish a favor?" she whispered.

"He has from the first moment he saw her," he breathed, bending his head to kiss her.

Their lips were cold from the icy night air, but the kiss soon flamed them with desire. She cast caution to the four winds, slipping her arms around his neck and allowing her body to melt yearningly against his. As her lips parted beneath his, she couldn't help pressing herself to the contours of his body—all the contours, especially the hardening at his loins, as he was aroused by the unexpected passion of her response.

His lips became more urgent, and his hands slid to enclose her buttocks, pulling her onto him so that the pleasure was heightened for them both. She felt his erection as it strained against the tightness of his breeches, and she could taste the need in his kiss. Her breath caught with gratification as wild sensations began to course through her. She moved her hips voluptuously against him and heard him gasp a little as her abandonment laid siege to his fast vanishing restraint. The wild sensations intensified, washing over her in wave after wave of elation. She didn't know who he was, but this unknown nineteenth-century Englishman had played havoc with her soul from that first moment in the courtyard.

Suddenly, the moment was broken by shouts from the stable yard, and they drew guiltily apart as the landlord and some of the men returned, after at last plucking up courage on hearing the pistol shot.

But then a dazzling electric light shone in her eyes, the chill of the winter orchard disappeared, and Chrissie grinned down at her as she lay confusedly on the sofa. "Come in, number six, your time's up," she said humorously.

Summer could have wept. The sensuous desire was still with her—the taste of his lips, the feel of his body, the wonderful security of his arms around her . . . But he was centuries away now, and she was alone.

Chapter Five

It was the small hours of the same night, and rain spattered against the apartment windows as Summer slipped out of bed, put on a wrap, and tiptoed along the passage toward the living room.

The digital lights on the TV and VCR cast a luminous glow over everything as she went to the sofa and felt underneath for the little cassette recorder. As she straightened, her glance fell upon Andrew's piece of medieval pottery, and for a guilty moment she felt as if he were sitting in his chair, looking accusingly at her.

Pulling herself up sharply, she went quietly from the living room to his study, pausing before going in to listen very carefully for any sound at all from the other bedroom. But all was silent, so she went into the study and closed the door behind her. There, with the volume turned down as low as possible, she tested the recording she'd made. She was interested only in the prompts Andrew used to put her into a trance, and what he said to bring her out of it again; everything else could be wiped clean, so she switched on his recording and editing system to rerecord the parts she wanted. She left a blank area between his commands, so she could lengthen or shorten things as she chose, but initially she set it at two hours. Provided all this worked, two hours in the past should be just about right.

Concealing the cassette and her portable recorder in her wrap pocket, she hurried back to her room and put everything into the drawer of her bedside table before lying back to think. Andrew would consider what she'd done to be a considerable crime if he knew about it, for although he recorded his sessions with clients and gave them the cassette afterward, he was very strict about *not* including the means by which the trance was induced or ended. This was a necessary precaution, for if a cassette containing these prompts were to be played while driving a car, for instance, the consequences of involuntarily entering a trance were only too obvious.

Of course, not everyone could be rehypnotized like this, but some people *were* susceptible, and it was her intention to find out if she was one of them. She wanted to be able to go back to being Olivia Courtenay whenever she felt like it, without having to wheedle with Andrew. She wasn't concerned about the recorder breaking down, because she knew she had eventually come out of the trance of her own accord. It was an old wives' tale that someone would remain hypnotized forever if the hypnotist were to drop dead. She felt very disloyal to Andrew, for she was being very underhanded, but regression to her previous existence was a welcome escape from the unhappiness of her life here in the present, and the kiss in the orchard had added a new dimension. She wanted to experience more, much more. To see if a trance could be triggered, all she had to do was turn the recorder on, but her conscience pricked again as she thought of Chrissie and Andrew's anger and hurt disappointment if they found out how deceitful she'd been.

Outside, the rain dashed against the window, and she could hear the crash of waves on the shore as the wind rose. It was almost as if the elements were daring her to do what her heart urged but her head cautioned against. *Press the button, Summer,* the sea hissed. *Press the button . . .*

The recorder lay there temptingly, its controls within inches of her fingers. She stretched out a hand, then hesitated again. Did she dare? Her forefinger trembled. Could she face Chrissie and Andrew if her sins were exposed? She bit her lip, then thought of the kiss in the orchard, and impulsively pressed the PLAY button.

She lay back with her eyes closed, going through the breathing exercises Andrew had taught her. His voice began on the cassette, and then followed the gentle music he always used. She felt herself relaxing, just as if he were in the room with her. The familiar warmth began to creep over her, and she sank into that deeper, even more relaxed state that was somewhere between sleep and consciousness.

Suddenly, there was absolute silence, and she opened her eyes uneasily. What had happened? Had the recorder switched off for some reason? But then once more she became conscious of the sparkling health and exuberance tingling through her veins. She sat up quickly, and heavy black curls tumbled forward over the shoulders of her white muslin nightgown. Her eyes parted excitedly. It had worked! She was Olivia again!

She glanced around. She was in her room at the Black Lion, and the only light was provided by the fire in the hearth and a night candle on the mantelpiece above. It was a simply furnished room, dominated by the faded blue brocade four-poster in which she'd been trying unsuccessfully to sleep. As inn rooms went in this age it was well furnished and comfortable, and it was certainly warm and clean, without any unwelcome insect life in the mattress. There were two doors, one into the passage in the inn, the other onto the first-floor gallery above the yard, and the only window looked onto the gallery as well. Everyone at the inn appeared to have retired now. The Twelfth Night celebrations were over, and the last stagecoach had departed. There wouldn't be another until just after dawn.

She was about to lie back again when she heard stealthy sounds on the gallery—footsteps, soft and creeping. Through the curtains she saw a shadow pass in front of the lantern that was fixed to one of the gallery posts. The footsteps stopped right by her door, and her frightened gaze went to the key. Had she locked it again after going out onto the gallery earlier? She couldn't remember! Her mouth ran dry. What if she'd forgotten? What if whoever it was could just open the door and come in?

Flinging the bedclothes aside, she hurried to the door, but as she reached it, to her horror she saw the handle begin to turn! Suddenly, there was a disturbance somewhere farther along the gallery. More footsteps sounded, but hurried and loud this time, and after a moment's hesitation, the shadow by the door fled past the light and vanished. Someone else shouted, and then she heard Lady Harvey's hysterical cries.

"My diamonds! My diamonds have been stolen!"

Doors opened, footsteps sounded on all sides, and as more voices joined the general alarm, Summer tried the door. It wasn't locked! She gave a horrified intake of breath. What might have happened if the alarm hadn't been raised? What if theft hadn't been the only thing on the intruder's mind? Suddenly, there was a loud knock at the door, and she was so startled she took an involuntary step backward.

"Are you all right?" asked the familiar voice of her gentleman.

With a flood of relief she hastened to open the door.

He'd flung his greatcoat on, and his golden hair was tousled from sleeping. He had a lantern, which he held up concernedly in order to see her face properly. "Are you all right?" he asked again.

For a moment she could only gaze into his eyes because memories of the kiss in the orchard flooded embarrassingly over her, as if she and she alone had been guilty of that resounding indiscretion.

He was clearly as conscious of her as she was of him. His glance took in her tumbling hair and her nightgown ribbons that weren't fully tied at the throat, so that the curves of her breasts were revealed.

She drew the muslin folds together. "I'd forgotten to lock the door," she said lamely, and couldn't prevent her lips from trembling a little with delayed shock.

He stepped inside, closed the door, and put the lantern down on the dressing table. He threw his greatcoat over the chair by the fire, then turned to face her again. He still wore his shirt and breeches, and seeing her surprise, gave another smile. "I fell asleep by the fire in my room," he explained, then became more serious. "After all, I had a great deal to think about," he murmured, coming to her. His hands were gentle on her shoulders, and she felt his warmth through the muslin. "What is your name?" he asked softly.

There was seduction in that soft note, just as there had been in the orchard, but this time there wouldn't be any interruption. Excitement had been stirring through her from the moment she saw him again, but now it became almost unendurable. She wanted to be taken, to be made passionate and abandoned love to. All thought of restraint had already vanished into the shadows. *Seduce me, please, oh please . . .*

"Am I not to know your name?" he inquired, tilting her face toward his just as he had in the orchard.

Her lips parted to answer, but then she hesitated as she remembered her cousin Caro's forthcoming betrothal. The prospect of being found innocently at the inn with Jeremy Fenwick had been bad enough, but there was nothing innocent about *this*! But it was only too easy to convince herself that any indiscretion in this room at the Black Lion would never spread beyond the confines of these four walls. She met his eyes. "My name is Olivia," she whispered.

"Just Olivia?"

"I think it best," she answered.

He took her left hand and raised it so that her wedding ring caught the light. "Is this the reason?"

"No. My husband has been dead two years."

He searched her face. "Very well, Olivia, I will not press you to tell me more, and I will introduce myself simply as Brand."

"Brand," she repeated softly, for at last he had a name. It suited him, for there was a flame running through him, a flame upon which she longed to burn her foolish Icarus wings. . . . At last the wanton words she longed to say came to her lips. "Make love to me, Brand," she whispered, undoing the remaining ribbon ties of her nightgown and allowing the garment to slide to the floor.

His dark gaze moved over her nakedness; then he smiled and began to untie his neckcloth.

She watched as he undressed. His timeless perfection crossed every century there had ever been, and that ever would be. He had a body that was smooth and leanly muscular, with broad shoulders, slender hips, and taut buttocks. The hair at his groin was thick and dark, and his virility sprang out in readiness.

He smiled again as he saw how she gazed at him, then held out a hand. "Come to me, Olivia," he breathed.

She walked toward him in a dream. Their fingers entwined, and he drew her into his arms. She felt the shaft of his virility pressing imperatively against her, then he swept her up into his arms and carried her to the bed.

Desire keened through her like a wild hunt as he placed her on the crumpled sheet and then lay with her. The smell of costmary lingered on his skin from his clothes, and his warmth was exciting as he leaned over her and put a hand on her thigh. He bent his head to kiss her breast, and she closed her eyes as he caressed the already stimulated nipple with his tongue.

He moved to straddle her, pinning her hands back against the pillow as he looked down into her eyes. "You are a woman to die for, my sweet Olivia," he whispered, slowly lowering his hips until his virility pressed between her parted thighs.

She felt his heat as he penetrated her. He took his time, pushing in slowly and luxuriously until he could push no farther. Then he looked down into her eyes again. "We are one now, Olivia, joined in the most exquisite way of all."

Tears stung her eyes. "Brand," she breathed. "Oh, Brand . . ." She was transported by an unbelievable tide of exhilaration. Her entire body felt as if it were floating, and the experience was almost too much. This felt so very right, as if it were meant to be, and she wanted it to last forever, wanted to be with him forever.

She shivered with gratification as he began to thrust, gently at first, but then more and more urgently. The wild hunt was coursing through them both now, bringing a tumult of pleasure that propelled them toward a final moment that promised every delight they could ever have yearned for. The prize shone before them, and at last the sheer force of climax swept them into the light.

She arched beneath him, her fingernails digging into his back as a thousand remembered, yearned-for, wept-for emotions sang through her entire being. Jack's face lingered for a beloved moment, but it was this man, this lover-stranger, who had brought her to life again. She clung to him, tasting the salt of her own tears on his lips and treasuring the firm warmth of his body against hers. A night like this might never happen again. He was a fantasy that for the moment was fact in her arms, and as his tender lips brushed hers again, she prayed the dawn would be a long time coming.

But she had forgotten the cold plain facts of time, and the cassette recorder that would bring her trance to an end because she herself had set the controls. He made love to her again, and again, but when the two hours had passed, the four-poster bed at the inn disappeared, Brand disappeared, and suddenly she was alone in the future.

She heard the cassette recorder switch off, then silence, except for the rain on the window.

Chapter Six

For a moment Summer's hand crept to where Brand would have been had she still been with him at the Black Lion. But he wasn't there, and the desperate loneliness of the past six months suddenly descended over her again. She could feel the glow of Olivia's health slipping out of her, leaving behind only Summer Stanway's fragility.

She turned over and hid her face in the pillows. Why hadn't she just played the beginning of the cassette? Why hadn't she omitted the end, and left herself to awaken naturally out of the trance? If she had done that, she would still be with Brand now! Tears of frustration stung her eyes, and her fists clenched, but gradually she calmed down. Common sense had to prevail. It was stupid to get angry; she was Summer Stanway, not Olivia Courtenay! Olivia had lived and died a long time ago, and becoming her again was, literally, a trick of the mind. But, oh, how good it would be to switch the cassette on and *never* become Summer again!

A little shocked by the force of this last thought, she sat up slowly, drawing up her knees and clasping them through the bedclothes as she gazed toward the window. It had come from the heart. She really did wish she could become Olivia forever, and the realization was a little numbing, for it brought home to her exactly how desolate Summer Stanway's existence had become. Six months ago, before Jack's death, she would *never* have felt or thought like this. Or would she? A few minutes ago—or was it centuries?—she had lain in Brand's arms, more satisfied and contented than she could ever remember being. And that included the time she'd been with Jack.

An awful feeling of disloyalty gripped her then, as if she'd been unfaithful. But Jack was dead. He was *dead*! Flinging the bedclothes aside, she got up, running her fingers agitatedly through her short hair. God, what an emotional mess she was. Guilt about Jack, guilt about illicitly recording Andrew, guilt about just everything under the sun, even—when it was conveniently too late and the deed had more than been done with Brand—guilt about Olivia Courtenay's cousin Caro! Oh, for heaven's sake, this was totally ridiculous! Was she about to shoulder the conscience of the entire world, present *and* past?

She needed a drink, and if it weren't for the darned diabetes, she'd have one. A large one! Instead, she'd have to content herself with water, but at least she could have half a ton of ice in it. Putting on her wrap, she slipped from the room and went to the kitchen. Then, with a large glass of ice and water clinking in her hand, she went to the living room, drew back the curtains, and sat gazing out at the sea. The rain didn't dash against the windows on this side of the apartment, and she could see the whites of the breakers on the shore.

She had to blame someone for the wretchedness her life had become, and the only person she could point a finger at was Jack. It was all his fault. If he'd taken more care behind the wheel, he'd still be alive!

"Damn you, Jack!" she cried, a little more loudly than she realized, for after a moment a door opened and Chrissie came in, her eyes still sleepy as she pulled on her cream silk negligee. "Are you okay, honey?"

"Yes. I'm sorry if I disturbed you."

Chrissie came closer and glanced at the window. "Not exactly a romantic moonlit night, mm?"

"Not exactly."

"Actually, I thought I heard you get up ages ago, must have been nearly two hours back."

"Oh?"

Chrissie eased herself onto the arm of Summer's chair. "You are *sure* you're all right, aren't you?" she asked gently.

"Yes, I'm fine," Summer lied.

Chrissie misinterpreted. "You *will* get over Jack, you know."

Summer didn't say anything, for Brand's reflection seemed to be smiling at her from the window.

"I'll be honest with you," Chrissie went on. "I heard what you shouted out just now. It's good, you know. Anger is part of the grieving process."

Summer felt awful. After what she'd done, she didn't deserve Chrissie's comfort.

Chrissie stayed companionably on the arm of the chair for a few minutes more, then got up. "Guess I'd better get back to bed, or I'll be a wreck for tomorrow evening."

"Tomorrow evening?"

"Andrew and I are going to that dinner at the Savoy in London. All Svengalis and wives welcome. Don't you remember?"

"It had quite slipped my mind."

"It hadn't slipped mine," Chrissie said dryly. "The only consolation as far as I'm concerned is getting a little Oxford Street shopping in first."

"So you're leaving at the crack of dawn?" Summer said, grinning.

"Of course. What else can a dedicated shopaholic do?"

"I'm really sorry I woke you like this, Chrissie."

"I'll survive. 'Night, then."

" 'Night."

Summer remained where she was. Chrissie's kindness made her feel worse than she did before. She leaned her head back then, for a stark, sobering truth insinuated itself firmly amid the jumble of guilt. Okay, so she had a conscience about what she'd done, but it wasn't going to stop her from doing it again. What she'd found in her previous life was far better than anything she had in *this* life, and she didn't intend to give it up. Now she had the ill-gotten means, she had every intention of becoming Olivia Courtenay as often as she could, so it was hypocrisy to wring her hands and don a hair shirt. She finished the water and got up. A minute later she was in bed, and two minutes after that she was asleep.

*   *   *

Chrissie and Andrew left for London at seven in the morning, with Chrissie brandishing her credit cards and Andrew looking sick at the prospect of trailing around store after store. Still, as Summer pointed out, it was the price he had to pay for his wife's company at the hypnotherapists' wingding.

Chrissie made her promise again to do everything she should as far as her diabetes was concerned. "You should have learned it all by heart by now, kid," she pointed out.

Summer replied like a seven-year-old. "Yes, I have, teacher. I'll nibble a snack on time, eat properly on time, and administer my insulin on time."

Even then Chrissie would have fussed around still more had not Andrew manhandled her into the car and driven off.

When they'd gone, Summer went for a walk along the beach. Her thoughts were taken up completely with Brand, as they had been from the moment she'd opened her eyes that morning. The sea was still rough, and the tide was beginning to come in when she returned to the apartment to take a shower. Then, as she had a cup of coffee and some toast in the living room, she knew she could no longer resist temptation.

She went into the bedroom and didn't wrestle at all with her conscience as she pressed the button, then lay back to begin her breathing exercises. Andrew's soothing voice and the music washed pleasantly over her, and once again she felt herself sliding into a dreamlike state. She could still hear the sea, but didn't want to, for it meant she was still in the present. Then suddenly a plate fell with a loud crash, shattering into what sounded like a thousand pieces. Was someone in the apartment?

She opened her eyes and found herself once more at the foot of the staircase in the Black Lion. Incongruously, the first thing she noticed was that the sporting prints and fireplace no longer boasted their rather withered Christmas greenery, then she saw the cause of the crash that had startled her so. A maid had tripped on an uneven flagstone, and greasy eggs, bacon, and sausages were everywhere.

The landlord, who was busy trying to placate two angry

guests who'd just discovered that they too had been robbed during the night by the intruder, rushed over to berate the poor girl for her clumsiness. The maid burst into tears, protesting that it wasn't her fault if she had too much to do and the floor was uneven. This enraged the landlord still more. He was suffering from the aftereffects of too much lamb's wool and was in no mood to be understanding.

Summer breathed in deeply as she felt Olivia's strength sweeping through her again, then thought about what had happened in this other life since last she'd been here. After several more hours of the most wonderful and rewarding lovemaking she had ever known, Brand had slipped from her room at daybreak and returned to his own room. Now they were to take breakfast together, but he wasn't yet in the dining room. What would happen after that she did not know. The only likely course seemed that they'd go their separate ways, ships that had passed in the night, but it wasn't what she wanted.

At that moment Sir Oswald and Lady Harvey came downstairs behind her. They looked a little incongruous in their evening finery, and her ladyship's eyes were red from the copious tears she'd wept. Her plump throat looked decidedly naked without the pink diamond sunburst, and her curly red wig was in need of more attention than could be provided by a mere inn maid.

"Good morning, Sir Oswald, Lady Harvey," Summer said, but as she greeted them, she was dismayed to recall having arranged to take breakfast with them as well, something she couldn't do if she was to see Brand again.

Lady Harvey hurried down toward her. "Oh, my *dear* Mrs. Courtenay, did you *ever* know such a night as this last? I vow I will never sleep easy in my bed again. It was terrible, quite terrible, and the villainous fellow escaped with my precious necklace. We might have all been murdered! Did you escape his vile attentions?"

"I'm relieved to say I did, Lady Harvey, but I'm terribly sorry you've had such a dreadful experience."

Sir Oswald took his wife's hand and patted it fondly.

"There, there, my dear, I will do what I can to acquire another such necklace for you."

She looked at him out of tear-filled eyes. "Oh, dearest Oswald, I do not deserve a husband as kind and considerate as you, but we both know there will never be another necklace like that one." She turned to Summer to explain. "It came from India, you know, and was once the property of a Hindu princess. Sir Oswald was a man of immense importance in the Raj and was highly respected by the Indian nobility. The necklace was a gift of thanks after he saved a prince from brigands, and my dear brave Oswald gave it to me. Now it has gone." A solitary tear wended its way down her rouged cheek.

Summer felt very sorry, for the necklace's sentimental value clearly made it irreplaceable.

Lady Harvey made a brave attempt to rally. "However, we must be thankful that our throats were not cut as we slept."

"We must indeed," her husband agreed, and then looked at Summer. "I trust you will still take breakfast with us, Mrs. Courtenay?"

"That . . . that would be most agreeable, Sir Oswald, but I fear I have something I must attend to first. Would you mind waiting, or shall we simply take coffee together before you depart?"

She was banking on his appetite making the latter a preferable course to the former, and she was right. He cleared his throat, then gave a quick smile. "My dear lady, do not let us impose upon your plans. By all means take coffee with us a little later, in fact that would be splendid. *À bientôt, madame.*"

"*À bientôt,* Sir Oswald, Lady Harvey." She dropped a little curtsy, and to her relief they went on into the dining room.

Meanwhile, the landlord had finished ticking off the unfortunate maid, who was on her hands and knees, gathering the mess into her hitherto spotless apron. It was all Summer could do not to allow her modern self to intrude by bending to help, but she knew that wouldn't do at all, so she edged around the poor girl, and made her way to the settles by the fire to wait for Brand to come down.

The landlord had returned to his two irate guests and was doing his best to explain that there was nothing he could say or do that would restore their stolen property. As the two disgruntled men left, the innkeeper heaved a sigh of relief, then glanced toward her as if remembering something. "Ah, madam, I have a letter for you," he said, searching in his pocket.

"A letter?" She was taken aback, for who would write to her here? Unless . . . Of course, it must be from Jeremy.

He came over to her and paused with a knowing grin that was only too reminiscent of the ostler's the day before. "It's from a Major Jeremy Fenwick, who I am informed you were to meet here yesterday evening. I fear it should have awaited your arrival yesterday, but it was sent to the White Hart instead, and they only dispatched a lad with it about half an hour ago."

Summer felt herself coloring just as she had in front of the ostler, for the man spoke in a voice that was easily loud enough to carry to the other four people in the hall. Wishing the landlord, the ostler, *and* Jeremy in Hades for causing her such unwarranted embarrassment, although if she were strictly honest she had no one but herself to blame for this particular predicament, she broke the seal on the letter, and began to read.

My dearest Olivia,

If you only knew how desperately I regret not being able to keep our assignation, but I fear the army has no finer feelings. I'm obliged to report to my barracks somewhat earlier than expected, and so this time will have to forgo the pleasure of gazing into your beautiful gray eyes.

I thank you from the bottom of my unworthy heart for being what you are, and I sincerely hope that on my return from Ireland we will resume what is for me the most precious of friendships.

You are a jewel among women, my darling Olivia, and if you have ever wondered what happened to that miniature of you that Roderick kept with him at all times, I fear the time has come to own up. Now *I* am the one who gazes upon your loveliness each night before going to sleep!

So, farewell for the moment, fair Olivia. Dream of me as I dream of you.

Jeremy

Summer gazed at the letter in utter astonishment, for it was couched in terms far more affectionate than the strictly platonic friendship that existed between Jeremy Fenwick and her. Gradually, the astonishment was replaced by anger. How *dared* he put pen to paper in such a way! And how dared he purloin that miniature!

She crumpled the letter into a ball, and then gradually calmed down a little. Jeremy's propensity for cognac was surely to blame for this. He must have been in his cups when he wrote it. Yes, that had to be the answer, for why else would he resort to such flowery, inappropriate phrases? Come to that, why else would he admit to having taken the miniature?

Then Jeremy went from her thoughts as she tossed the letter into the fire and got up. What was keeping Brand? She returned to the foot of the staircase again, not realizing that the letter she thought the flames had consumed had actually bounced against an andiron and fallen into the ashes in the hearth, where the only portion to burn at all was that upon which her full name was written.

The dining room door opened as a waiter hurried out with a tray of empty plates, and she caught a glimpse of the crowded room behind him. Lady Harvey was in floods of tears at her table because a jug of milk had been knocked over and spilled in her lap. Poor Sir Oswald was doing what he could to soothe her after this latest disaster, and he happened to glance up just as Summer glanced in. Their eyes met, and he beckoned imploringly. There was nothing she could do except respond, so she hurried into the room.

But as she bent to comfort Lady Harvey, who was by now quite hysterical, Brand's tall figure emerged from the shadows at the top of the staircase, from where he'd heard and seen everything from the moment the landlord informed her of the letter and its author. A nerve flickered at his temple, and his blue eyes were dark and angry as he looked at the dining room door. His mouth was set, and there was no softness about him at all as he strode to the fireplace and retrieved the singed ball of paper from the hearth.

He read, and his blue eyes became like ice. Slowly he folded the letter and pushed it into his pocket, then turned to collar a passing waiter. "I wish to speak to the landlord."

"Yes, sir."

The man hurried off, then returned with the reluctant landlord, who feared another guest with a theft to report. Brand turned swiftly toward him and raised the singed paper. "What is the lady's name?" he demanded.

"Name? I don't know, sir."

"You must know, you gave her this letter!"

"I don't know, sir, I can't read. I only know it was from Major Fenwick, because that's what the boy from the White Hart said when he brought it, and the lady asked for the major on arriving yesterday." The landlord spread his hands.

"It doesn't matter. Here's what I owe you; now just have my carriage brought to the yard without delay." Brand thrust some coins into the man's hand.

"Yes, sir."

"And I mean without delay!"

The landlord almost ran out into the yard, and Brand returned to his room, where he gathered his few overnight belongings, before going onto the gallery. It wasn't long before his coachman tooled the carriage carefully through the archway from the stable yard, and then drew the team to a standstill.

It was at this moment that Summer looked up from ministering to Lady Harvey and recognized the carriage in the yard. Brand? She straightened in puzzlement. Surely he wasn't leaving without at least saying good-bye? Then she saw him swiftly descending the wooden steps opposite, his overnight valise in his hand.

Dismayed, she gathered her skirts and hurried to the door into the yard. She emerged into the cold winter morning. "Brand?" she called.

He paused, then turned.

"You surely aren't leaving without saying good-bye?"

Their eyes met just as they had on his arrival, but this time she saw cold loathing in his gaze. Then he walked on toward his carriage, flung the valise inside, and climbed in. A second later the whip cracked, and the coachman urged the team forward. The vehicle swept out beneath the archway into the market square, and within moments all sound of it had gone.

Shaken, Summer stared after it. Nothing could have been more tender and loving than their last kiss just before dawn; now he'd spurned her. He hadn't even had the grace to say good-bye. She felt cheap and used, and more hurt than she could ever have dreamed possible.

But as she stood there in the chill yard, she suddenly became aware of other eyes upon her. She turned quickly toward a travel-stained carriage that had arrived a few moments before she emerged from the dining room. The thin, black-clad, almost cadaverous occupant had alighted and was gazing at her with a rather surprised, if not to say disapproving expression in his rather small eyes. It was Mr. George Bradshaw, the London lawyer brother of her late Aunt Merriam. He'd acted for her when Roderick died, but she didn't like him. Now he was not only here at the Black Lion, but quite clearly on his way to Oakhill House for his niece Caro's betrothal, just as she herself was, and unkind fate had been spiteful enough to bring him into the courtyard at the very moment she made a fool of herself!

She froze in unutterable dismay. How much had he seen? How much might he have deduced? Swiftly, she snatched her wits together and hurried toward him. "Why, Mr. Bradshaw, what a happy surprise this is!" she cried, forcing a smile to lips that were stiff.

His thoughtful glance flickered toward the market square

archway and then to her. "A happy surprise indeed, Mrs. Courtenay," he murmured, inclining his head. He had a thin voice to match his appearance.

"I vow I sometimes cannot credit the foibles of chance. I was in the dining room with Sir Oswald and Lady Harvey when I was absolutely *certain* I saw one of my near neighbors from Kensington. I rushed out to greet him, but instead it was a total stranger! Can you imagine how very foolish I felt? And now I find you instead, so my excursion into the cold morning air hasn't been entirely in vain!" She gave a tinkle of laughter that she trusted didn't sound as false to him as it did to her.

"It, er, would seem not, Mrs. Courtenay," he said, the tone of his voice suggesting he was now less sure than he had been a moment before.

"And how happy too the reason for us both to be en route for Oakhill House. You *are* en route for Oakhill House, aren't you?"

"I am indeed, Mrs. Courtenay."

"I'm so pleased for dear Caro. A love match is surely the most felicitous thing in the world, is it not?"

"I, er, imagine so, madam, but being a bachelor, I cannot claim personal experience," he murmured.

She rattled on. "Do come inside, sir, for I'm sure you must be feeling the chill. Do you know Sir Oswald and Lady Harvey?"

"I do not have that honor."

"Then I must introduce you. Oh, there have been such dreadful happenings here. We have had a villainous thief, and her ladyship's necklace was stolen during the night . . ." She began to walk him toward the dining room door, and by the time they went inside, it was her fervent hope that he'd forgotten anything he may have observed on alighting from his carriage.

But as she presented Mr. Bradshaw to Sir Oswald and the now recovered Lady Harvey, her misery over Brand returned. Oh, how she wished she hadn't succumbed to temptation the night before. Not only had she been badly hurt by the experience, but now Caro's unlikable uncle had witnessed her indiscreet conduct in the courtyard!

Suddenly, she was no longer enjoying the past. The very thing that had made it so wonderful, now made it awful. She wished she hadn't set the cassette recorder for as long as two hours, but she had, and she had no option but to wait until the trance was brought to an end.

One thing was certain, after this she didn't want to sample 1807 again!

Chapter Seven

Summer returned to the present at the allotted time, and after lying unhappily in her bed for a while, eventually fell into a restless sleep. She felt ragged the next morning, although Chrissie and Andrew didn't notice when they returned from London. They'd had an excellent time and were in good spirits as they regaled her with all that had happened, from Chrissie's success on the shopping front to the unexpectedly high quality of the dinner.

Somehow Summer managed to evince the necessary interest, but behind her brave smiles she was empty. It was as if she, Summer Stanway, not her previous self, had been so cruelly let down by Brand. It was always bad enough to return to the present and forfeit Olivia's health and vitality, but this time the feeling was far worse because she felt unbelievably hurt.

She was so upset that she didn't feel at all like eating at the regulation times, and then realized she'd forgotten her insulin too, but Chrissie's alarmed fussing soon put her on track again. She then had to endure her sister's wagging finger on top of everything else, but knew that on this occasion at least, the telling off was more than justified. She glanced outside as Chrissie lectured her. Lowering clouds raced endlessly above an unfriendly, slate-colored sea. It looked exactly how she felt, she thought resignedly.

At midmorning she decided to escape to Chichester for a while to see if shopping for new clothes would provide the necessary tonic, but even that failed her this time. After several hours of fruitless browsing, followed by a snack she didn't want but had to have, she returned to Bracklesham empty-handed. The weather now helped even less. It started to rain again, and as she drove to the constant rhythm of the windshield wipers, she felt close to tears.

At the apartment she found Andrew making a cup of tea in the kitchen. He glanced over his shoulder at her. "How goes it?" he asked.

"Oh, all right, I guess."

"Chrissie's taking a shower."

"Right."

He turned. "What's up?"

"Nothing. Why?" She attempted to look bright.

"Well, in all the time I've known you and Chrissie, neither of you has *ever* returned from shopping without at least one purchase!"

She gave a quick laugh. "I guess Chichester didn't come up to scratch this time. Or maybe I just wasn't really in the mood."

He leaned back against the table, studying her more closely. "Something's wrong, isn't it?" he said quietly.

"No, I'm fine," she insisted, going to the window and gazing out at the sea.

"You're a lousy liar, Summer Stanway."

"I'm just feeling low, that's all."

"Well, perhaps a little visit to 1807 would cheer you up," he suggested suddenly. "Maybe I'm wrong, but it seems to me that both trips so far have brought a considerable smile to your face. Am I wrong?"

"No, you're not," It's the trips you *don't* know about that are the trouble, she thought contritely.

"Would you like to go back again?"

"Well, I . . ." To say no was going to seem peculiar, and she knew it.

"Don't be coy. Come on, we'll do it now, before your mouth turns down even more." With a quick smile, he picked up his cup of tea, then held out a hand to her.

Feeling as guilty as hell, she managed a smile as she accepted.

* * *

Olivia's unhappiness over Brand was the first sensation that engulfed Summer this time. The second was the motion of her carriage as it drove along a narrow country road.

Andrew's voice intruded from the future. *"What's happening? Are you still at the Black Lion?"*

"No, I'm in my carriage on my way to Oakhill House, my relatives' residence. The weather is still dry and bitterly cold, and I'm well wrapped up in my hooded cloak. There's a warm brick on the floor under my feet, and a smaller one in my muff to keep my hands warm."

"Central heating, eh? Describe what you see."

"Well about half an hour ago we drove south out of Berkeley, and—"

Andrew interrupted. *"We?"*

"Yes. There are two carriages, mine and the one belonging to my cousin Caro's maternal uncle, Mr. George Bradshaw. He arrived at the Black Lion, and we've driven in convoy from there." She spoke carefully, because her first meeting with George Bradshaw had taken place during an illicit visit to the past that Andrew didn't know about.

The lawyer hadn't said anything else to her about the courtyard incident, and she was fairly certain he'd dismissed it from his mind. She prayed so, for she'd begun to form the unsettling impression that for some unknown but compelling reason he would prefer Caro's betrothal not to take place.

"Go on," Andrew prompted.

"Mm? Oh, yes. Sorry, my mind was wandering. Well, we're approaching the gates to the grounds of Oakhill House. To my right, that's the west, the countryside is very low and level because the Severn estuary is only about half a mile away. It's a landscape of streams, ditches, hedgerows, apple and pear orchards, and farms. I know from Caro's letters that in medieval times there used to be a forest here called the Forest of Horwood, where the lords of Berkeley hunted, but now only fox coverts remain because the Berkeley Hunt is still one of the most famous in England."

She looked out the other window. "To the east there's rising land. Not too high, but I guess it would have been an island back in the mists of time. Now it's all been laid out as a huge park, not belonging to Oakhill House I hasten to add, but to Bevincote, Lord Lytherby's country seat, which is out of sight on the far side. There are beautiful specimen trees that have been carefully tended, and I can see a herd of red deer moving across some more open land." She glanced along the road ahead. "Oh, I can see the gates of Oakhill House now!" She knew a great deal from Caro's letters and had been told how the gates would suddenly appear on a bend, so she continued to describe everything to Andrew as she lowered the window glass and leaned out.

Uncle Merriam's new property lay at the very southern end of the rising land, its grounds taking a modest rectangular piece out of otherwise exclusively Bevincote land. There was a little lodge, gray stone with a tall chimney, and a man came out to open the wrought iron gates and wave his hat as the carriages swept past into the small rather open park.

Oakhill House itself stood amid gardens halfway up the incline ahead. It was a six-bayed stone building with a central pediment and hipped roof, and parts of it dated back to the fourteenth century. Through a wicket gate from one of the gardens there was a church, which served the scattered cottages and farms that dotted the countryside.

The door of the house opened as the carriage drove up, and Summer's—or rather Olivia's—uncle and cousin emerged to greet their guests. Caro Merriam was that most rare of creatures, a redhead with a flawless skin. She was slightly built, with wide green eyes, full lips, and an infectious smile that seemed to light up her whole face. Her leaf green fustian gown had a gauze-filled neckline, and she clutched a warm pink shawl around her shoulders as she waved.

Uncle Merriam was still a good-looking man, although his wiry gray hair had thinned to leave a bald patch in recent years. His financial problems had left their mark on his health, for there was a new frailty about him that his concerned niece noticed straightaway. His penchant for old-fashioned clothes hadn't changed, however, for his blue velvet coat, gray brocade waistcoat, silk breeches, and buckled black shoes would not have been out of place in the last two decades of the previous century.

As a manservant came to open Summer's carriage door, she spoke briefly to Andrew. "I don't want to say anything more for the moment."

"All right, I'll leave you to it, and bring you out of the trance in half an hour, okay?"

"Okay." She alighted from the carriage, and Caro ran to hug her.

"Oh, Olivia, I'm *so* glad you've arrived at last. I have so much to tell you I really don't know where to begin."

Summer returned the hug, then turned to Uncle Merriam as he came over too.

"Olivia, my dear, how good it is to see you out of mourning, I've always loathed black." He embraced her, then he held her arms to study her face. "I vow you look more and more like my dear brother every time I see you," he murmured, his eyes filling with easy tears.

"I hope I may take that as a compliment, Uncle," she replied with a smile.

"Oh, you may, you may. Would that I was fond of *all* my kinsfolk," he muttered as his brother-in-law approached, but then gave a brisk smile as he took the lawyer's hand and pumped it. "George, m'dear fellow, it's excellent to see you again," he said untruthfully, then clapped the lawyer on the back and ushered him into the house.

Caro moved closer to Summer. "Where did you encounter Uncle Bradshaw?"

"At the Black Lion in Tetbury."

"Poor you." Caro smiled. "To be truthful, I wish we didn't have to invite him, but as he's Mama's brother, we couldn't really leave him out." She shivered, for the hillside was exposed to the wind from the estuary, which from here was visible as a wide silver ribbon that curved inland between the flat eastern shore and the much steeper hills of the Welsh borderland on the other side. She linked Summer's arm. "Come on inside before we freeze."

They hurried toward the house and laughed with relief as

they entered the hall, where a huge log fire flickered in the hearth of an impressive carved and gilded chimneypiece.

A maid had already assisted George Bradshaw with his outdoor clothes, and as she came to take Summer's cloak and muff, Caro spoke to her. "Have tea brought to my room," she said, then caught Summer's hand to lead her toward the straight stone staircase at the far end of the hall. "Come upstairs, for I wish to tell you all about Francis."

Having no desire to take tea in Mr. Bradshaw's gloomy presence, Summer made no complaint as she accompanied her cousin up to a dark-paneled passage that led to the bedrooms at the front of the house, all of which enjoyed magnificent views toward the estuary.

Caro's room was firelit and comfortable, with chairs and sofas that were upholstered with blue-and-cream tapestry, and matching hangings on the four-poster bed. There was a mullioned bow window with a fine seat to which Summer was ushered as her cousin went to bring an ivory-framed miniature from her bedside, before joining her in the window.

"Well? What do you say, Olivia? Is Francis not the most adorably handsome man you ever saw?" she breathed, her green eyes shining with love as she pressed the little portrait into Summer's hands.

With dark hair, soft brown eyes, and sensitive lips, the Honorable Francis Lytherby gazed almost wistfully out of the frame. He was indeed romantically handsome, and clearly a man of high fashion too, for his high-collared mustard coat was very stylish, and there was something undeniably à la mode about his large, intricately knotted neckcloth.

"Well?" Caro prompted impatiently.

"Yes, he's *very* good-looking indeed," Summer agreed, thinking that Brand was more handsome by far, but then beauty was in the eye of the beholder, was it not?

Caro took the miniature and clasped it to her breast. "Oh, Summer, I'm more happy than I could ever believe possible, and yet six months ago I hated coming here. After the grandeur of Merriam Park this house seemed odiously poky, and I was brought so horribly low by poor Father's reduced circumstances that I thought I'd never be happy again. Then we received an invitation to a ball at Berkeley Castle, I met Francis, and that was that. It was love at first sight, truly it was, and I cannot believe I am so fortunate as to be the object of his love too."

"He's clearly a paragon."

"Oh, he is, he is!"

"Good heavens, he really has got you all at sixes and sevens, hasn't he?" Summer observed with a tolerant smile.

Caro met her eyes seriously. "I'd *die* if I could not marry him, truly I would, and now I live in dread that his father will find some reason to forbid the match. I *certainly* can't believe that the betrothal will still go ahead in two weeks' time."

Summer fended off her own guilty conscience. "What's all this about, Caro? You've hinted in your letters that you think Lord Lytherby has changed his mind, but you haven't said why."

"I believe he now wants Melinda Huntingford as his daughter-in-law."

"Who?" It was the first time Summer had heard the name.

"His ward, the Honorable Miss Melinda Huntingford." Caro sighed. "Oh, Olivia, she's so beautiful, and she loves Francis, I *know* she does! You should see how she makes up to him whenever she can. She's always touching him, smiling at him, and giving him warm glances . . . I feel drab and inadequate in comparison."

"Drab and inadequate are things you'll never be, Caro Merriam," Summer said, putting a quick hand over her cousin's. "Besides, Francis loves you, not this Melinda person."

"I know, and he has no idea that I suspect his father of changing his mind."

"But does Francis himself suspect his father?"

"No, of that I'm quite certain."

Summer was puzzled. "Then why are *you* so convinced? And besides, why would Lord Lytherby *suddenly* want Francis to marry his ward? Surely, he would have pressed for such a match *before* agreeing to let Francis marry you?"

Caro looked helplessly at her and shrugged. "I can't answer

any of those questions, Olivia, but I still have this . . . this *awful* feeling deep inside."

"I'm sure you must be wrong. If the Honorable Melinda were his lordship's choice, he'd have said so from the outset. You're seeing bugbears where there are none, and the betrothal will take place, I'm certain of it, so stop worrying."

A small smile crept to Caro's lips. "Yes, I mustn't let my fears run away with me."

"Correct."

"Well, you'll soon see for yourself, for it's the annual Bevincote masked ball in two days' time, and you'll meet them all then, including Melinda Huntingford. Oh, I loathe her, Olivia, for recently she has become the most *odious* creature that ever was, and yet when we first met, I really liked her. Now, in front of me, all she does is give Francis longing looks, smiling at him, flattering him, and generally flirting with him in the most outrageous way. She behaves as if I don't exist!"

Summer smiled. "Then we'll present a united front and behave as if *she* doesn't exist either."

Caro managed a laugh. "Oh, it's good to have you here, Olivia."

"So come, let's change the subject to something more agreeable. What did you do over Christmas?"

Caro's eyes took on a gloating gleam. "What did I do? Why, I was presented to His Royal Highness, the Duke of Clarence," she declared lightly, as if it were the most ordinary thing in the world.

Summer stared, then laughed. "Caro Merriam, for a moment I actually believed you!"

"But it's true. The Duke of Clarence, and the Duke of Chandworth, and the Earl of . . . oh, I don't know what, and many more. They all came to the castle for the coming-of-age celebrations of Lord and Lady Berkeley's firstborn son." Caro leaned forward conspiratorially. "Actually, their firstborn isn't their first *legitimately* born," she whispered.

"Caro, I'm shocked at you!

"It's true. Anyway, that's another story, for I was telling

you of the celebrations. Well, everyone in the county attended, including we humble Merriams, and I was one of those who were presented to the Duke of Clarence, much to dear Melinda's fury, for she was not so fortunate, although she *did* dance with the Duke of Chandworth, who—after Francis, of course—was easily the most handsome gentleman present."

Summer smiled, for the duke was reckoned one of England's most eligible young aristocrats. Handsome and *débonnaire,* he was the object of much conspiring by predatory mamas, anxious to see their daughters become the Duchess of Chandworth.

Nothing more was said because at that moment the maid brought the tray of tea and set it on the window seat between them. Then, just as Caro leaned over to pick up the dainty silver teapot, Summer suddenly found herself back in the beach apartment because Andrew brought her trance to an end.

He smiled down at her. "Better now?"

Summer just hadn't remembered how short this trance was to be, therefore the transition from past to present came as quite a shock. For a moment or so she still expected Caro to press a cup of tea into her hands, but the window seat and her pretty redheaded cousin were far away in 1807.

Andrew looked inquiringly at her. "Well? *Are* you better now?"

"Yes, much," she answered truthfully. "I was just so engrossed in what Caro and I were talking about that I clean forgot I had to return to the future. Then there's this business of not feeling so full of beans here in my own time. Darn it, I wish I had Olivia's constitution!" She sat up and looked across at Chrissie, who was curled up on a nearby chair in a peach toweling robe, her hair fluffy because it was freshly dried.

Chrissie grinned. "Hi, there, oh mighty time traveler."

"Hi."

Andrew was pleased Summer's mood had lightened. "It's good to see you smile again. Now then, tell us all about it, because we have no idea what went on after you drove up to Oakhill House. Did you like your relatives?"

"Oh, yes." She began to recount it all.

When she'd finished, he raised an eyebrow. "So I guess you want to attend this masked wingding, mm?"

The ball at Bevincote? Oh, yes, she wanted to be there, for apart from wanting to meet Caro's Francis, she was filled with curiosity about Lord Lytherby and the Honorable Melinda Huntingford. She grinned at Andrew. "I sure do."

"Then Cinders, you *shall* go to the ball," he declared in a pantomime voice.

They all three laughed, but the past was still only the press of a button away, and Summer knew she was too interested in Caro's woes to be patient enough to wait until the night of the ball.

For a while she'd set aside her hurt over Brand, but her next secretly taken excursion to 1807 was going to supply a very sharp and disquieting reminder of the indiscretions at the Black Lion.

Chapter Eight

The following morning, having taken time off to be with Summer during her stay, Chrissie and Andrew had to return to their respective places of employment, he to his Chichester practice, Chrissie to the small real estate office she and a friend had opened nearby. Alone in the apartment, Summer immediately and without any nod in the direction of conscience, resorted to the cassette recorder.

This time her journey back in time found Olivia riding alone toward the estuary. Her horse was a bay hunter, and she was wearing a rose woolen riding habit with black braiding on the jacket. Her hair was pinned up beneath a top hat, and her face was partially concealed by a net veil. It was a cold but bright winter morning, and the sun had yet to melt the overnight frost. Seagulls called overheard, and from time to time she heard the lonely cry of a curlew.

She was riding along one of the deserted tracks that led toward the estuary through an isolated area she now knew was appropriately named the End of the World. A barely perceptible breeze rippled the water in the dikes on either side of the track and whispered through the elms and willows that were the most common wild trees in these parts. A few hundred yards ahead of her was the grassy medieval embankment that was all that stood between these bleak low-lying acres and the Severn estuary, which was nearly two miles across at this point.

She meant to ride as far as a little derelict chapel she'd seen from her bedroom window that morning. Fourteenth-century monks had built it on the embankment, together with its fellow on the opposite shore, to guide ships through the treacherous sandy channels and submerged rocks of the estuary, and that was a function they both still served, even though they had both long since fallen into ruin.

She reined in at the bottom of the embankment to look back at Oakhill House and the church, but instead her astonished gaze was drawn to the hilltop above which peeped gilded tops of domes and pinnacles very like those her modern self knew would soon adorn the Royal Pavilion in Brighton. It was Bevincote, which by any standard was an example of amazing extravagance. Caro had told her that Lord Lytherby had spent much of his youth in India, and that on inheriting the estate in England, he'd razed the original house to the ground to put an eastern palace in its place. The lengthy business of building a portion of the Orient in this otherwise quiet corner of Gloucestershire had only been finished two years ago, and must have cost a very large fortune indeed.

After gazing at it for a minute or so, Summer turned to the front again and urged the hunter to the top of the embankment. The tide was out, and the estuary was a wasteland of mud, rocks, channels, and sandbanks, at the far side of which lay the fertile patchwork hills of the Welsh borderland. She rode along the path that led along the top of the embankment toward the ruined chapel, a few hundred yards beyond which lay one of the fox coverts that had once formed part of the vanished Forest of Horwood.

At last she reached the chapel, which afforded a little shelter from the icy salt-laden air coming off the estuary. She dismounted in the lee of the ruin, tethered the horse to a thick stem of the ivy that had grown over much of the ancient stone walls, then went around the front into what remained of the building. Because of the shaft of pale daylight that fell through the arched doorway onto the wall directly opposite, she noticed that over the centuries people had carved dates and their initials. Graffiti, even here, she thought.

Then one carving in particular caught her eye. It was at eye level by the entrance, on an otherwise untouched surface. S & S 1719. She wondered who S & S had been. Lovers maybe?

As she went closer, a tender whisper breathed softly through the chapel, as if someone—a man—were in the shadows behind her. *I, Stephen, adore thee, Susannah . . .*

Long gone joy filled the chapel, and her eyes flew to the initials. Stephen and Susannah! As Summer Stanway she'd never been psychic, but Olivia Courtenay clearly was. For a second or so the whisper continued to echo softly among the stones. *I, Stephen, adore thee, Susannah . . .*

Then the breeze got up suddenly, and the ghostly sound was lost in the rustle of the ivy that grew so profusely around the ruins. She leaned against the doorway to gaze across the estuary, hoping that Stephen and Susannah remained as happy all their lives as they'd been when they carved their initials. Then her eyes lowered as she wished Olivia Courtenay's life were still as joyous as it had been for those few hours in Brand's arms at the Black Lion. But he had left her feeling like a whore. So much for happiness . . .

She didn't hear the other horse approaching from the fox covert farther along the embankment. The gentleman was riding at a slow canter as he too made for the chapel, a natural landmark on the estuary. He wore a pine green coat, leather riding breeches, and highly polished boots, and his top hat was tilted back on his head. His horse was a mettlesome gray, but he kept it effortlessly under control, hardly seeming to do a thing as he reined in about twenty feet away. He had no idea anyone was already there, for she was out of sight in the doorway, and her own mount was tethered at the rear of the building.

It wasn't until his horse snorted and shook its bridle that Summer became aware of him. She straightened uneasily to peep toward the sound, and her heart almost stopped with shock and dismay, for the rider was none other than Brand! Shaken, she stared at him. How could he *possibly* be in this isolated spot in the middle of nowhere!

Almost as if he sensed someone's eyes upon him, he turned suddenly toward the chapel. She drew hastily out of sight, pressing back against Stephen and Susannah's initials and praying he didn't decide to investigate the building. Her heart was thundering, and her mouth had run dry. Of all the unkind tricks fate could play upon her, this was surely one of the worst. He couldn't be here, he *couldn't*!

She tried to marshal her spinning thoughts. Maybe he was just passing through! But even as this improbable hope struck her, she eliminated it. No one *passed through* the End of the World, which was well and truly off the beaten track, and besides, he was riding now, and had been in a carriage the last time she saw him, so at the very least he had to be staying somewhere in the neighborhood. Maybe he even *lived* in the area! Her heart sank. Perhaps he knew Caro and Uncle Merriam, or, more likely, he knew the Lytherbys! She closed her eyes tightly. Please don't let this be happening, *please*! But when she opened them again, she knew it was. Her shocking misconduct at the Black Lion had followed her, and suddenly she had the most awful premonition that it was going to harm Caro's betrothal.

Brand's horse snorted again, and to her horror her hunter whinnied in reply. Knowing Brand was almost certain to investigate, she edged into the shadows away from the daylight by the chapel doorway. She heard him ride a little nearer, and then the squeak of leather as he dismounted. His shadow crossed the entrance as he went to see what other horse was nearby. He couldn't help but know it was a woman, for the sidesaddle would tell him as much, and the quality of both horse and saddle would tell him it was a lady. She closed her eyes again. *A lady!* No doubt that was the last way he would ever describe her.

She heard him murmur to the horse and pat its neck, then he called out. "Hello? Is anyone here?"

She didn't reply.

"Hello?"

Still she remained silent, and after a moment his tall figure blotted out the sunlight in the doorway.

"I know someone is here," he said then.

To her dismay he came farther in.

As his eyes grew accustomed to the darkness he saw her pressing back against the wall, but was unable to make out her face because of her veil. "Please don't be afraid, for I mean you no harm, madam. I just wish to be sure you are all right," he said gently.

"I'm quite well, sir," she said, altering her voice slightly in the hope he wouldn't recognize it.

There was a moment's silence, then suddenly a flame burst into life as he took a little bottle of luminaries from his pocket and held one up.

Quickly, she turned her face away. "I wish to be left alone, sir," she said, still disguising her voice.

But he came a little nearer, his face demonic in the flame light. "I believe I know you, madam," he said then, trying to see her face behind the veil.

She made to walk past him, but he caught her arm, holding the flame closer, and in the few seconds before it went out he at last recognized her.

"You!"

"Please let me go!" she cried, trying to wrest herself away.

"What in God's name are you doing *here*?" he demanded, keeping his grip.

"It's none of your concern, sirrah! I wish nothing more to do with you, and request you to let me go!"

"Not until you've answered my question. What are you doing here?"

"It's none of your concern," she said again.

"I'm making it my concern," he replied, dragging her closer to the doorway and pushing her veil back in order to see her properly. His blue eyes were piercing as they gazed down into hers. "Now then, Olivia, what are you doing here?" he demanded a third time.

She didn't reply, but pressed her lips mutinously together.

"Damn you, I demand an answer!"

His arrogance provoked her. "Oh, *do* you! Well, I seem to recall hoping for an answer from you when last we saw each other, but I did not receive one then, so you certainly will not receive one now!"

"Believe me, madam, I bitterly regret what passed between us at the Black Lion," he snapped.

"*You* regret it? Sirrah, what you feel can be as nothing to the disgust and self-loathing I feel for having sullied myself with you! I can only put such lack of taste and moderation down to a sip too much of cider punch!"

Fury flashed into his eyes. "Have a care, madam!" he breathed.

But something swept her beyond caution. "Have a care? Why should I? You are beneath contempt, a so-called gentleman who is really nothing of the kind. I think you are the most base and shabby creature I ever met, and if I could turn the clock back, believe me I would not give you a second glance! I wish I could scourge myself free of every vile kiss you gave me!"

Her furious words caught him on a nerve. "So you found my kisses vile, did you? I doubt that very much, my dear, but what I do *not* doubt is that you are a woman of considerable experience, very far from the innocent widow you purported to be at the Black Lion. How many lovers have you had, Olivia? Or should I call them clients, for that is probably closer to the mark!"

"How *dare* you!" she cried, raising her riding crop to strike him, but he caught her wrist, then pushed her roughly back to the wall.

"I could almost believe such a fine display of outrage, but unfortunately it doesn't quite ring true. You're a whore to your fingertips, my dear, and if I were to take you against this wall, I have no doubt it wouldn't be the first or last time you've known the experience."

He put a hand to her thigh through her riding habit skirt, and suddenly bent his head to put his lips over hers. He was too strong for her to push away, and although she struggled, he continued the kiss at his leisure, moving his hand over her leg and then gripping her buttock to force her against his loins.

Anger gripped him, but he was aroused by the writhing of her body against his. She felt his virility stiffening like steel, invoking memories she wished to forget, but his lips, harsh and cruel though they were, were almost too much to resist. She wanted him! Even like this, she wanted him! Just as happened in the orchard, she was swept almost to climax just to feel his masculinity pressing her though their clothes. Then she recalled other things too, like the cold loathing in his eyes as he'd left without speaking to her in the courtyard, and the way he'd called her whore!

With a huge effort she raised her riding crop to strike him furiously again and again until he pulled away to stop the rain of blows. In a trice she'd gathered her cumbersome skirts to run to her horse.

She heard him come after her, but managed to haul herself on to the saddle before he reached her. As she tried to urge her mount away, Brand lunged forward and seized the bridle, but she beat him wildly with the crop until he let go again. The moment his grip loosened, she kicked her heels furiously, and the hunter jerked away at headlong pace. She glanced back, and saw Brand dashing toward his own horse. He was going to give chase!

She flung her frightened mount down the embankment toward the track, then galloped at full stretch toward the road. On reaching it, she didn't turn toward the gates of Oakhill House, but went in the opposite direction toward the crossroad she knew lay a hundred yards or so beyond a bend. From there, instead of taking one of the other roads, she urged the hunter through an open gate into a field and hid behind a barn.

She heard the clatter of his approaching horse, for he'd seen her turn left on leaving the track. At the crossroad he reined in, and she saw him glancing around. She might have taken any of the roads, and he knew it. For a long moment he remained where he was, controlling his capering mount with consummate ease as before. Anger darkened his handsome face as he decided to choose the road to Berkeley.

As the sound of his horse gradually diminished into the distance, she emerged from her hiding place and quickly returned to Oakhill House. At last she reached the sanctuary of the stables, and on dismounting rested her forehead weakly against the hunter's neck. She could feel punishment for her wantonness creeping inexorably closer. Oh, why, *why* had she been so irresponsible at the Black Lion? She'd *known* how harmful her conduct could be to Caro, but she selfishly went ahead anyway. And all for a few stolen hours between the sheets with a man who now clearly despised her! She deserved to suffer the consequences of such foolhardiness, but poor Caro didn't.

Tears stung her eyes. "Oh, Caro, I'm sorry, I'm sorry . . ." she whispered, but then light steps hurried toward her, and she turned to see Caro herself approaching, looking very sweet and pretty in white-dotted lime dimity.

As Caro's lips parted to speak, the visit to the past ended, and Summer found herself lying on her bed in the beach apartment.

A key was turning in the main door, and she sat up with a gasp.

Chrissie hurried in. "Summer? Summer, are you okay? Where are you?"

Puzzled, Summer called out to her. "I'm in here, Chrissie. What's wrong?"

Chrissie almost ran in. Her face was pale and tense as she halted at the bedside. "What's wrong? Are you having a hypo, or something?"

Summer stared up at her. "Am I *what*? Why on earth do you think that?"

"Because I've been trying for ages to call you on the phone, and you haven't answered! After you forgot your insulin yesterday, I thought you might be ill, and . . ." Tears filled Chrissie's eyes, and she sat down abruptly on the bed.

Dismayed with guilt, Summer scrambled over to put her arms around her. "Please don't cry, Chrissie. I'm fine, truly I am. I just came to lie down, and I must have fallen asleep."

"I can't believe you didn't hear the phone at all."

"I didn't, honestly."

Chrissie dabbed her eyes, and then gave a sheepish smile. "Now I've mussed my eye makeup, right?"

"Just a tad. Nothing a minute in front of the mirror can't put right." Summer felt awful.

Chrissie drew a long breath. "I *know* I shouldn't get in such a state over you, but I just can't help it."

"You'll *have* to help it when I go home to Boston," Summer pointed out gently.

"I know," Chrissie got up. "Well, I guess I'd better tidy myself up and get back to the real estate grindstone." She went through to the bathroom.

Self-reproach flooded through Summer, and she lowered her eyes to the floor. As Olivia she was at fault because of Caro, and as herself she was at fault because of Chrissie! Guilty on both counts.

After a few minutes Chrissie called from the door. "See you later!"

"Okay!"

The outer door closed, and Summer got up to look out at the sea. She could still taste Brand's contemptuous kiss and feel his body pressing harshly to hers, and shame crept into her heart as she recalled how much she'd wanted him, how much she'd probably always want him from now on. The damage was done; Olivia Courtenay was in love with him, and so, God help her, was Summer Stanway.

Chapter Nine

Summer gave her adventures in time and memory a wide berth for the rest of that day, but by the following morning—in 1807 the day of the annual masked ball at Bevincote—the temptation once again proved irresistible. She knew what she intended to do as soon as Chrissie and Andrew had gone to work, so before they left, she reassured Chrissie she'd be a very good girl. She also said she intended to take a long walk along the beach, so not to worry this time if the phone went unanswered.

The apartment was very quiet as she lay on the bed and pressed the button. Then Andrew's voice spoke softly into the silence of the bedroom, the music washed over her, and she felt herself drifting pleasurably away into that other world she'd begun to crave so much.

The rattle of wheels on cobbles made her open her eyes this time. It was a sunny but cold morning, and an ox wagon was lumbering along the narrow Berkeley street where she and Caro were laughing happily as they hurried arm-in-arm on the pavement. Caro was wearing a sea green cloak with a hood that was trimmed with white fur; Olivia wore a royal blue velvet pelisse and a wide-brimmed gray gypsy hat with gray-and-blue striped ribbons. She'd chosen the hat with great care today, because when wearing it she had only to lower her head slightly to conceal her face, which *had* to be a consideration now she knew Brand was somewhere in the vicinity. Her greatest fear—or was it secret thrill?—was that he would attend the ball tonight, for although she'd be masked, she still felt he might recognize her. She'd certainly know him, if only by his distinctive golden hair.

Uncle Merriam and George Bradshaw had come into town to conduct a little business, and the cousins had accompanied the men in order for Caro to purchase some last-minute trimmings for the Bevincote ball. She had belatedly decided to adorn her mask with little green beads to match her gown, and there was an excellent haberdasher's shop in the town, so they were en route there right now.

Berkeley Castle dominated the little town. It was a medieval fortress that had not suffered greatly from the ravages of time, and the same family had occupied it throughout the centuries, gradually turning it from stronghold into gracious home. The *beau monde* of London flocked across its drawbridge, and it was seldom there wasn't a gathering of very superior guests enjoying its renowned hospitality. The frequent presence of so many persons of quality meant there was a demand for high-class haberdashery, and as a consequence the seemingly insignificant shop nestling in the shadow of the castle walls was filled to bursting with all manner of fashion notions, from ribbons and lace of every description, to the sort of buttons, sequins, and spangles that would have held their own at any Mayfair assembly.

As the cousins hurried along the pavement, they could hear the Berkeley Hunt foxhounds in their kennels about a quarter of a mile along the road to Oakhill. There was to be a hunt tomorrow, so the famous pack was being prepared. Practically the whole of Gloucestershire society would converge on Berkeley, gentlemen *and* ladies, although the latter would either keep company at the castle or watch the sport from vantage points. The hounds sensed they'd soon be in full cry across the countryside, and their excited yelps and barking carried clearly on the almost still winter air, but then one hound gave a long howl, and Summer came to an abrupt halt.

Caro stopped too and looked quizzically at her. "What's wrong?"

"That howl makes me shiver." Summer gave a rueful smile

then and explained about the "werewolf" at the Black Lion, omitting all mention of Brand, of course.

Caro's eyes widened. "Oh, how horrid."

"It was," Summer agreed, beginning to walk on.

Suddenly, there was a commotion behind them, and they saw a carriage and four negotiating the corner from the market square. Summer gazed at it with dismayed recognition, for there was no mistaking the team of four perfectly matched chestnuts, the superb green-lacquered bodywork, and the gleaming brass of Brand's carriage.

The street was so narrow that the cousins had to press back for the vehicle to pass, and Summer caught a brief glimpse of Brand. He wasn't wearing his top hat, and his arm was resting along the window ledge, his gloved fingers drumming impatiently. She lowered her gaze quickly in case he should look out, and as the carriage drove on, she looked quickly at Caro. "Do you know whose carriage that was?" she asked, trying not to sound overinterested.

"I have no idea."

Summer was both relieved and frustrated. Relieved that her cousin wasn't acquainted with Brand, frustrated that she herself still didn't know who he was. "You didn't recognize the crest on the door?"

"No." Caro glanced curiously at her. "Why?"

"Oh, I just wondered. I thought I saw the same carriage as I was leaving Tetbury, and I was just curious."

Caro pursed her lips knowingly. "Hm, well, having observed the peculiarly handsome gentleman inside, I can well understand your desire to know his identity."

Summer colored. "It isn't like that at all."

"No?"

"No!"

"You don't have to snap my head off, you know."

Summer lowered her eyes. "I didn't mean to."

"I forgive you. Now come on, if we don't get on with my purchase, we'll be late meeting Father and Uncle Bradshaw to eat at the Crown."

They reached the haberdasher's shop and went in. Soon

they were poring over the vast selection of beads, and as Summer inspected some particularly pretty pink ones with a view to buying them herself, she glanced thoughtfully at Caro. "What do you think of Mr. Bradshaw?" she asked lightly.

"He's more disagreeable than ever," Caro replied, pulling a face. "Do you know, I actually begin to think he doesn't want me to marry Francis?"

"Oh?" Summer looked intently at her. "Why do you say that?"

"He pours cold water on anything to do with it, but I suppose he pours cold water on absolutely *everything*."

"Yes, he does," Summer murmured. So Caro thought the same as she did. Her brow furrowed a little as she pondered what possible reason George Bradshaw could have for not wishing his niece to marry Francis Lytherby.

They left the haberdasher's shop and hastened back through the town to the Crown Inn, where they were to meet the two gentlemen. Almost immediately Summer became aware of a change in Uncle Merriam. On the way from Oakhill House he'd been in good spirits, but now he was oddly quiet, as if something momentous were suddenly weighing on his mind.

"Is something wrong, Uncle?" she asked concernedly as they all four sat down at the table d'hôte.

He gave George Bradshaw a surreptitious glance. "No, of course not," he replied swiftly. Too swiftly, she thought, following his glance.

The meal was hearty—a tasty chicken soup, followed by Severn salmon with oyster sauce, then lamb and all the trimmings, and apple pie. Summer smiled a little wryly as she ate, for as her real self she wouldn't have dared to eat so much, but as Olivia there were no restrictions on her diet, and did it feel *good*!

As the two gentlemen took glasses of mulled ale at the end of the meal, something made Summer look up at the smoky mirror above the mantelpiece. To her immense shock, she saw Jeremy Fenwick's face gazing back at her from the doorway behind her. She whirled about, but there was no one there. For a moment she was too startled to move, but then she murmured an excuse and got up to hurry out. The door led into a passage, and then into the street, but of Jeremy there was no sign.

Caro came out after her. "Aren't you feeling well, Summer?"

Summer gave her a quick smile. "I'm fine, it's just . . ."

"Yes?"

"You'll think this foolish, but I was *sure* I saw Jeremy in the mirror."

Caro was blank for a moment. "Jeremy? Oh, you mean Major Fenwick, Roderick's friend?"

"Yes." Summer glanced along the pavement again. "It *was* him, I'm certain it was, although . . ." She paused. "He wasn't wearing his uniform," she said then.

"Which means you *must* be mistaken, for during this endless war with France all soldiers must wear their uniforms, and besides, what on earth would he be doing here in Berkeley?"

"I have no idea."

Caro linked her arm. "That mirror in the Crown *is* very smoky; in fact, I doubt if it's ever been cleaned, so don't give it another thought. Whoever you saw, it can't have been Major Fenwick. Come on, I've persuaded Father to leave now, for I wish to get back so I can sew all these wretched beads on my mask, and I fear it's going to take an age." She drew Summer back into the inn, then through into the yard at the back, where the two gentlemen were waiting impatiently by the carriage.

But as they drove out of Berkeley, Summer's thoughts returned to Jeremy. Nothing Caro said would really persuade her she hadn't seen him, for she knew him too well to be mistaken. She also knew him too well not to accurately read the expression on his face when he'd realized she was there. He'd been startled, then dismayed; in fact he'd been very anxious indeed *not* to be seen! But why? What possible reason could he have for being in this part of the world without at least *speaking* to her? She was still mulling over the mystery when the carriage turned in through the gates of Oakhill House, but then the cassette recorder brought her abruptly back to the present.

She lay where she was for a few minutes before getting up to make herself some coffee. Then she leaned against a table to dwell some more on the many unanswered questions that had now arisen in her previous existence. Why was Jeremy in Berkeley, and at such pains to avoid her? What had upset Uncle Merriam? Why did George Bradshaw oppose Caro's match? Was Lord Lytherby equally opposed to it, or was Caro imagining it? Would Olivia encounter Brand again? Would her indiscretions come to light? The list seemed as endless as it was intriguing, and oh, *how* she wanted to know the answers!

She glanced at her cup and suddenly remembered it was one she'd seen Jack use when they'd been here last year. Remorsefully, she put it down, for she'd hardly thought of him at all for a day or so now; yet for the last six months she'd thought of nothing else. Now it was Brand who crept unbidden into her waking thoughts—Brand whose smile she longed for, Brand whose lovemaking she needed, Brand whom she loved.

Tears filled her eyes. "Oh, Jack, I'm so sorry," she whispered and almost ran to the bedroom to get out all the photograph albums. She took them into the living room and put them on the sofa, but before she sat down to browse guiltily through them, her glance wandered to the bottles of spirits on the corner table. To hell with diabetes just this once, she thought, and poured herself a very generous glass of Chrissie's vodka, then settled down to resurrect her neglected memories of Jack.

Page after page of cherished snapshots passed before her eyes, and the vodka affected her because she was no longer accustomed to it. Tears trickled slowly down her cheeks as she ran a loving fingertip over a favorite close-up of Jack, but even now she couldn't put Brand from her thoughts.

The photograph album slid from her lap as she hid her face in her hands and gave in to heartbreak. How long she sobbed she didn't know, but she was still weeping quietly when Chrissie came home.

Chrissie glanced at the albums and telltale empty glass. "Oh, Summer!" she cried.

Wiping her eyes, Summer sat up penitently. "I'm sorry, Chrissie . . ."

"So you should be! Can't you be trusted at *all?* The albums

I can sympathize with, but not the vodka! You're not supposed to have alcohol, so it was a stupid, stupid thing to do!"

"I know, I just felt bad about Jack . . ."

Chrissie was too mad to say anything more. Instead she conveyed the offending glass into the kitchen, where she then gave another angry exclamation as she found that Summer had forgotten to switch on the oven. She banged the oven door closed. Now they'd have to eat salad instead of the beef ragout she'd so painstakingly prepared, and she wasn't pleased.

There was an atmosphere when Andrew came home later, but he tactfully said nothing, although he must have felt as if World War III were in the offing. Chrissie picked away at Summer all evening, but it finally came to a head when Andrew casually remarked that he fancied a Chinese carryout.

Chrissie replied to him, but looked darkly at Summer. "Well, you wouldn't be so hungry if we'd had the beef ragout we were supposed to!"

Summer leapt irritably to her feet. "What makes you think your darned ragout's so special? You never season it enough!"

"At least I can make one, which is more than can be said of you!" Chrissie fired back.

"Oh, for God's sake, give it a rest, Chrissie! You've been on my case for hours now, and I've just about had it!"

"If I'm on your case, it's because you deserve it!"

"You're getting to be a real pain, Chrissie Marchant!" Summer cried, venting her fury by throwing a cushion across the room.

Andrew had been toying uncomfortably with his piece of pottery, wishing to God he'd never heard of China, but as the cushion flew past him, he got up hastily. "Look, this is getting out of hand. I don't know what it's about, but I'm sure there's no need for—!"

"Oh, no?" Summer's bright gaze flew to this new target. "We haven't even *started* yet!"

Chrissie was outraged. "Don't you *dare* pick on him!"

Summer flung from the room and slammed the door behind her.

Andrew sighed and sat down again, giving Chrissie an inquiring look. "Well? Are you going to let me in on this, or must I guess?" he asked patiently.

Some time later, Summer was leaning out of her window, watching the sea, when she recognized her sister's hesitant knock at the door. She straightened warily and turned. "Yes?"

Chrissie came in slowly. "I'm sorry," she said quietly.

Summer's anger dissolved. "I deserved it," she conceded. "It was irresponsible to drink that vodka, spiteful to turn on Andrew, and dumb to forget the ragout."

"Oh, to hell with the rotten ragout!" Chrissie ran to her, and they held each other close.

Summer gave a wobbly smile. "I promise I won't do it again, Chrissie, so *please* don't fret about me tomorrow."

"I'll do my best, but I guess I'm just a natural-born fussbudget. Are you coming back to watch TV a while?"

Summer drew back and shook her head. "Don't take this the wrong way, but I think I'll go to bed now. I've had a few lousy nights recently and need a long laze, and as it's Saturday tomorrow, I can have a good lie-up in the morning as well."

Chrissie smiled. "Okay. Sleep well."

"I will. Oh, and tell Andrew I'll grovel suitably tomorrow."

Chrissie smiled, and the door closed behind her.

Summer drew a long breath. Sleep was the last thing on her mind, for tonight was the night of the masked ball at Bevincote, and she was no more capable of staying away than she was of flying.

Chapter Ten

Summer turned the recorder volume down because she didn't want anything to be heard accidentally from the passage. Then she lay back and commenced her breathing exercises. She knew a moment of alarm because the cassette sounded distorted, as if the recorder's batteries were almost spent, but then it seemed okay again, so she relaxed and began to sink into the trance.

The tinkle of hairpins told her she was Olivia again, and she opened her eyes to find herself seated before the dressing table in her room at Oakhill House. A lighted candlestick stood beside the mirror before her, and the room was also firelit. It was a large, very beautiful room, with dark oak paneling on the walls, and a low ceiling of richly patterned plasterwork. The bed had a cream silk canopy and was so large that a little set of steps was required to climb into it, but it was very comfortable, and close enough to the fire to never be cold.

Like Caro's room, this one also had a window seat that enjoyed a fine view toward the estuary, but the maroon damask curtains were drawn because the winter night was very cold and dark. It had become windy now, and from time to time she heard the scratch of ivy on the front of the house as it was blown against the glass.

Caro's maid was combing her hair for the ball. Her name was Gwenny, and she was a local girl, the daughter of a plowman on one of the End of the World farms. She had straight brown hair, which she piled on top of her head beneath a hand-embroidered mobcap, and her full-bosomed country figure was neat in a simple blue woolen dress and crisp white apron. The position at Oakhill House was not her first; indeed before coming here she'd been employed at Berkeley Castle itself, where she'd acquired great skills when it came to fashionable coiffures, but her mother's ill health required her to work closer to home, and so she'd taken the post with Caro, whom she'd already attended tonight. Caro was now virtually ready in her room, but still agonizing over the final detail of which jewelry to wear.

Gwenny had pinned Olivia's black hair into the style known as *à l'Égyptienne,* which consisted of a froth of little curls at the front with the rest of the hair pulled back and tightly plaited before being coiled into a corkscrew shape that was adorned with a jeweled comb. It was an intricate style, but very à la mode, and was worn with a circlet of two dainty gold chains that held a turquoise-studded ornament in the center of her forehead. The ornament would be shown off to great advantage when she donned her domino, a gold velvet eye mask with a little gauze veil that concealed the lower half of her face. Her gold-embroidered turquoise silk evening gown was very décolleté and high waisted, with tiny sleeves and a lavishly trimmed hem.

Gwenny put the comb and last pins down, then met Summer's eyes in the mirror. "Will that do, madam?"

"It's excellent, Gwenny, thank you. Berkeley Castle's loss is definitely Oakhill House's gain," Summer replied, smiling and then smoothing her long white evening gloves so there wasn't a wrinkle in sight.

There was a tap at the door, and Caro's green-masked face peeped in. "Are you nearly ready? Father has instructed the carriage to be brought to the door."

"Yes, I'm ready, Caro. Come in and let me see you."

Summer nodded at Gwenny. "That will be all now. I'll attend to my cloak myself."

"As you wish, madam." The maid bobbed a curtsy and withdrew, closing the door softly behind her.

Caro turned for her simple emerald satin slip and gauze overgown and elegant coiffure to be admired, and Summer smiled approvingly. "You look absolutely beautiful," she declared truthfully.

"Do you really think so? I don't know what to think anymore, for I'm so nervous I feel positively sick," Caro confessed. "I wondered if the rose taffeta would look better after all, and if my pearls——"

Summer got up quickly and interrupted. "Believe me, Caro, you look exquisite. Francis will adore you all over again," she said reassuringly, squeezing her cousin's fingers. "Francis Lytherby is a very fortunate fellow to have snared you, and I trust he knows it."

"*I'm* the fortunate one, Olivia, as you'll realize when you meet him."

"So you keep insisting."

Caro laughed self-consciously. "Forgive me for thinking only of myself," she said, and then glanced enviously at Summer's gown and hair. "You look very lovely too, Olivia. Oh, how I wish I had a figure like yours."

Uncle Merriam's voice echoed along the passage from the top of the staircase. "Come on, ladies, or it will be time to come home before we've even left!"

As Caro hurried out to get her cloak, Summer put on her own cloak and looped her reticule and fan over her wrist, and then went back to the dressing table to don the domino. She gazed at her masked reflection in the mirror. If Brand were there tonight, surely he couldn't *possibly* recognize her now! She turned away. The longer she stayed here at Oakhill House, the more likely it was that Brand would find out exactly who she was, so for Caro's sake it would be better if within the next day or so cousin Olivia found some pressing reason to return to Kensington. But Brand filled her heart as well as her fears, so knowing what was best and actually bringing herself to do it were things that were poles apart.

She left the room and joined Caro, and together they went down to the entrance hall, where Uncle Merriam and George Bradshaw were waiting. Both men wore plain black velvet eye masks and formal evening clothes, but even on an occasion like this the lawyer managed to look more like an undertaker than someone setting out for a ball. Summer's glance moved to Uncle Merriam. How inordinately low and anxious he seemed, she thought. Until this morning in Berkeley he'd been looking forward to tonight's ball, but now she felt he'd rather break a leg than go to Bevincote.

A manservant opened the front door, and the wind gusted icily over them all as they hurried out beneath the lamplit porch to the waiting carriage. A few moments later the whip cracked, and the coachman tooled the restless team away from the house, down through the grounds, and then out onto the road that led around the foot of the hill to Bevincote.

Seeing the tops of the domes and pinnacles of Lord Lytherby's incredible house during her ride hadn't prepared Summer for the brilliantly illuminated scene of Oriental splendor that greeted her astonished eyes as the carriage turned through the gates of Bevincote. A procession of gleaming vehicles was making its slow way along the drive that led between an avenue of magnificent specimen trees, and she pressed close to the window to gaze at a building that was the Taj Mahal and the forbidden city of the Chinese emperors rolled into one. The brilliance of the illuminations was wondrous, for not only was the house itself lit from top to bottom by a thousand lamps or more, but every nearby tree was lavishly hung with variegated lanterns that trembled in the wind so they resembled fireflies. Lord Lytherby's residence shone miraculously through the January darkness, as if vast invisible doors had opened to allow a glimpse into an eastern treasure cave.

Caro glanced at Summer. "Is it not the most breathtaking sight in all the world?"

"It is indeed," Summer murmured, then gave her a sly smile. "And to think that one day *you* will be its mistress."

Before Caro could respond, George Bradshaw broke in. "A terrible responsibility, one might say," he said coolly.

Caro lowered her eyes, but Summer's flashed toward him.

"Or a great honor, depending upon one's point of view," she said tersely.

"What other view can there be other than that being mistress of Bevincote will be a difficult task that may even prove an impossible burden?" he replied, his little masked eyes sliding to Uncle Merriam and then away again.

Summer's lips pressed angrily together. What was the matter with the odious fellow? He was like a death's-head at a feast! Why couldn't he hold his tongue entirely if he didn't have anything pleasant to say? Oh, how she'd like to lean across and jab him with her closed fan, if only to see the look of astonishment on his sour face!

Uncle Merriam shifted uncomfortably on his seat, cleared his throat, and said nothing, which angered her still more. *He* was the proper person to put George Bradshaw in his place, but instead he just sat there. She fiddled with her fan, wishing she knew what had gone on while she and Caro had visited the haberdasher's shop.

The carriage had slowed to snail's pace now, caught up in a jam of vehicles close to the main entrance, where oil lamps shone beneath a porch of elegant Indian arches. As the coachman at last maneuvered his team to a halt before the steps, menservants dressed in golden Chinese silk hastened to open the door and lower the rungs, and a small boy got up like a Tartar emperor brought a huge basket containing floral wrist favors for the ladies.

The party from Oakhill House alighted, and as the little emperor tied a favor to Summer's wrist, she heard the faint melodic sound of windbells somewhere in the park, but it was almost drowned by the music and voices in the house. Summer took a deep breath to compose herself and was very glad indeed of the anonymity afforded by her domino, for now that she was here, she could almost *feel* Brand somewhere close by!

She avoided George Bradshaw's grudgingly offered arm to follow Uncle Merriam and Caro toward the dazzling red-and-gold entrance hall, where the crush of elegant guests seemed almost impenetrable. It was very warm inside because log fires burned in two huge marble fireplaces carved with dragons, and everything was lit by half a dozen lotus-shaped lusters which added to the heat. Doorways adorned with scarlet bamboo trelliswork were set in walls decorated with Chinese river scenes, and there were flowers everywhere, as was expected at a grand ball, but added to their fragrance was the sweetness of Oriental spices in open potpourri jars in the hearths.

From the far end of the entrance hall rose a splendid staircase, and Summer and her party joined the queue of masked guests making its slow way up to a landing on the next floor, where the triple-arched entrance to the ballroom could be seen. Progress was very slow, and the farther up the stairs they went, the more uneasily she glanced around for any sign of a gentleman who might be Brand, but she saw none. In the ballroom a minuet gave way to a polonaise, and then to a country dance, but still Summer and her party had not reached the top of the staircase. The heat from the entrance hall rose all around, and both she and Caro had to resort to their fans.

As the queue moved up a step or so, Summer and her uncle were momentarily separated from Caro and George Bradshaw, so she seized the opportunity to speak to her uncle. "Uncle Merriam, I asked you at the Crown if something was wrong, and you said not, but clearly there is. Can't you tell me what it is?"

He forced a smile. "You're quite mistaken, my dear, for there's nothing wrong at all."

"But—" She broke off because Caro and George Bradshaw rejoined them, but as she continued to watch her uncle, she saw how anxiously his tongue passed over his lower lip. All was far from well, and she wouldn't leave it alone until she found out what it was.

At last they reached the landing, and Summer was able to look through the archways into the ballroom. It was another breathtaking scene of eastern opulence, a shimmering vision of blue and gold, lit by chandeliers that resembled immense clusters of Chinese lanterns. The domed ceiling glittered with gold mosaic, the walls were alternately paneled with blue silk and hand-painted mirrors, and the elegant gold-cushioned sofas around the edge of the floor were studded with ivory and mother-of-pearl. There were potted ferns everywhere, and more on the dais where a fashionable London orchestra played. A small army of gold-clad footmen hurried to and from the adjacent supper room with iced champagne and fruit cup with which the overheated guests could quench their thirst.

The queue from the staircase edged across the landing, then through the arches to the small flight of white marble steps that led down into the ballroom. At the foot of these steps Lord Lytherby and his son were waiting to receive everyone.

The Honorable Francis Lytherby was exactly like his portrait, romantically handsome, with dark hair, brown eyes, and sensitive lips. Few gentlemen present tonight appeared to greater advantage in the close-fitting evening clothes that were de rigueur for such occasions. A solitaire diamond flashed on the knot of his starched neckcloth, and a quizzing glass swung idly from one white-gloved hand as he diligently endeavored to show interest in each new face presented before him. But he kept glancing at the bronze chrysanthemum clock on the wall nearby, and Summer knew he was anticipating Caro's arrival. Seeing him in the flesh, she could understand only too well why her cousin had fallen so head over heels in love.

Lord Lytherby was tall and stout, with fair skin that flushed easily, and he was so tightly laced into his clothes that he looked very uncomfortable indeed. His manner was abrupt, and even from where she stood Summer could hear how staccato his voice was. It was hard to believe Francis was his son, for they could not have been more dissimilar—the one so slender, dark, and sentient; the other so overweight, fair, and brusque.

Uncle Merriam and George Bradshaw were presented first, and Summer watched her uncle. He greeted Lord Lytherby with becoming grace and civility, but when it came to Francis, he hesitated visibly before inclining his head at all. A puzzled look passed through Francis's dark eyes, but then Uncle Merriam moved on and George Bradshaw took his place.

Summer wondered if Caro had noticed anything, but her cousin's adoring gaze saw only the object of her heart's desire, until suddenly she had to drag her eyes away from Francis as Lord Lytherby addressed her.

"Miss Merriam," he said in his odd, almost disjointed manner.

Caro sank into a hasty curtsy, and he raised her hand briefly to his lips, releasing it with almost undue haste. As Caro quickly moved on to her beloved Francis, Summer hung a little to one side, hoping to sidle past without being presented to Lord Lytherby, to whom she'd taken an instinctive dislike. It was a ploy that worked, for he hardly noticed her as his glance moved on to the next group in the queue.

She had no such reservations about meeting Francis, with whose warmth and charm she was quite taken as Caro introduced them. "Mrs. Courtenay?" he said smilingly, drawing her hand fully to his lips.

"Sir." She returned the smile.

The country dance had ended, and as a *ländler* was announced, Francis glanced surreptitiously at his father, before drawing both ladies away from the staircase. Then he looked at Summer again. "Would you mind very much if I stole Caro for this dance?"

"Mind? Me? No, of course not."

"It's just that I feared she would never get here, and—"

"There is no need to explain, sir, for I quite understand," she interrupted.

He gave her a grateful look, then seized Caro's hand to lead her on to the fast-filling floor.

Summer watched them until they disappeared in the sea of dancers, but then, quite suddenly, another couple caught her eyes. The somewhat elderly gentleman was of no interest, but his young lady companion most definitely was. Tall, willowy, and very elegant indeed in a shell pink satin ball gown that must have cost a great deal, she wore a domino that was similar to Summer's, and her hair was completely concealed beneath a silver brocade turban. Nothing would really have set her apart in Summer's eyes, had it not been for the eye-catching necklace at her throat.

Summer stared at the black velvet choker and sunburst of pink diamonds. Surely there couldn't be two such pieces of jewelry? It *had* to be poor Lady Harvey's necklace!

Chapter Eleven

The *ländler* carried the lady and her partner farther toward the center of the ballroom, and Summer moved along the edge of the floor, trying to keep an eye on them. It was difficult, for there were so many people standing around that she was constantly having to apologize for accidentally nudging someone. The dancers swept around and around the sanded floor, and at last Summer had to pause by one of the large potted ferns because she lost sight of her quarry.

She scanned the heads, trying to catch a glimpse of the silver turban, but it seemed nowhere in sight. She snapped open her fan and wafted it before her suddenly hot face. Maybe she was mistaken; maybe it *wasn't* the stolen necklace. But even as she mulled over this possibility, she dismissed it. Lady Harvey's diamond sunburst was far too distinctive; unless, of course, someone had admired it so much they'd had a copy made. Her fan paused. That was a possibility she could not dismiss, but even so, was it not a peculiar coincidence that within days of the original being stolen at the Black Lion, an exact copy should appear here, only twenty or so miles away? Yes, that was far too *much* of a coincidence!

A determined glint entered her eyes, and she glanced around for a position from which to observe the floor more clearly. The only place appeared to be the orchestra dais, where numerous ferns, some of them very tall, also offered a little concealment, and so that was where she made her way next.

From her new vantage spot she had a much better view of the ballroom, but for a few tense moments she thought the lady in the silver turban must have left the floor. Then, quite suddenly,

Summer saw her almost directly below the dais. The diamond sunburst winked and flashed at her throat as she threw her head back to laugh at something her partner had said, then the dance carried them away again.

At last the *ländler* came to an end, and Summer kept her gaze firmly fixed upon the silver turban. The lady and her partner moved to the side of the floor, where they parted. The lady glanced around for a moment, then went into the adjacent supper room. Summer hastened down from the dais, once more pushing her way through the throng to follow her quarry.

The supper room, with its costly Chinese silk wallpaper and alabaster statues of mandarins, was crowded with guests gathered around the feast of fine food, but as Summer reached the entrance, once again there was no sign of the silver-turbaned lady.

There was a trellised door across the room, so she hurried toward it, and on the other side discovered a candlelit passageway that led to another door. It was clearly part of the house that had not been opened up for the ball, but since she could only presume the lady had come this way, she went swiftly along the passage to inspect what lay beyond the other door. She found herself looking into a richly carpeted inner hall, off which opened several darkened rooms. The hall itself had a fireplace, where a log fire flickered brightly, and directly opposite a staircase led up to the next floor. Two girandoles on either side of the chimneypiece provided a little additional light to that supplied by the fireplace, but after the brilliance of the ballroom, it seemed almost dark.

Slowly, she went inside, and as the passage door closed behind her, a strange almost muffled silence seemed to descend. She listened carefully for any sound of voices, but there was nothing. Thinking the lady couldn't have come this way after all, she was about to leave when she heard voices approaching along the passage from the supper room. Not wanting to be caught in what seemed likely to be the private apartments, she drew hastily into the nearest of the darkened rooms and closed the door. Darkness engulfed her for a moment, but to her relief there was a lamp-festooned tree just outside the uncurtained window, and as her eyes swiftly became accustomed to the faint spangled light that swayed because of the wind, she realized she was in Lord

Lytherby's billiard room. She pressed her ear to the door and listened as the passage door opened. She immediately recognized Lord Lytherby's voice. He was with another gentleman, and they paused for a moment, speaking in low tones, but then Lord Lytherby's words carried more clearly.

"This is not something I wish to be overheard. Come, we'll be more private in the billiard room."

Horrified, Summer cast around for somewhere to hide. There didn't seem to be anywhere at all, but then she noticed a tall cupboard next to the rack of billiard cues and ran over to step inside. She closed the doors just as Lord Lytherby and his companion entered. Through a crack she was able to see as Lord Lytherby lit a luminary. His plump face was lit from below as he held the flame to a candle on a side table, then dropped the luminary into a silver dish where it continued to burn for a few moments before going out. The candle flame leapt as he brought it to the billiard table and set it down on the smooth green baize, where he was lit by the dancing light but not his companion.

"What have you tell me?" Lord Lytherby demanded curtly.

"Nothing much as yet."

Summer's brows drew together, for the other man's voice was known to her, but on only four words she couldn't place it, except to say it wasn't a young man's voice.

The reply hadn't pleased his lordship. "Don't be mistaken enough to think that delay will avail you of anything."

"You misjudge me."

Again the response was too brief for Summer to come to grips with the voice.

Lord Lytherby drew a long breath. "There are less than two weeks in which to find a justifiable reason to halt this match, one that will not estrange my son from me, so you'd better get on with it or it will be the worst for you!"

Summer's lips parted. Caro was right, Lord Lytherby *did* now oppose the match!

Lord Lytherby continued. "I wish to God I'd never agreed to it in the first place, but circumstances were different then. I can't afford to tolerate a nonentity like your niece as my daughter-in-law when there is a much more fitting bride to hand!"

At last Summer knew who the second man was, for there was only one person to whom Caro was niece—George Bradshaw! So the odious lawyer *was* against the match, in fact he was actually aiding and abetting Lord Lytherby!

Lord Lytherby hadn't finished. "If I'm to see my son married to my ward, this has got to be done quickly, do I make myself clear? All you have to do is find a way to convince that fool Merriam that this match is *not* in his daughter's best interests. I don't care what you say to him, provided my involvement doesn't come to light. I warn you, if that should happen, I'll tear your heart out with my bare hands. Fail me any way, and I'll use your debts to ruin you."

"I'll do everything to your satisfaction," the lawyer said quickly. "I began the task this morning, but there simply isn't any progress to report as yet, except that I believe the seeds of doubt have taken root."

Summer inhaled slowly. This morning. Yes, in Berkeley! But what had the odious man said to poor Uncle Merriam?

For a moment it seemed Lord Lytherby might press for precise details, but instead he nodded. "Very well, I'll leave it with you."

George Bradshaw's relief was almost palpable. "All will be accomplished in good time, my lord. You may be certain that the betrothal will be broken off, and Miss Huntingford will be your son's bride, just as you wish."

Lord Lytherby grunted. "Just handle it carefully." He picked up the candle again. "Well, that's all for the moment. No doubt you and Merriam will join the Berkeley Hunt tomorrow?"

"We will."

"If you have anything further to tell me, you may do so then, but discreetly."

"Very well, my lord."

Lord Lytherby went to open the door, and as the light from the hall shone palely into the room, he extinguished the candle, returned it to the side table, then strode away toward the passage that led back to the ball. After a moment George Bradshaw followed, closing the door meticulously behind him.

Summer remained as quiet as a mouse in the cupboard, fearing that either man might return and realize she'd overheard their conversation, but as the minutes ticked by, she felt safe enough to emerge from hiding. The spangled light from the tree swayed dimly over her gown as she tiptoed to the door. There wasn't a sound, so she went quietly into the hall, then paused to adjust her domino. But as she undid the little ties to quickly do them up again, the domino fell to the floor.

At that precise moment the passage door was opened by a masked gentleman in a black corded silk coat and white silk knee breeches. In spite of his mask, his golden hair gave his identity away in a moment. It was Brand.

Startled, he halted. "Olivia?"

She stared at him in such great alarm that for a second or so she couldn't think or move, but then she regained her wits, snatched the domino from the floor, and fled up the nearby staircase.

"Olivia!"

She reached the top of the staircase and glanced around at the brightly lit passages that led away on all sides. Choosing one, she ran along it as fast as she could, then saw some large double doors and slipped hastily through. It wasn't a room on the other side; instead she found herself in a two-hundred-foot-long gallery that led from one end of the house to the other. There was another set of double doors at the far end, but they seemed a very long way away, and since every candle, lamp, and chandelier had been lit, she couldn't possibly hope to avoid being seen. She heard Brand's steps behind her, so for the second time that night she cast around desperately for somewhere to hide.

One side of the gallery was taken up by floor-to-ceiling windows with heavy mulberry silk curtains that had been left undrawn so the light inside would shine out into the night. She ran to the nearest window and pressed among the rich folds of silk just as Brand flung open the doors.

For a few seconds there was silence, then he spoke. "I know you're in here, Olivia, so you may as well show yourself." An echo took up his voice and carried it along the gallery.

She held her breath, praying she wasn't shaking so much that the curtain would tremble visibly. She wished the recorder would bring a halt to this visit to the past. Surely it was time now? Yes, it was at least two hours since she'd found herself seated before the dressing table at Oakhill House. *Take me back now, please—* Her unvoiced entreaties came to an abrupt halt as Brand spoke.

"This is foolish, Olivia, for there is no other way out of here; the other doors are locked."

Locked? That single word dashed any lingering thought she had of making a bid to escape. She closed her eyes.

He came farther in, his steps slow and intimidating. "I have no intention of leaving, madam, so the sooner you have the grace to face me, the better."

She made no sound.

There was a long silence, and she began to feel unnerved. Why was he just standing there? Why didn't he at least start searching?

Suddenly, the curtain was jerked aside, and she screamed as he seized her. "We meet yet again, sweet Olivia," he breathed, his dark blue eyes angry behind his mask.

Chapter Twelve

The domino slipped from Summer's fingers as she struggled with all her might, but he merely laughed, for her efforts were futile against his superior strength. "Don't waste your energy, madam, for without the advantage of a riding crop, you stand no chance."

"What do you want of me?" she cried, still trying to wrench free of him.

He snatched off his mask and tossed it aside. "*I* will ask the questions, madam. To begin with, I wish to know *exactly* who you are."

She pressed her lips together stubbornly.

"Tell me, Olivia."

"No, for it is none of your business."

"It's very much my business."

"Why, because you belatedly wonder with whom you shared a bed?" She met his eyes squarely.

He relaxed his hold a little and moved back, although still without allowing her any chance to escape. "Yes, we did indeed share a bed, and a very pleasurable experience it was too, but then as I said at our last encounter, I suspect you've had vastly more teachers than just your late husband, if indeed there ever *was* a late Mr. Courtenay."

"Someone of real experience would have detected at a glance that you were no gentleman, sir, but I was too naive to realize the truth about you until the following morning, when your shabby conduct revealed your true low colors."

He gave a cool laugh. "Ah, yes, *you* are the sweet little innocent, *I* am the beast who used you to satisfy his base male lust before casting you aside like an old rag."

"That's *exactly* how I'd describe it," she said levelly.

"Well, let's get to the truth about your presence at the Black Lion, shall we? You weren't simply staying there on your way anywhere. You had very particular reasons."

She stared at him. Did he know about Jeremy? No, that was impossible!

He gave a contemptuous laugh and put his hand to her cheek in a parody of a caress. "Ah, sweet, sweet Olivia, you're really quite perfect for the task, aren't you?"

"Task? I really don't know what you're talking about."

"Do you deny that you went to the Black Lion expecting to meet someone else?"

Her lips parted. He *did* know about Jeremy! But how? *How?*

"Guilt is written all over you, Olivia, so please don't insult me with this pretense of being the wide-eyed innocent!" he snapped, taking her arms and pushing her against the curtain. "What a fool you made of me! Your lover Fenwick let you down, so you took me to your bed instead. Oh, how passionately you gulled me, how sensuously and cleverly you made me believe you knew nothing of what had been going on. You were even convincing with the Harveys the next morning, being the soul of solicitous concern, when all the time . . ." He didn't finish.

At last she thought she knew what he was accusing her of, and she was both indignant and alarmed. "I had *nothing* to do with those thefts!"

"Liar! You and Fenwick are lovers, and you went to the Black Lion to steal what valuables you could."

"No!" she cried.

In reply he took from his pocket the crumpled letter he'd retrieved at the Black Lion and held it up in front of her. "Oh, yes, my dear, the tenderly expressed evidence survived, albeit without your name," he said, returning it to his pocket.

Caught completely off guard, she could only stare at it. "I can explain . . ."

"I have no doubt of that, Olivia, for your kind are always proficient liars."

"My kind? My *kind*?" Suddenly, her stunned disbelief transformed into fury. "How *dare* you stand there calmly accusing me of lies and villainy! I don't deny an exceedingly misguided intention to meet Jeremy Fenwick for dinner at the Black Lion. *Dinner,* sirrah, not a night of lust and thieving! Believe me, I was very thankful indeed when he failed to arrive. He was my late husband's close friend and helped me when Roderick died, but that is the *full extent* of my friendship with him, no matter what the tone of the letter may suggest to the contrary! I had nothing to do with those thefts, and since Jeremy wasn't even in Tetbury that night, I fail to see how you can accuse him either."

"Major Jeremy Fenwick is a felon who has gone absent without leave from his regiment after stealing from his fellow officers."

Her eyes widened, then she shook her head. "No, I won't believe it."

"Your playacting is becoming tiresome, Olivia, for the letter establishes that Fenwick is your lover, and I *know* that you and he are fellow thieves! Which brings me to tonight. Where better than a masked ball for a light-fingered intruder to move without detection, not only in the ballroom but in the private apartments too."

Her mouth began to run dry. "No," she whispered. "I'm not an intruder. I'm here by invitation and have no purpose other than to enjoy the ball . . ."

"Don't lie! Fenwick's here as well, isn't he? *Isn't* he?"

"No!" she cried. "At least . . ."

His eyes sharpened. "Yes? At least what?"

"This morning I thought I saw him in Berkeley. It was only a reflection in a mirror, and when I turned, he'd gone. He wasn't in uniform, and I'm certain he was dismayed that I'd caught a glimpse of him." She was confused and a little frightened. What if Jeremy *had* been the thief at the Black Lion? If Brand believed the letter was compromising evidence of her involvement in the crimes, might not a court of law take the same view?

Brand gave a disdainful smile. "You're almost believable."

His scorn caught her on a nerve, and suddenly she found her spirit again. "And why should *I* believe *you* about anything?" she challenged. "I wasn't the only one at the Black Lion that night, was I?"

Now his lips were the ones to part in amazement. "You have the gall to accuse *me*?" he asked.

"Why not?" A new thought occurred to her. Lady Harvey's diamonds! The stolen necklace and this man were under the same roof. She knew *she* was innocent of stealing it at the Black Lion, but she didn't know anything at all about *him,* except that he was the most wonderful lover she'd ever had.

He searched her face. "Out with it, madam, for I might as well hear the whole of your preposterous countercharge."

"Someone here tonight is wearing Lady Harvey's diamonds," she said.

Now it was his turn to stare, but then he recovered. "Oh, come *on* now, you'll have to do better than that!"

"I'm telling you the truth. I tried to follow the woman who was wearing them, and that's how you discovered me."

"Who was she, this Jill-o'-the-wisp?" he demanded caustically, emphasizing the "Jill."

"I don't know; she wore a domino like mine and a turban!"

"Olivia, *all* the women here tonight are masked or dominoed, and at least a third of them are wearing turbans."

"I'm aware of that, but this one was also wearing Lady Harvey's necklace, and both you and she are here tonight," she added coolly.

"The implication being that I gave her the item *I* stole?"

"Or that you and she both stole it."

"I wasn't with anyone at the Black Lion except you," he pointed out.

"So you say, but that doesn't signify anything. You didn't see me with Jeremy, but you've still seen fit to accuse me of being his accomplice. Who knows *what* you were up to when you weren't with me?"

He gave an incredulous laugh, then leaned a gloved hand against the wall close to her head to look deep into her eyes, his lips only inches from hers. "Dear God, what a resourceful mind you have! For a moment I came close to swallowing your turbaned fairy tale. You haven't seen any necklace here tonight; you're merely attempting to throw me off the scent."

"I'm innocent, Brand."

He straightened again. "Are you? Then what of the letter? It proves that you were expecting to meet a felon at the Black Lion on the night that, among other things, Lady Harvey's necklace was stolen."

"It also proves that he didn't keep the appointment. You are the one who knows all about his so-called crimes and absence without leave, so maybe *you* are his accomplice!"

He smiled at that. "My dear Olivia, I would rather be his murderer than his accomplice," he said quietly. "I hold your friend Fenwick in utter contempt and loathing, and if he were here right now, I would take great delight in putting a shot between his vile eyes."

Knowing he carried a pistol, she had no doubt he meant every word. She stared at him. "Why? Brand, what is between you and Jeremy?"

"I have no intention of telling you, but not out of consideration for myself. Suffice it that his conduct has been despicable in every way, and if you are as innocent of complicity as you claim, you would be well advised to break off all dealings with him."

"Does that mean you accept that I may be innocent?"

"Possibly."

"I *am* innocent, Brand."

Again he leaned a hand against the wall in order to look down into her face. "Then tell me your full name," he said softly.

She hesitated. "I will resort to your own words, Brand. I

have no intention of telling you, but not out of consideration for myself."

"This conversation begins to resemble the art of foils. You, madam, are a verbal swordswoman, parrying with consummate skill."

"Not willingly on this occasion, I promise you," she replied frankly. "Brand, if I could tell you who I am, I would, but I dare not."

"Because you don't trust me?"

She gave an ironic smile. "If you were me, sir, would *you* trust you?"

"Possibly not," he said softly, gazing down into her eyes.

She glanced hastily away. "Don't look at me like that, for it will avail you of nothing. I will not tell you who I am, so you waste your time with silken words and warm glances."

"I'm looking at you like this in acknowledgment of a realization we've both been endeavoring to ignore for some minutes now."

"What realization?"

"That in spite of everything, what we both want to do right now is make love."

Her cheeks flamed and her pulse quickened. "Your vanity is as towering as your odiousness!"

"Really?" He smiled. "And your indifference is as convincing as a six-guinea banknote."

"You flatter yourself if you think my indifference is counterfeit."

He straightened once more in order to slowly tease off the fingers of his white gloves. "Oh, Olivia, if only you knew the effect your flashing gray eyes have upon me," he murmured.

She couldn't reply, for her traitorous body was letting her down again. When he looked at her and spoke softly like this, all her anger and mistrust melted away, leaving a woman who was completely vulnerable to any advance he chose to make.

He put warm fingers to her chin and made her look at him. "Do you want to walk away from me right now?" he asked.

Tears stung her eyes. "No," she whispered.

"Then stay," he murmured, bending his head to kiss her.

Chapter Thirteen

Once again Summer came alive to him. She closed her eyes as Brand's mouth teased and trifled with hers in a way that led her further and further into temptation. His kiss was hard, then soft, then hard again, and she could taste champagne on his lips. It was as intoxicating as if she herself had sipped from his glass, and she felt her senses beginning to steal all thought of resistance.

At last he pulled her into his arms, crushing her close as once again the wild hunt of passion began to surge through them both. He allowed her no quarter, nor did she seek it, for she knew she would never feel like this with any other man. Her arms slid helplessly around his neck, and her lips moved needfully against his as she surrendered to waves of wanton emotion.

Kiss followed kiss, and their caresses became more and more ardent. Desire had them both in its power, sweeping them on and on with its promise of that most ultimate of pleasures. She was imprisoned by her own sensuality, fettered by a passion that transcended all other considerations. There was no thought now of Caro, no thought of anything except possessing and being possessed by this man. She was plunging into the very abyss of scandal she'd been at such pains to avoid, and she was doing it right here at Bevincote.

He pressed her to the wall, and she felt the hard mound of his maleness pushing against her through the thin silk of her gown. "If you would say no, then say it now," he breathed.

"I cannot say it," she whispered, her whole body trembling with anticipation as he began to unbutton his breeches.

Then he gently raised her gown and lifted her slightly in order to enter her. She wrapped her legs longingly around his hips and gave a soft moan as she sank onto him. It was sweet impalement, and her parted lips were warm and clinging as they met his again. He withdrew slightly, then pushed in deep again, and she cleaved helplessly to him as a torrent of delight pounded through her veins. She felt both weak and strong, prey to every erotic sensation of which her body was capable.

The climax was shattering in its intensity, and they held each other tightly afterward, savoring every last moment until their heartbeats were slow and relaxed again. Then, and only then, did he withdraw from her and lower her gently to the floor.

When he'd straightened his clothes and then pulled her into his arms once more, she leaned her forehead against his shoulder. Suddenly, all she could think of was how he'd taunted her in the chapel about taking her against a wall. "I've never behaved like this before, you must believe me. What you said in the chapel . . ."

He knew what she was thinking and made her look at him again. "I didn't mean what I said then; all I could think of was that damned letter from Fenwick."

She put her fingertips to his cheek. "That dinner at the Black Lion would have been innocent, you *must* believe me. I cannot answer for his overaffectionate tone, except to suspect he was in his cups. There has never been anything but friendship between him and me, I swear."

He looked into her eyes. "I believe you, Olivia."

"I pray that you do, for I could not bear it if you still doubted me. I was very unwise to agree to meet him like that, but I've been much more unwise with you," she said softly.

"So where do we proceed from here?"

"Proceed?"

"You will not divulge your name to me, and I'm certain you will be equally as secretive about your address."

She looked up again. "I don't know who you are either," she pointed out.

"That's easily rectified. My name is Brand Huntingford, Sir

Brand Huntingford, and I'm staying here at Bevincote for a while."

She stared at him. "Huntingford?" she repeated. "Would you be any relation of Lord Lytherby's ward?"

"Melinda is my half sister."

Summer's dismay was so complete she had to pull out of his arms. *Melinda Huntingford's brother?* For all she knew he might be party to Lord Lytherby's wish to see Francis betrothed to Melinda instead of Caro; in fact he probably was!

He caught her wrist, renewed suspicion beginning to cast a cool shadow across his eyes. "Why does my being Melinda's brother affect you so?"

"I . . . I think I should go now," she said haltingly, wresting her wrist free, then bending to retrieve her domino, but as she straightened he seized hold of her again.

"I demand an answer, Olivia. What difference does it make that I am Melinda's brother? Unless—" The shadow in his eyes became ice cold. "Of course! What a fool I've been, I should have *known*! You're right, madam, you *should* go now," he said abruptly.

The change in him was almost frightening. "Brand?"

"Just go, Olivia, for I fear there will always be an insurmountable barrier between us."

She stared at him through tear-filled eyes, then gathered her skirts to hurry from the gallery.

He remained by the window. His face was pale, and a nerve fluttered at his temple as he suddenly tightened his hand into a fist and brought it crashing against the wall.

Trying to retie her domino. Summer hurried confusedly back through the passage to the inner staircase, but her fingers shook too much, and as she reached the blue-carpeted hall, she paused to tie it properly before returning to the ball. She breathed in deeply in an effort to steady the conflicting feelings that spanned sickeningly through her. Of all the people in the world, Brand had to turn out to be part of the inner sanctum of Caro's enemies! Why couldn't he have been someone who'd been invited to the ball simply because he was staying with a household associated with the Lytherbys? Instead, he had to be the half brother of the woman Caro suspected of wanting Francis for herself, and who Lord Lytherby *definitely* wished to see married to his son.

Tears stung Summer's eyes. "And you've just given yourself to him against a wall like a common whore!" she whispered to herself, feeling so dreadful she didn't know how she was going to carry the rest of the evening off. Now more than ever she knew the best thing she could do would be to cut short her stay at Oakhill House, for if she remained, the time was bound to come shortly when she and Brand would be formally introduced.

She was glad of the domino, for it hid her tears as she made her way back along the passage to the supper room, which was still crowded with guests. In the ballroom the orchestra was playing another minuet, and she watched from the side of the floor as the sets moved gracefully through the formal steps, but she was still too distracted to do anything but think of the shocking scrape she'd so wantonly gotten herself into, and into which Caro might yet be dragged too. She was relieved not to see her cousin anywhere, for now it would be very difficult indeed to face her.

The minuet ended, and a cotillion was announced. A short, middle-aged gentleman with thinning light brown hair, a blue silk mask, and an overabundance of lace at his throat bowed to her. "Would you honor me with this dance, madam?"

Her gaze moved absently toward him. "I . . . I beg your pardon, sir?"

"This dance. Will you honor me?"

In a daze she nodded and slipped her hand over the arm he offered, and as the dance began, she was almost glad of the diversion it offered, for there seemed to be extra anonymity in the succession of figures that wove the couples to and fro, but when the cotillion was nearing the end, she happened to glance toward an adjacent set. Francis was among its number, but instead of Caro for a partner, he was dancing with the silver-turbaned lady in shell pink satin!

Summer's steps faltered, and she almost collided with her

unfortunate partner, for her gaze was riveted to the sunburst of diamonds at the lady's throat. From that moment on, her attention wasn't on the cotillion at all, but upon Caro's intended husband and the mysterious lady. Whoever she was, she either knew Francis rather better than she should, or she was the most inveterate flirt that ever was, for her domino did not hide the provocative warmth in her eyes, and when its delicate veil lifted, it revealed lips that were curved into a too-warm smile.

The lady danced with a subtle voluptuousness that invited Francis to make advances, and to Summer's dismay, it seemed that he wasn't quite as indifferent as he should have been. He returned every smile, and when they came together because of the dance, he quite clearly whispered something in her ear. The worst thing of all, though, was that when the cotillion demanded the giving or taking of a favor from one's partner, the lady held up her veil for a kiss. As their lips brushed together, Summer's heart sank. Was Francis Lytherby perhaps not quite as devoted to Caro as she was to him?

Somehow Summer managed to get through the remainder of the cotillion, for her attention was constantly upon the adjacent set and the dubious conduct of her cousin's husband-to-be. As the dance came to an end, she once again lost sight of the telltale silver turban in the confusion of everyone leaving the floor.

Uncle Merriam suddenly appeared at her side. "Ah, there you are, my dear. I've been wondering where you'd got to. I trust you are enjoying the ball?"

She gave him a smile she was sure was unconvincing. "Yes, very much indeed," she fibbed, for right now she felt as if purgatory itself would be more agreeable than the Bevincote masked ball.

He surveyed the floor, where dancers were assembling for an allemande. "I suppose one has to concede that Lord Lytherby knows very well how to give a ball," he murmured in the sort of tone one might use if gazing upon something for the last time.

Summer looked anxiously at him. "Why do you say it like that?"

"Like what, my dear?"

"As if you don't expect to see another ball here."

"What nonsense. No, truth to tell, I'm just not looking forward to accompanying the hunt tomorrow, but since to refuse would cause offense at the castle, I fear George and I must show our faces. No doubt I'll be tipped into the first ditch, and that will be that."

"So you'd have me believe your low spirits are solely due to the hunt?"

"Yes, my dear, but it's kind of you to be concerned."

"Forgive me if I point out that hunting has never bothered you before, and under any other circumstances you'd revel in riding to hounds as famous as the Berkeley, so something else is wrong." For the first time it struck her that it might be something to do with her. Her mind whisked back to the billiard room and George Bradshaw's assurance to Lord Lytherby that he had already commenced something to bring about the end of Francis's match with Caro. In spite of her efforts to disguise the truth, had the lawyer after all placed an only-too-accurate interpretation upon what he'd seen in the yard of the Black Lion?

Hot color flooded Summer's cheeks. "Uncle Merriam, it isn't anything to do with me, is it?" she asked then, hardly daring to hear his answer.

He met her eyes. "You? Oh, no, my dear, whatever makes you think that?"

"Well, I . . ." she swallowed. "I . . . I don't know really, I just wondered."

"There is no need to fear on that score, and since you clearly will not leave the matter alone, I will admit that there *is* something wrong, but before you ask, there's absolutely nothing you can do to help."

"It concerns the match, doesn't it." she said quietly.

He met her eyes. "No, my dear."

She didn't believe him.

He went on. "It's something which I and I alone have to deal with, Olivia, so please do not mention anything to Caro, for the last thing I wish to do is worry her."

"Of course I won't say anything."

He smiled. "Thank you, my dear. Ah, I see George over there. He and I have agreed to indulge in a little cribbage, so if you need us, we'll be in the card room. I believe it's somewhere off the main landing. If you'll excuse me?"

Her glance flew toward the lawyer, who had just emerged from the supper room, and she put a quick hand on her uncle's arm. "Uncle—"

"My dear?"

"Beware what you believe if it comes from Mr. Bradshaw's lips."

He was clearly startled. "Why do you say that, my dear?"

She could hardly tell him what she knew. "It—it's just a feeling, Uncle."

He smiled and patted her arm fondly, then pushed away toward his waiting brother-in-law. Summer's heart was heavy as she watched the two men make their way toward the ballroom steps, but then Caro spoke right behind her.

"Where on earth have you been, Olivia? Francis and I have been looking everywhere for you."

Summer managed to smile as they came up to her. "Oh, I've been here and there, mostly there," she said.

Francis gave her an open smile. "What do you think of Bevincote, Mrs. Courtenay?"

"It's a wonderful house, sir."

"It's either wonderful, or an abomination, according to which school of thought one subscribes."

"And to which do you subscribe?" she asked.

He smiled. "Oh, without a doubt the former. I love every pinnacle, archway, and square inch of wildly expensive painted silk." His gaze moved beyond Summer. "There's Melinda. Melinda, join us for a moment, please," he called.

Summer turned, then froze as she found herself confronted by the woman in the shell pink satin gown and silver turban.

Chapter Fourteen

Francis presented Summer. "Mrs. Courtenay, may I present my father's ward, Miss Huntingford?"

Lady Harvey's diamond sunburst was dazzling as Melinda gave a slight smile and inclined her head. Behind her domino her eyes were an arresting shade of lilac, and although she directed her reply to Summer, it was upon Francis that her gaze was turned. "I'm honored to make your acquaintance, Mrs. Courtenay."

Summer was shaken to realize who her quarry had turned out to be. "And . . . and I yours, Miss Huntingford."

At last Melinda's eyes moved to her. "I trust you are enjoying the ball?"

"I am indeed." Summer saw how fondly Francis smiled at Melinda, and how anxiously poor Caro watched them both.

"I vow I admire your coiffure greatly, Mrs. Courtenay, and I am especially envious of your Egyptian circlet."

"Thank you, Miss Huntingford." It was the opening Summer sought. "May I say in return that your necklace is quite the most beautiful I have ever seen?"

A slender gloved hand crept to the sunburst, and Melinda nodded. "Yes, it is, isn't it?"

"Is it a family heirloom?"

Melinda paused. "Er, no. It was a gift from my brother."

Summer felt cold inside. "Indeed? How fortunate you are to have a brother who thinks so highly of you."

"Brand is very generous."

Isn't he just, Summer thought miserably. Had she been closer to the mark than she realized when she accused him of being the thief at the Black Lion? Oh, please she thought, don't let that be so, and yet—what other explanation was there? How else could Melinda have come into possession of the necklace? Oh, what a gull she'd been to allow him to seduce her yet again . . .

Francis spoke. "Actually where *is* Brand? I haven't seen him tonight."

Melinda smiled at him. "Oh, he's probably playing billiards with Lord Lytherby; you know how thick they've become of late."

Summer's heart reached the lowest ebb possible. More and more she feared that Brand had to be party to the plot to force Francis from Caro's arms into Melinda's.

Caro toyed with her fan, then glanced at Francis as the orchestra struck up another *ländler*. "Oh, please, let's dance," she begged, determined to get him away from Melinda.

"But we've already broken the rules a little too much by dancing three dances in succession," he replied with a smile. "You know it simply isn't the thing for a gentleman to dance so frequently with the same lady."

Caro fell silent, but her crestfallen glance turned briefly toward Melinda.

Summer spoke up. "Caro, have you had any supper yet?"

"Supper? Er, no . . ."

Summer tapped Francis's arm. "Sir, it does not do to neglect the inner woman, or the inner man, for that matter. Why do you not adjourn to the supper room? I vow the spread looks most choice."

He immediately turned to Caro. "Forgive me, my dearest, I should have thought earlier. Come." He offered her his arm, and Caro's little face lit up again as they inclined their heads and left Summer and Melinda.

Melinda's lilac eyes followed them. "How very happy they seem," she murmured.

"Seem?" Summer took up the invisible cudgels she was increasingly suspicious were necessary on Caro's behalf.

"Well, Francis is so charming with everyone."

"Does that mean he also proposes marriage to *everyone*?" Summer inquired coldly.

Melinda flushed behind her domino. "Of course not. Please don't misunderstand me, Mrs. Courtenay, for it wasn't my intention to cast doubt upon his commitment to the match."

Oh, yes it was, you *chienne*, Summer thought, but she said, "No, of course it wasn't, Miss Huntingford, and I wouldn't *dream* of thinking otherwise."

Melinda fingered Lady Harvey's diamonds and changed the subject. "The ball is indeed a press, is it not?"

"And therefore a great success," Summer observed.

Melinda glanced up at the golden mosaic on the ballroom's domed ceiling. The Chinese lantern chandeliers shone brilliantly as they moved slightly in the heat. "I love this house very much," she murmured.

"I can quite understand that, Miss Huntingford," Summer replied.

"I wish it were mine," Melinda said then.

Which it will be if you marry Francis, Summer thought, angrily snapping her fan open and closed.

Melinda watched her. "Is something wrong with your fan, Mrs. Courtenay?"

"Nothing at all, Miss Huntingford."

The two women eyed each other from behind their dominoes, and it was Melinda who looked away first. "Oh, dear, I have *such* a headache, I fear I may soon be obliged to retire," she sighed, putting a languid hand to her forehead.

"How very disagreeable for you," Summer murmured insincerely, hoping the headache became incapacitating.

"Yes, most disagreeable. Well, it was most pleasant speaking to you, Mrs. Courtenay. I trust we'll meet again soon, but for the moment I must circulate a little. Lord Lytherby expects it."

Summer inclined her head. "Please don't let me detain you."

Melinda moved away through the crowds, and Summer gazed sourly after her. There seemed little room for doubt that Melinda Huntingford wanted Francis for herself, she thought, absently taking a glass of champagne from the tray of a passing footman.

The taste reminded her of Brand's kisses and of how wonderfully passionate his lovemaking had been; then of how suddenly again he'd become cold and distant . . . It was a repeat of what had happened at the Black Lion. First the sensuous ecstasy, then the hurtful congé. Oh, how she wished tonight were over . . .

Suddenly, she lowered the glass at the return of the unsettling thought about the length of time she'd been here in the past. It was now *far* too long; something must be wrong!

The disturbing train of thought was interrupted as Brand suddenly plucked the glass from her hand and gave it to a rather startled gentleman standing nearby, before forcing her to join the *ländler* with him. "I will have words with you, madam," he breathed, twining his arms around hers as demanded by the dance.

"Well *I* have no wish to have words with *you!*" she replied, her cheeks reddening behind her domino.

"What were you saying to my sister?" he demanded, gripping her arms even more tightly as she struggled a little.

"I was admiring the stolen necklace you gave to her," Summer replied accusingly. "What a complete fool you made of me tonight. Why such a gift, Brand? Is it in anticipation of the moment she wins Francis and—" She broke off hastily, for she'd almost betrayed her closeness to Caro by using the latter's pet name.

His hold became more harsh, and he drew her closer as permitted by the *ländler.* "Wins Francis? What do you mean? I will have an answer, Olivia!"

"Don't try to turn the tables, Brand, for this isn't about me! *You* are the villain in all this! Your sister has just informed me that you gave her the necklace!"

"It may interest you to learn that I don't know Lady Harvey, nor have I ever seen her diamonds."

"Liar!" she breathed angrily.

His steely fingers dug into her arms. "If you were a man, I'd call you out for less!"

"And if I were a man, I'd accept!"

"Be wary, madam . . ."

"I know what manner of low creature you are behind that mask, Sir Brand Huntingford! You are a vile seducer, a thief, a liar, and a conspirator against the happiness of others! You are beneath contempt, a maggot masquerading as a gentleman, and I wish I had never set eyes on you!"

She didn't realize how much her voice had risen, but suddenly some nearby dancers halted in astonishment, and she glanced around in dismay to see everyone staring.

Then the rest of the floor came to a standstill as well, and the orchestra dwindled away on a few discordant notes. All eyes were riveted upon Brand and her as they stood in bitter confrontation, their arms still linked for the *ländler* that was no longer in progress.

Horrified to have caused such a monumental scene, Summer wrenched herself free and fled toward the steps leading up out of the ballroom. She didn't dare halt at the top for fear Brand might pursue her to demand an apology for the prodigious insults she'd dealt him in front of the entire ballroom. As she made her escape onto the landing, she was thankful that her uncle and George Bradshaw were in the card room, and Caro and Francis in the supper room, for there was no one else to know *exactly* who she was!

Intending to quit Bevincote without further delay, she dashed down the main staircase to the hall, where she asked one of the footmen to bring her cloak, but as she nervously awaited his return, glancing constantly toward the top of the staircase for Brand, it was Caro and Francis who appeared there.

"Olivia? Oh, Olivia, what a dreadful thing to have happened!" Caro cried, hurrying down toward her with Francis following.

Summer was greatly perturbed that they had witnessed the scene. "I thought you were in the supper room," she said as they reached her.

Francis explained. "It was such an unbearable crush we decided to wait a while. We . . . er . . . couldn't help but see and hear what happened."

Caro looked curiously at her. "Olivia, wasn't that the gentleman we saw in the carriage in Berkeley? I know he's wearing a mask tonight, but his golden hair is rather distinctive, is it not?"

Behind the domino, color flared into Summer's cheeks, then she pulled herself together as best she could. "Yes, it *was* the same gentleman," she confirmed.

Francis was bemused. "You and Brand are acquainted, Mrs. Courtenay?"

Caro's eyes widened. "Brand? Sir Brand Huntingford?" she said in surprise, for she had yet to meet Melinda's brother.

Summer nodded and kept her reply low because she was conscious of another footman nearby. "To be truthful, Sir Brand and I encountered each other at the Twelfth Night celebrations at the Black Lion in Tetbury. Although we were not introduced, we didn't hit it off then, and we certainly didn't tonight. Now, to avoid further embarrassment, I intend to plead a headache and return to Oakhill House without further ado." It was the truth, if only a portion of it.

The footman returned at last with her cloak, and when the man had withdrawn again, Francis paused before placing it around her shoulders. "Please don't feel obliged to leave the ball, Mrs. Courtenay. I assure you that Brand isn't at all as disagreeable as you may think, and I'm certain that if I use my good offices to mediate—"

"Oh, no, please, for that would embarrass me still more!" Summer interrupted hastily. "Truly, all I wish to do is escape anonymously, and since Caro's father and uncle are in the card room, and Sir Brand still doesn't know who I am—" She broke off. "He doesn't, does he? I mean, you haven't spoken to him in the last minute or so since I . . . ?"

Francis shook his head. "No, as it happens we haven't, and you may be assured that Caro and I will say nothing at all, but I fear you may have forgotten that I introduced you to Melinda. I saw her watching the incident, which means that she knows it was a Mrs. Courtenay who so publicly told her

brother exactly what she thought of him. Then there is my father, who may recall you from when you first arrived and were
introduced to him. He is likely to remember anyone in Caro's
party."

Summer felt sick. Every time she thought she'd wriggled
clear, something else happened to trap her. Heads she lost,
tails she lost too! But at least she was a little reassured by
Francis's manner now, for there wasn't any hint of concealed
relief that her misconduct had offered him a solution to anything.

Caro's eyes brightened. "As I recall, Olivia, you weren't actually presented to Lord Lytherby at all, and you were only introduced to Melinda as Mrs. Courtenay, without any mention
at all of being my cousin. Is that not so, Francis?"

He nodded. "Yes, it is."

Summer breathed out with relief, but then looked urgently
at Caro. "Uncle Merriam and Mr. Bradshaw are in the card
room, but if by any further misfortune they should hear of the
incident and realize that the lady described could have been
me, will you fib by saying I had already left by then?"

"Yes, of course we will, won't we, Francis?"

"Certainly," he replied, gently placing Summer's cloak
around her shoulders.

Summer fiddled awkwardly with her fan. "For your sakes,
the only proper thing for me to do is return to Kensington as
soon as possible, in the hope that no one will connect Oakhill
House with tonight's regrettable incident."

Caro's face fell. "Oh, please don't go back to Kensington,
Olivia. You've only just arrived here, and I do so love having
you with me!"

Francis was concerned too. "I'm sure there's no need to
do that, Mrs. Courtenay. Whatever has gone wrong between
you and Brand must, I'm convinced, be a misunderstanding."

"It's best, believe me," Summer replied, feeling her face go
hot as she thought of what else she'd done with Sir Brand
Huntingford tonight apart from argue with him in public.

"Anyway, for the moment I'll go home in the carriage, but I'll be sure to see it returns in time for the end of the ball."

Caro hugged her, and Francis raised her hand to his lips. "Your wish for anonymity will be closely observed, Mrs. Courtenay," he said gently.

Her fingers closed briefly over his. "Thank you, Mr. Lytherby," she said, suddenly knowing that no matter what the Honorable Melinda Huntingford wished to the contrary, it was Caro that he loved.

"Allow me to escort you to the carriage," he said.

"No, please. I'd rather you and Caro just returned to the ball." Then, before he could protest, she hurried out into the windy night to search along the double line of waiting vehicles for the one belonging to Oakhill House.

She found it at last and called the reluctant coachman from the game of dice he was playing with some of his fellows. Within five minutes of the dreadful scene on the dance floor, she was being driven away from Bevincote. She removed her domino and leaned her head back as tears slid down her cheeks. *Oh, what a dreadful scrape all this was, what a dreadful, dreadful scrape . . .*

She gazed out at the snowy darkness and thought of the September night in the future. Why was she still here in 1807? Belatedly, she recalled the strange distortion of the recording as she was relaxing. Had the recorder broken down? A pang of alarm shot through her, but then she took a grip on herself. Something may have gone wrong in the future, but here in the past all was well. Or at least, she herself was physically and mentally well, even if all else had fallen into chaos around her.

It seemed the return journey took three times as long as the outward, but at last the carriage swung in through the familiar gates of Oakhill House and the coachman urged the team up the drive. Uncle Merriam's servants were startled when she alighted alone from the carriage, and glances were exchanged as she hurried up to her room with a candle she'd taken from the hall. It was with some relief that she closed the door behind her and leaned back against it, protecting the flickering candle with her hand.

"Olivia?"

Jeremy's urgent whisper made her give a start of fright. Hot wax splashed over her gloved hand, and she dropped the candlestick. The room was immediately engulfed in darkness, except for the soft glow of firelight from the hearth.

Chapter Fifteen

Summer searched the shadows. "J . . . Jeremy?" she breathed, wondering if she'd imagined it. Then there was movement by the wardrobe, but as he started to emerge from hiding, Gwenny's light steps approached.

Jeremy retreated hastily into the shadows again, and Summer turned quickly toward the door as the maid entered with another candle. "It's alright, Gwenny, I won't be needing you."

"But, your hair—" The maid broke off, realizing the room was in darkness except for the candle she'd brought with her.

Summer hastily retrieved the one she'd dropped. "I'm afraid I tripped on the rug," she said, lighting it again from the maid's, then placing it on the mantelpiece.

Gwenny looked curiously at her. "Is something wrong, madam?"

"No, I'm quite all right. I just have a headache, that's all."

"Oh, madam, I'm so sorry, for it must have spoiled the evening for you."

"Just a little."

"Shall I bring some lemon to apply to your temples, madam?"

"No, there's no need."

"Your hair—" the maid began again.

"I can attend to it myself," Summer said quickly.

"As you wish, madam." Gwenny curtsied, then left again.

Summer turned toward the shadows where Jeremy was hiding. "You can come out now."

He emerged once more. He wasn't in uniform, but wore a

plain brown coat and fawn breeches, and his light brown hair
was unkempt. His roguishly good-looking face was pale in the
firelight, emphasizing the sword scar on his right cheek, the
result of a past encounter with an irate husband.

"So it *was* you I saw at the Crown in Berkeley! What are
you doing here?" she demanded, her voice trembling with a
mixture of anger and unease.

He came slowly toward her. "Forgive me for frightening
you, Olivia."

"I have a great deal more than that for which to forgive you,
sir, namely a letter of unconscionably familiar tone, which you
had no business whatsoever to write," she replied coldly.

"Ah, the letter . . . Well, I confess I put pen to paper after
nearly a whole bottle of brandy. Not that I haven't entertained
such desirous sentiments toward you from time to time," he
added.

"I assure you, they have always been unrequited."

"Oh, I realize that." He gazed at her in the candlelight.

"I'm told you've gone absent without leave from your regiment, and that you've also been accused of theft from your fellow officers."

"My, my, how swiftly bad news travels," he murmured,
flinging himself on the bed and folding his hands behind his
head.

"So it's true?"

"That I've been accused and therefore obliged to flee? Yes.
But it isn't true that I'm guilty." He stared up at the bed
canopy for a long moment, then looked at her again. "I hope I
haven't made a huge mistake by deciding to trust you, Olivia,"
he said softly.

"And what is that supposed to mean?" she asked, offended.

"Simply that I mislike some of the people with whom you
now mix."

"Who, in particular?"

"Well, shall we start with the person who no doubt told you
about my, er, difficulties? To wit, one Sir Brand Huntingford,
who just happens to be a bosom friend of the man who really

did steal from the army. It *was* Huntingford who told you, wasn't it?"

"How do you know I'm acquainted with him?"

He allowed his eyes to slide over her. "Let's say I observed an exceedingly interesting Twelfth Night kiss in the Black Lion orchard. Lucky Huntingford, although to be sure the fellow does not deserve you."

Hot color washed into her cheeks, but then realization crept slowly over her. "*You* were the horseman with the hound! How else could you know about the orchard?"

He gave a faint smile. "The hound's name is Jasper, and he's really very amiable, except if he's cold and hungry, at which times he's inclined to grumble long and loud."

She recalled the mournful howl that had so frightened the Black Lion wassailers.

Jeremy drew a long breath. "Huntingford cannot be trusted, Olivia, and I therefore hope that you will not tell him you've even seen me, let alone spoken to me."

Before she could say that she'd already mentioned seeing him at Berkeley, Jeremy went on. "Huntingford is no friend of mine, Olivia, nor, I believe, can he possibly be any friend of yours. You do know he's Melinda Huntingford's brother, don't you? And like Lord Lytherby, he's intent upon doing all he can to break up the match with your cousin so that Francis can marry Melinda instead."

"You seem to know a great deal."

He smiled again. "If you're consorting with Huntingford, maybe you too have reasons to wish the match to be stopped. Poor Caro, surrounded on all sides."

Summer's eyes flashed indignantly. "How *dare* you suggest such a thing! I only want Caro's happiness, and as for Sir Brand, he doesn't even know who I am! Nor, if I have my way, will he ever find out."

Jeremy was dumbfounded. "He doesn't know who you are?" he repeated.

"I've been at considerable pains to keep my identity to myself," she said, avoiding his gaze.

"Those were *anonymous* caresses in the orchard?" he said disbelievingly.

"Yes."

He raised an eyebrow. "Now why would you wish to keep your identity from him, I wonder? What *have* you been up to, sweet Olivia? More than just kisses, I'll be bound."

"It's none of your business." She eyed him. "It doesn't really matter what *I* was up to that night, Jeremy, but what were *you* doing? I happen to know that a highwayman with a savage hound tried to hold up Sir Oswald and Lady Harvey on their way to Chavenage, and that later that same night at the Black Lion a thief stole Lady Harvey's diamond necklace, as well as other items."

Indignation lit his eyes, and he clapped a hand to his heart. "Not guilty, I vow, and it ill becomes you to even think it! As it happens, my purpose that night was simply to speak to you, but you were, er, otherwise engaged."

"So there were *two* mysterious horsemen at large in and near Tetbury on Twelfth Night, each accompanied by a large hound? That stretches credulity."

"I may have had the opportunity to play the thief, but I didn't have the motive!" He got up from the bed. "Please don't suspect such ill of me, Olivia. Rogue I may be, but I've always kept inside the law, you *know* that to be so."

"Yes, I do, Jeremy, but you have to admit that the circumstantial evidence against you would be pretty damning were it to be placed before a court, martial or otherwise." It would indeed, she thought, for Jeremy would find it virtually impossible to prove himself innocent, even though it was certain that Brand was the real thief.

He nodded resignedly.

"Anyway, I know you are innocent, for something happened at the ball tonight that proves it. Melinda Huntingford was wearing Lady Harvey's necklace, and said her brother had given it to her. That can only mean that *he* was the thief at the Black Lion. But that being said, the fact remains that you *were* there on Twelfth Night, and you *have* already been accused of theft."

His lips twisted into a wry smile. "So, light fingers are among Huntingford's many attributes, eh?"

"It would seem so," she said unhappily, then she drew a long breath. "Anyway, what did you want to see me about that night? I can't imagine you intended to take dinner with me after all."

"I came to seek your help, but then saw you with Huntingford and deemed it prudent not to make my presence known. That's why I've come here instead." Jeremy looked at her. "Olivia, the colonel of the regiment is the real thief, and he and Huntingford belong to the same St. James's club and are like that." He held up a hand and crossed his fingers. "You must help me, Olivia. Huntingford is eager to blacken my name in order to protect his friend, but I want to prove my innocence. I'll flee the country if I can't, for I'm damned if I'll go to jail for something I didn't do."

"Help you? In what way?"

"I want the use of your carriage. I still have one or two friends in Cirencester who may be persuaded to speak up for me."

"My *carriage*? But—"

"To go anonymously to and from Cirencester, and if necessary to Southampton, from where I can take passage for America."

"I don't know, Jeremy, this has all come as such a shock."

"I suppose you prefer to believe what Huntingford tells you?" he accused.

She glanced away. "As it happens, I wouldn't believe *anything* he told me now."

His hazel eyes were speculative. "A lovers' tiff?" he murmured. "Well, I suppose that's one small mercy."

"I know I've made a fool of myself with him, so please refrain from saying so. About the carriage . . ."

"If I have to stoop to reminding you of all the help I rendered you at the time of Roderick's death, then I will."

She faced him again, searching his face earnestly in the firelight. "Do you *vow* that you are innocent?" she asked quietly.

He met her eyes. "Yes."

Her mind was made up suddenly. "Then I'll help you," she said.

"Oh, Olivia!" He hugged her tightly.

She pulled away. "I'm returning to Kensington tomorrow, but you can have the carriage any time after that."

"But I need the carriage tomorrow!" he cried in dismay.

"If I stay, there's a real chance of Brand finding out who I am. I believe Brand is as eager as Lord Lytherby to prevent Francis from marrying Caro, and I have no doubt that if he were to learn my true identity, he'd inform Lord Lytherby of my misdemeanors at the Black Lion."

"All I'm asking is a week at the most. Then by all means return to Kensington if you so desire. In the meantime, I'm sure you have to concede that Huntingford may *not* find out who you are. Can't you stay inside and plead illness for that short time?"

"Jeremy, I—"

"Can you reasonably say that a mere *possibility* concerning him is more important than my freedom?" he interrupted quietly.

She hesitated, then shook her head. "No, I suppose not. Very well, I'll stay here."

He smiled with relief. "Thank you, Olivia. Now then, I've considered how to do this without causing comment. The nearest coachbuilder is in Gloucester, so I suggest you instruct your coachman to say he's discovered some fault or other in the axle. Then he is to set off first thing in the morning as if for Gloucester, but instead, just before reaching Berkeley, if he takes the lane that leads to the estuary embankment, I will be waiting by the fox covert. Carriages will converge on this area from all directions tomorrow because of the hunt, and a number of ladies and elderly or injured gentlemen always watch the sport from various points, so no notice will be taken of another vehicle."

She nodded. "Very well. I hope you prove your innocence and don't have to flee the country, Jeremy."

He drew a long breath. "So do I, but I have to fear the worst."

"You'd better go now," she said, glancing toward the door as she thought she heard a sound in the passage.

"You *will* send the carriage as agreed?" he pressed.

"Of course."

He opened the window and climbed over the ledge to let himself down the sturdy ivy against the wall, which was clearly the way he'd gained entry in the first place.

She watched his shadowy figure slip away into the darkness, then closed the window again and sat before the dressing table to let down her hair. But after one or two pins had tinkled into the dish, she gazed thoughtfully at her reflection in the mirror.

The more she learned about Sir Brand Huntingford, the more despicable he seemed. Fresh tears stung her eyes, for in spite of the anger she felt toward him, there were other feelings that would never be easy to shed. When she'd given herself to him tonight, she'd known what true love was, for no other word could describe the way she felt toward him. But he was a man who did not shrink from treating her with great cruelty.

Not even trying to blink back the tears, Summer went on unpinning her hair and ten minutes later climbed the little steps into the huge bed. All thought of her overlong hypnotic trance eluded her now, for as Olivia she had so much to contend with here in the past that the future and Summer Stanway hardly seemed to exist. Everything kept whirling around and around in her tired head, but gradually her eyes closed and she fell into an uneasy sleep. But uneasy or not, it was a very long sleep indeed.

Chapter Sixteen

It was dark when Summer at last awoke and immediately realized she wasn't in her bed at Oakhill House or in the beach apartment. It was nighttime, and she was in a room she didn't recognize.

Shaken, she gazed around the unfamiliar surroundings. Opposite the bed she could just make out a wooden-armed chair and a table with a TV on it. Then she stared up at what looked like a control panel above her bed. It had earphones wrapped around it, and there were four labeled buttons: BBC Radio, Commercial Radio, Hospital Radio, and Nurse. With a shock she realized she was in hospital.

Why? What had happened to her? Physically she felt lousy. It was always bad when she became her modern self again because of the diabetes and the slow recovery from pneumonia, but this time was infinitely worse. Through the venetian blinds at the window she could see across to a brightly lit ward where nurses were hurrying to and from an emergency at a curtained bed, but where she lay all was quiet. Subdued lighting slanted through the open door from the corridor outside, where she could hear nurses talking softly together.

Weakly, she raised a hand to press the button for a nurse, then realized she was attached to a drip. Leads from some machine or other were fixed to her chest as well, and after a moment she recognized it as an electrocardiograph. Had she had a heart attack? No, that couldn't be . . . Her glance returned to the drip. Glucose? Yes, and insulin. Hypoglycemia! But she'd done everything she should before going to bed! She stared at the drip. Yes, she'd done everything she should, but how long ago? Her diabetic regimen was very strict and precise, and something had gone wrong the last time she'd gone back to the past. Had she missed her insulin shot?

A soft sigh drew her attention back to the chair opposite, and as she looked more closely, she saw her sister sleeping there. "Chrissie?" she whispered.

Chrissie's eyes flew open. "Summer? Oh, thank God, you're awake at last!"

Before Summer could say anything more, Chrissie leapt to her feet and dashed to the door to call the nurses.

Footsteps hurried, and the night sister came in. She was a small woman in her thirties, with brown curls tucked up beneath one of those strange starched caps that perched awkwardly right on the top of the head. "Ah, you're with us at last," she said, switching on the light over the bed and then smiling down. Her uniform was dark blue, with a crisp starched apron that reminded Summer of Gwenny's at Oakhill House.

Summer blinked in the sudden light. "What happened? Have I had a hypo?"

"You certainly have, my love, but we've stabilized you again now."

"But I've been doing everything I was told to do."

The sister took her pulse and checked the ECG. "Yes, you probably have, but it happens, especially when you haven't long been stabilized. I gather from Mrs. Marchant that the doctors in America had some difficulty getting you sorted out."

"Yes, but I was all right by the time I came here."

"And all your tests have been okay?"

"Yes."

"Nothing borderline?"

"Nothing at all. How . . . how long have I been here?"

"Well, it's now about three a.m. on Sunday morning, and you came in about two o'clock yesterday afternoon."

Summer stared at her, for it had been Friday night when she'd last gone to the past.

Chrissie edged to the bedside. "I feel a bit responsible, Summer. You see, after you'd gone to bed on Friday, Andrew and I stayed up very late watching old movies and having a glass or two of that wine we brought back from Burgundy last summer. We slept in the next morning, I mean *really* slept in, and by the time we got up at midday, you were completely out. We got the doctor who lives opposite, but although he tried all the usual things, he couldn't bring you around, so we had to get you here to Chichester."

The sister smiled again. "You've been a stubborn one, Miss Stanway, but we won in the end."

"Can I go home now?"

"Go home? Certainly not. We've got to make certain you're properly balanced again before we allow that."

"But I *am* properly balanced," Summer insisted.

"Then what has all this been about?" The sister raised an eyebrow.

"I don't know." But Summer *did* know. It was suddenly only too clear to her what had gone wrong. The distortion of sound when she'd last played the cassette was due to the recorder's batteries running low. They'd given up completely before the playing of the prompts that would have brought the trance to a close, and so she'd been left in the past. If it weren't for the diabetes, she'd have awoken normally in due course, but because she was diabetic, instead of waking up she'd gone into a coma.

The sister watched the expressions crossing her face. "Is there something we should know, my dear?" she prompted gently.

"No."

"Are you quite sure, because if there is, it might be best if you tell us."

Somehow Summer managed to look the woman in the eyes. "There isn't anything, truly there isn't."

"All right. Now then, you just lie there quietly, and I'll get the doctor."

The sister hurried out, and Chrissie came quickly to take Summer's hand. "I really do feel guilty about this, Summer," she said again.

Summer squeezed her fingers. "There's no need, for it isn't

your fault. In future I'll know to set about six alarm clocks by the bed, so at least one of them goes off and wakes me. All right?"

But Chrissie wasn't consoled. "It's just that I feel really awful for quarreling."

"Stop this right now, Chrissie Marchant. I'm as much to blame as anyone for not waking up, so that's the end of it." Summer's thoughts ran guiltily on. I'm ten times *more* to blame, if you did but know it, for all this is definitely down to me, and only me.

Chrissie searched for a handkerchief and wiped her eyes. "God, this has been the longest day of my life. They kept telling me you'd be okay, but I was convinced you'd never wake up again. In the end Andrew persuaded me they knew what they were talking about, and I felt a little better, but it wasn't until you actually opened your eyes that I really believed."

"Well, here I am again, as large as life and twice as ugly," Summer said fondly. "Where's Andrew now?"

"He stayed as long as he could, but something important came up, and he's had to fly to Dublin—something about a seminar after Christmas. He'll be back tomorrow." Chrissie managed a smile. "He said to tell you he'd bring you back a leprechaun."

"If he can squeeze one in along with all the bottles of poteen," Summer murmured.

"Probably." Chrissie sniffed.

Summer smiled fondly. "Go home and get some sleep. You'll feel better then."

"I don't want to leave you."

"I'm okay now, so go."

"But—"

"Go! They'll do everything for me in here, so there's no danger of my forgetting anything!"

"That's true." Chrissie relaxed enough to give a little laugh and get her coat from the hook behind the door. Then she returned to the bed and bent to kiss Summer's cheek. "I'll come back in the morning, and as soon as Andrew's home, he'll come in as well."

"I hope to be out of here by then," Summer said determinedly.

"I hope so too. Night."

"Night."

Alone, Summer drew a long breath and gazed at the control panel. When she first started using the cassette to bring on the time travel, she took account of the recorder failing by relying on waking up naturally, as people always did if they weren't brought out of the trance after being hypnotized. But she *hadn't* reckoned with the trance lingering long enough to take her past the time for her insulin, thus triggering her diabetes and turning the self-induced trance into a diabetic coma!

Her brows drew thoughtfully. All the time she'd been in the past she hadn't sensed anything going wrong; in fact she'd felt fine. It was an interesting point. No, more than that, it was positively engrossing. She'd gone to sleep in 1807 as Olivia Courtenay, but had awoken here in the future as Summer Stanway, not because the cassette had prompted her as usual, but because the doctors had succeeded in stabilizing her. Olivia hadn't been affected at all by Summer's medical crisis, which posed a very interesting question—if Chrissie and Andrew hadn't found her when they did, and she'd remained in a diabetic coma, would her existence in the past have continued undisturbed?

The next logical question was to wonder what would have happened if they had been too late, and her present-day self had died? Would she *still* live on in the past? If she wished, could she escape to become Olivia forever? She smiled a little wryly, for now that Brand had been revealed in all his true despicable colors, what reason could she have for wanting to stay as Olivia? She still wanted to go back again to see the outcome of everything, but as to staying there . . . No, it wasn't even on the agenda anymore. Footsteps approached again as the sister returned with a young doctor. Summer submitted to their ministering and put her fascinating theories temporarily to one side.

*   *   *

Summer was allowed to leave the hospital a few days later. The weather was particularly fine that evening, and as the September sun sank beyond the horizon in a blaze of glory, she curled up in an armchair in her robe to watch it.

She sipped a cup of hot milk and smiled at Chrissie. "God, am I looking forward to a decent bed tonight. British hospitals should be reported to the Court of Human Rights, for I'm convinced their mattresses were devised as a means of torture."

Andrew laughed. "And those in American hospitals are worthy of the Ritz?" he remarked, folding the newspaper he'd been reading.

Summer pursed her lips. "Mm, well, maybe not quite," she conceded.

Chrissie had been lolling on the sofa, but now she sat up. "I don't know about you two, but I'm bushed. I haven't slept in days and will have to hit the sack soon."

Summer nodded. "I won't be long either. What is it about hospitals? All that time in bed, and *still* I'm tired."

Chrissie looked at her. "Just make sure you set those new alarm clocks before you go to sleep."

"I will." Summer chuckled. "I still don't believe you actually went out and bought those things."

"I'm not taking any chances with you from now on."

"Okay, but did you have to choose a model of Big Ben that's so loud it sounds like the real thing, and a green plastic frog that croaks *Wake up, rise and shine*? I'll wake up all right, but only long enough to die of shock!"

"I thought the frog was cute, and the Big Ben seemed an appropriate souvenir of England."

Andrew chuckled and eyed Summer slyly. "Yes, and it makes up for those dreadful musical eggcups you and Jack gave us last year."

Summer grinned. "Tacky, weren't they? We thought of you two as soon as we saw them."

"Gee, thanks," Andrew replied, leaning across and tapping her on the head with his folded newspaper.

Chrissie got up. "Enough of this witty banter. I've just got to get some sleep."

Andrew rose. "I may as well turn in too, I've got a heavy day tomorrow." He looked at Summer. "Will you be okay?"

"I *can* finish hot milk unaided, you know," she replied.

"Night then."

"Night."

Alone, she gazed out at the remains of the sunset. In spite of what had happened, she had every intention of returning to 1807 tonight. She'd bought some new batteries in the shop in the hospital, and on getting back to the apartment had checked the recorder thoroughly. It worked perfectly again now, and to be absolutely certain there wouldn't be a repeat hypo performance, she would set those darned alarms too.

She finished the hot milk and went through into the kitchen to wash the cup. A few minutes later, all mandatory medical rituals complete, she went to bed. Putting out the light, she lay there for a long time, to see if Chrissie or Andrew stirred from their room to double-check on her, but as the minutes passed, she knew they'd gone to sleep.

She smiled as she glanced at the bedside table. Big Ben and a green frog! Typical Chrissie, she thought as she set them for the morning. Then she opened the drawer containing the recorder. Her finger paused above the button. After all her sins of late, she really shouldn't be doing this, but she *had* to find out what happened next in the past, she *had* to! So she pressed it and lay back.

Breathing in deeply, she commenced her exercises as the soothing music washed over her. She felt the familiar drowsiness stealing through her body, as warm and sensuous as Brand's caresses. "Oh, Brand," she whispered, but the words seemed to be whipped away, as if by a playful breeze.

She opened her eyes in puzzlement, then closed them again quickly because everything was so white and bright after the dark bedroom. Slowly, she looked once more. She was in the garden in front of Oakhill House. It was two days after the ball, and fresh snow had fallen overnight, but the sun was out now. She wore her ankle boots and dark green cloak, her hands were warm in her muff, and the black fur framing her hood fluttered against her cheeks in the breeze that swept along the vale. In the distance the estuary shone silver beneath the January sun, and she could just make out the ruined chapel on the embankment.

Her boots crunched in the snow, and she shivered, for it was very cold, but after two days of observing Jeremy's advice that she stay inside in order to avoid all chance of coming face-to-face with Brand, she was glad to be in the fresh air again. She wasn't the only one to have come out, for George Bradshaw had left the house immediately after breakfast in order to go for a long walk in the park. There was no sign of him anywhere, and she couldn't help the unchristian hope he'd fallen in a drift somewhere.

Nothing of great consequence had taken place since the last visit to the past. The carriage had been there for Jeremy as planned, and as it hadn't returned, she could only suppose it had mingled successfully with the numerous other vehicles that had cluttered the neighborhood lanes because of the hunt. Jeremy must be in Cirencester now, and she prayed he would succeed in gaining the help he needed to prove his innocence.

The hunt itself, from which Uncle Merriam and George Bradshaw had returned unscathed, had proceeded without event. She and Caro had watched from the upstairs windows as hounds and horsemen streamed south across the End of the World.

Caro assured her that no one at the ball had discovered who the lady was who'd caused the scene, but there had been one further strange incident after her departure, and that was the disappearance from Melinda's throat of Lady Harvey's diamonds. Caro had commented upon it at breakfast the following morning, observing that it was strange the necklace should have been discarded halfway through the ball when it went so very well with Melinda's gown. Summer, of course, read a great deal into its sudden absence. Because the diamonds had been recognized, Brand had decided it was wiser for his sister not to flaunt stolen property at so public an event as a ball.

She brushed the snow from a stone bench in a rose arbor,

and sat down, pushing her hands further into her muff as she gazed toward the house. Francis was shortly expected to ride over from Bevincote to call upon Caro this morning, and since breakfast that young lady had done nothing but change from gown to gown in an effort to look her very best for her beloved.

Footsteps crunched through the snow, and Summer glanced up to see George Bradshaw returning at last from his walk. He wore a voluminous black cloak, and the sunlight caused his top hat to cast a sharp shadow across his thin face.

He didn't realize she was there until the last moment, and halted in surprise. "Why, good morning again, Mrs. Courtenay," he murmured, for they'd faced each other across the breakfast table.

"Sir." Her reply was curt because her intense dislike for him was now very hard to hide.

"An excellent morning, is it not?" he declared, glancing around and deeply inhaling the sharp winter air.

"Indeed, sir."

Her tone precluded any further attempt at polite conversation, so he muttered something about having been out in the snow for long enough, and walked on toward the house.

Summer watched him. Gambling debts or not, it was impossible to feel an iota of sympathy for such an unpleasant, mealymouthed insect. How he could ever have had a sister as lovable as Caro's late mother she couldn't imagine. One or other of them had to be a changeling, for to be sure they could not have been more unalike!

She hunched her shoulders against the chill as the breeze gusted slightly. The leafless rose branches around the arbor swayed, scattering some of their load of white over her, and a little whirlwind of dusty snow sped along the path, blunting the sharp edges of the footprints she and the lawyer had left. It was much more cold out here than she'd realized, and the thought of returning to the house for a cup of hot sweet chocolate began to appeal. Summer smiled, for such a drink would definitely be *verboten* for her modern self.

Hoofbeats sounded on the drive, and she saw Francis riding

toward the house, but he wasn't alone, for at his side on the same mettlesome gray as before, was Brand. She rose agitatedly from the seat and pressed back out of sight by the arbor as the two horsemen passed only about fifty feet away.

She was glad her cloak was dark green, for it did not catch the eye, but neither of them so much as glanced in her direction. They reined in before the porch, and a groom hurried to take their mounts to the stables. As the two men were admitted to the house, Summer emerged uneasily from the arbor. How long would the visit last? An hour? Two? Maybe longer? She'd freeze if she had to stay out here that long, but what else could she do?

Then she thought of the two remaining carriages in the coach house, Uncle Merriam's and George Bradshaw's. It seemed sensible—and much warmer—to wait in one of them until the two men's horses were sent for, a moment she'd be aware of because the coach house opened onto the stable yard.

Gathering her cloak close, she hurried along the path, then skirted the side of the house to make her way to the stables by way of the kitchen gardens. No one saw her slipping across the cobbles, which the stable boys had spent all morning clearing of snow, and she was able to reach the coach house without anyone realizing she was there.

The doors swung to behind her, and the shadows advanced. For a moment it was hard to see after the brightness of the snow, but then her eyes adjusted, and she saw the carriages. The latter was drawn up close against the far wall, and she climbed in through the only accessible door and made herself as comfortable as possible for what might prove to be a disagreeably long wait. She flung back her hood and undid her cloak ties, then leaned her head against the upholstery and closed her eyes. It was strange to think Brand was only yards away in the house, without any idea at all that she was here. Strange, and a little exciting.

She smiled to herself. What was it about villains that drew women? There was no doubt that Sir Brand Huntingford was very far from being the soul of chivalry, and yet her Icarus wings would still be in danger of burning if she were to be confronted by him again. The thought of his kisses made her tremble, and the thought of actually making love with him again was . . .

Slow footsteps made her start. She peered out of the carriage window, and her heart stopped, for Brand was standing about six feet away! His top hat was tipped back on his golden hair, and he wore a maroon coat and close-fitting gray breeches. There was a plain golden pin in his neckcloth, and his riding crop swung idly in his gloved hand as he glanced around the shadowy coach house. Because the carriage was against the wall, she knew she could not escape, so all she could do was entreat fate not to betray her presence.

But fate was in no mood to protect her, for suddenly he seemed to sense her secret gaze upon him. His eyes flashed directly to hers, and he gave a cool smile.

Chapter Seventeen

Brand advanced toward the carriage, and Summer edged uneasily away until her back was pressed to the window by the wall.

He opened the door and faced her. "So, Mrs. Courtenay, you are unmasked at last."

Her heart sank. In spite of all her efforts, he'd identified her anyway. "How did you—?"

"Discover who you were? By the base tactic of questioning the footmen at Bevincote. I fear you, Francis, and Miss Merriam didn't lower your voices quite enough. Once furnished with the necessary details, I insisted on accompanying Francis here today. I casually questioned Mr. Bradshaw, who kindly informed me that he had not long since seen you by the rose arbor. From there I followed your footsteps to the stable yard. The rest you know."

She lowered her eyes. "I begged Francis not to divulge my identity, so please don't blame him if he said nothing to you."

"How little faith you have in my integrity, madam. It may interest you to know that it is *not* my primary intention to act the town crier with your reputation."

Her eyes flickered, and she looked away disbelievingly.

He drew a weary breath. "Olivia, I can well imagine your horror when I came upon you at the chapel, for until that moment you hoped your misconduct at the Black Lion would remain a secret. Am I right?"

"*Our* misconduct," she corrected. "Yes, that *was* what I'd hoped."

"Have it as you wish, *our* misconduct."

"I didn't want my foolishness to damage Caro's betrothal."

He removed his top hat and casually hung it on one of the carriage lamps, then he placed a booted foot upon the rung and leaned forward to look at her more closely. "Well, I suppose tardy considerations about one's nearest and dearest are better than none at all," he murmured, slowly removing his gloves.

"You surely aren't about to pretend that your conscience is as clear as the driven snow?" she countered.

"I haven't denied gracing your bed at the Black Lion," he reminded her, tossing his gloves onto the carriage seat.

"No, but you've denied everything else!"

His blue eyes were shrewd. "Ah, yes. I'm not only a vile seducer, but a thief, a liar, and a maggot masquerading as a gentleman. Oh, and you wish you'd never set eyes on me. That was the gist of it, I seem to recall."

"If you expect me to retract a single thing, you're mistaken!"

A glimmer of wry humor played upon his lips. "Oh, I wouldn't expect *you* to retract anything, madam. Heaven forfend that Olivia Courtenay could be wrong!"

An angry brightness lit her eyes. "I'm not wrong about you, sirrah! You are everything of which I've accused you, and if you require an instance of your sins, let me remind you of the necklace Miss Huntingford wore at the ball. No, allow me to correct that statement. The necklace Miss Huntingford wore at the ball until *you* discreetly requested her to remove it. What was it you said just now? I suppose tardy considerations about one's nearest and dearest are better than none at all? After all, it wouldn't do for one's sister to be discovered wearing stolen diamonds that you gave to her, would it?"

He was silent for a long moment, then to her horror climbed into the carriage, slammed the door behind him, and sat directly opposite her. He stretched his long legs out, resting them on the seat beside her, thus trapping her in her corner, then folded his arms. "You have it all solved, don't you? Sir Brand Huntingford is the monster of the piece, and that is the end of it."

"That was the gist of it, I seem to recall," she replied with as much poise as she could muster.

The humor returned fleetingly to his lips. "More verbal fencing, and this time you can also cry *'Touché!'* as you thrust your noble blade into my vile heart. End of pantomime, bring down the curtain. Take a bow, Miss Courtenay."

"I do not regard this as a pantomime, sir," she said stiffly.

"Nor do I, Olivia, which is why I intend to keep you here until we sort this out."

"Until you've persuaded me to believe you again, you mean."

"No, Olivia." He removed his legs from the seat and sat forward suddenly. "I want to know *exactly* what I'm charged with, apart from stealing that damned necklace, of course."

"Apart from the necklace? Very well. I believe that you and Lord Lytherby are working hand in glove to destroy Caro's match so that your sister can marry Francis instead. I believe that you know your friend the colonel is the one who really stole from his officers, and that you are assisting him to incriminate Jeremy instead. Finally, contrary to being a man of integrity, you have every intention of informing Lord Lytherby that Miss Merriam's cousin is a loose woman with whom it would be a catastrophe for the Lytherbys to be associated."

"My, my, what a very disagreeable fellow I am, to be sure," he murmured.

"Yes, sir, you are," she said quietly.

"And if I deny it all?"

"Do you?"

He met her eyes. "Yes, Olivia, I do."

"Then how did Miss Huntingford acquire the necklace?" she challenged, knowing that this was the one solid thing she had to go on, the rest being little more than intuition and informed guesswork.

"You will not believe me if I tell you," he replied.

"From which I take it you cannot answer because anything you say will be quite obviously a fabrication," she declared scornfully.

Brand leaned back wearily against the upholstery. "There is

no fabrication. You're right about one thing, though, I *did* order her to remove it at the ball because I had no desire to risk her being implicated in a crime, but *I* didn't give her the necklace in the first place, Fenwick did."

For a moment she was dumbfounded, but then the scorn returned. "Oh, of course, it would *have* to be Jeremy!"

"Be as disdainful as you wish, madam, it still happens to be the truth. For over a month now Melinda has been head over heels in love with Fenwick."

Summer was startled. "I don't believe you . . ." But she remembered the conversation in her bedroom after the ball, when Jeremy had known all about Sir Brand Huntingford and his sister. *How* had he known about them?

"It's the truth, Olivia."

"She told me the necklace was a gift from *you*!"

"And when I admired it before the ball, she told *me* she'd purchased it eight weeks ago in Bristol. Two vastly different stories, you will admit."

She searched his face. "Neither of which contain a single reference to Jeremy Fenwick."

"He is the only reason she ever lies. It was careless of her to give two separate explanations, but then she didn't think an occasion would arise when her lies would become evident. Well, it did arise, and my suspicions arose with it. From there it was a simple matter to deduce that Fenwick was secretly at the Black Lion that night after all."

She toyed with the fur on her cloak.

"What are you thinking?" Brand asked suddenly, watching the expressions on her face.

"Jeremy *was* there that night," she admitted reluctantly.

He sat forward sharply. "How do you know?"

"He told me."

"When?" he demanded.

"He was waiting here at Oakhill House when I returned from the ball."

"So he's in the area! I *knew* it!" Brand ran angry fingers through his hair.

"He came to seek my help, but then saw us in the orchard, and—"

"He was the horseman in the orchard!" Brand said suddenly.

She nodded.

He gave a bitter laugh. "And I had him in my sights! If I'd squeezed the trigger, I'd have been rid of him there and then!"

"And been guilty of murder," she pointed out.

"Possibly. Well, I didn't put a bullet in him, more's the pity, and he survived to give my sister the necklace, which I'm now more certain than ever was stolen by him." He leaned back again almost resignedly, except she sensed he was a man who would never resign himself to anything that didn't suit.

"Brand, the Jeremy I know isn't at all as you describe him. He's kind, a good friend, and—"

He started forward furiously. "Damn it, Olivia, he's a common little nobody who seeks to advance his fortunes through my sister!"

She found his words offensive. The Honorable Melinda Huntingford wasn't exactly royal, although one might think so to listen to her brother, and Jeremy's social standing was exactly the same as her late husband Roderick's, so when Sir Brand Huntingford spoke contemptuously of Jeremy as a common little nobody, he implied the same of Roderick.

Brand gave an ironic laugh. "Olivia, your precious friend Fenwick is an adventurer in pursuit of a fortune, and Melinda has recently become an heiress. Do I need to spell it out further? He has already endeavored to seduce her. Why else do you imagine I'd put an end to him if I laid hands upon him?"

"I cannot believe that Jeremy would—"

He interrupted. "You clearly don't know him as well as you'd like to think. Just over a month ago, when Melinda stayed with me at my house in Hanover Square, she went riding with friends in Hyde Park and was introduced to Fenwick. He learned of her inheritance and immediately began dancing attendance, so I banned him in no uncertain terms. But it didn't end. Two evenings later I saw her slipping out and followed her to Grillion's Hotel in Albemarle Street, where I found her taking dinner with Fenwick. He fled immediately through a back entrance, and I subsequently discovered, although Melinda never knew, that he'd taken a private room in the names of Major and *Mrs.* Fenwick. I lost no time in bringing Melinda back here to Bevincote and protected her reputation by saying nothing to Lytherby. Now do you believe me?"

"I hardly think you would invent such a tale," she conceded unhappily, but it *still* didn't sound like the Jeremy she knew. "If he's really in search of a fortune, and if he did steal the necklace, surely all he had to do was sell the latter to achieve the former!"

"Dear God, woman, do you imagine he wants to settle for hundreds when he can have hundreds of *thousands*?"

Summer stared at him.

Chapter Eighteen

"Hundreds of *thousands*?" Summer repeated in amazement.

Brand nodded. "It isn't widely known yet, but due to various unexpected deaths in her late mother's family, Melinda has become a great heiress. That's why Fenwick is pursuing her so relentlessly, and also why Lord Lytherby probably regrets permitting Francis to make a match with your cousin, although if he *does* regret granting that permission, I know nothing of it. I'm certainly not his accomplice in any plot to drive a wedge between Francis and Miss Merriam in order to put Melinda forward instead. The Lytherby coffers were emptied by the astronomic cost of turning Bevincote into an Oriental extravagance, but Lytherby wasn't concerned, because he expected a vast inheritance from a dying cousin. Then a month or so ago—coinciding with Melinda's great elevation in wealth—that inheritance went elsewhere, leaving his lordship with threadbare pockets."

Summer's lips parted. At last she knew why Lord Lytherby had changed toward the match, and what he'd meant in the billiard room when he said he couldn't *afford* Caro as his daughter-in-law.

Brand continued. "The annual masked ball was an extravagance Lytherby's finances couldn't really rise to, but cancelling it would have meant admitting his predicament to the world—and to Francis, who knows nothing of the true situation. I only know because I happened to catch Lytherby a night or so ago when he was maudlin after a little too much cognac. But maudlin or not, he still made me swear to hold my tongue, so what I've said to you is in the strictest confidence. Is that understood?"

"Naturally."

"I can conceive that Lytherby is probably pinched to the quick that Francis is in love with your financially humble cousin, but at least theirs is a true and honest love, which is more than can be said of Fenwick's pursuit of my foolish sister. I'll see him dead before I permit him to marry her."

Summer looked at him again. "If she really loves him, bringing her here to Bevincote won't make the slightest difference. Love always finds a way," she observed.

"She isn't a fool; sooner or later she *has* to see him for what he is, and I would much rather it were sooner. It was in order to discredit him that I kept the letter he wrote to you, for its affectionate and suggestive contents seemed likely to convince Melinda that the fellow wasn't as faithful, noble, and flawless as she thought." He broke off for a moment, his lips pressed together as he met Summer's eyes again. "Discovering that you and he were probably lovers was a double-edged weapon, Olivia, for if it suggested Fenwick's unfaithfulness to my sister, it also suggested that you were rather less than I'd hoped."

"Jeremy and I are not and never have been lovers," she said stiffly.

He sat forward again. "Look, Olivia, I don't want to keep quarreling with you. I'm *desperately* worried about Melinda, who is much more headstrong and determined than even I anticipated. I want to protect her from the likes of Fenwick, but since Hanover Square she has become as wily as a fox."

Yes, Summer thought, recalling how Melinda had seemed so completely infatuated with Francis at the ball. If Brand was to be believed, that young lady's affections were actually directed at Jeremy!

Brand gave a caustic laugh. "And to think that when I arrived at Bevincote, I actually expected to find her full of praise and longing for the Duke of Chandworth!"

"What has *he* to do with it?"

Brand explained. "I encountered him just before leaving

town. The manner in which he inquired after her suggested they may have formed a mutual *tendresse* at Berkeley Castle recently, and I was well pleased, for he is *definitely* suitable. In the event, however, I arrived at Bevincote to find that she seemed to have warmed to Francis instead. I was relieved Fenwick was no longer on the scene, so did nothing with his billet-doux."

"That letter wasn't a billet-doux," she said coldly. "Jeremy was in his cups and being mischievous when he wrote it."

"I'd dearly like to believe that, Olivia."

"Then do so, for it is the truth."

"Truth being something you clearly think I would not recognize if it too had a label attached to it," he murmured wryly.

"You chose to say it, sir," she replied tartly.

"So I did," he said with a sigh.

Summer was beginning to find it difficult keeping disbelieving him, but Sir Brand Huntingford had taken her in twice before, treating her shabbily after both occasions.

Brand was silent for a long moment, then his dark blue eyes met hers again. "You say Fenwick accuses me of being friendly with his colonel. Olivia, I don't know any colonels, let alone that particular one. Can't you see that *Fenwick* is the liar in all this, not me? Oh, damn the fellow's vile eyes! He's ruining my sister's life, and there seems precious little I am able to do about it! After you'd identified the necklace at the ball, I realized she must have seen him during the last few days, so for the sake of her safety I was obliged to tell Lytherby about the liaison. Now he's confined her to Bevincote and its grounds, and I have to agree that he has no real choice. At least for the moment we can be sure she is safe." He looked away, for a moment almost overcome.

His obvious distress was too touching to be anything other than sincere, and Summer suddenly felt her distrust finally slipping away. She was hardly aware of the beguilingly different emotion that took its place; indeed she didn't realize anything until she suddenly sat forward to put her hand over his. "I'm so sorry all this has happened, Brand," she said softly.

His firm fingers enclosed hers. "I haven't lied to you at all, Olivia, and now I deny the last charge you have made against me. A gentleman *never* tells tales on a lady, least of all a lady with whom he's shared such sweet intimacies as I've shared with you."

Her heart almost turned over. "I believe you, Brand."

He made to put his other hand to her cheek, but she drew back a little guiltily. "I . . . I haven't yet told you everything I know." She related what she'd heard in the billiard room.

He was silent for a moment when she finished, then he looked at her. "Have you any idea what Bradshaw has begun?"

"No, except . . ." She thought for a moment. "Well, he may have said something to Uncle Merriam, although I can't be sure, nor do I know what it could be." She related her exchanges with her uncle.

"Have you said anything to Miss Merriam?"

"No. Uncle Merriam was at pains to make me promise not to. Will you tell Francis and Melinda?"

He shook his head. "I think not. We can't be certain that your uncle's problem derives from anything Bradshaw has said, and rather than cause unnecessary upset, it's best we find out all we can first."

"We?" She smiled a little. "Are we conspiring together, Sir Brand?"

"Yes, Mrs. Courtenay, I believe we are, unless, of course, you still nurture deep doubts about me?"

He put his hand to her cheek again, and this time she didn't move away. "I don't doubt you at all anymore," she whispered.

He slid his fingers gently into the soft hair at the nape of her neck to draw her lips toward his. Their mouths moved lovingly together, and the passion that smoldered constantly between them began to ignite again. Angry words and accusations hadn't damped it, suspicion and mistrust couldn't extinguish it, and to touch one another fanned it into instant flame. His tongue caressed hers gently, and his hand moved sensuously over her thigh through the thickness of her cloak and gown.

Then he drew her across the carriage onto his lap before kissing her again.

She sank willingly against him, sighing softly as he slipped a hand inside her cloak to stroke her breast. Her cream woolen gown was thin and delicate, and her nipple eager beneath his knowing touch. He enclosed the entire breast, and his lips became more urgent as his fingers slid between the tiny ribbons fastening her bodice. Her skin was warm and pliable, the swelling of her breast inviting.

She could feel his erection pulsing beneath her, and she felt almost weak with pleasure as she moved against it. He moaned softly, and she leaned back a little as he undid the ribbons of her gown and put his lips to her upturned nipple, teasing it with his lips and tongue as he took it deep into his mouth.

They both knew they would make love here in the carriage; their desire swept them along too fiercely for there to be any other outcome. Her cloak parted as he lifted her onto the seat opposite, and she lay there, her exposed breasts soft and pale in the shadowy light. As he knelt beside her to slip his arms around her and put his lips to hers again, neither of them gave any thought to the possibility of discovery. Anyone could have entered the coach house and caught them in their stolen passion, but they paid no heed to such a danger.

Her hands roamed adoringly over his back and taut buttocks, and then more hesitantly toward the fierce arousal that strained his breeches. Slowly, oh, so slowly, her fingers slid over it. His kiss immediately became more ardent, and after a moment he drew slightly away to unbutton his breeches and free the shaft that pounded with preparedness. He paused as her trembling fingers circled the hilt before moving slowly and wonderingly along its length, then he closed his eyes as she leaned up a little to put her lips to the tip. His hand slid into her hair as she took him deep into her mouth, her arms wrapping around his hips to hold him close as for the first time ever she indulged in this most exhilarating of intimacies. Even with Jack she had never done this, but with Brand, oh, with Brand it was the most perfect and exquisite pleasure . . .

Fearing her lips would prove too much, at last he drew away, and she lay back again as he raised her gown and prepared to make her his. She drew him down into her arms, and his erection slid tantalizingly between her thighs, but without penetrating her. She craved full union, but he knew how to prolong her pleasure. His caresses were skillful and more sensuous than ever before, and she was so lost in excitement that she almost feared she would lost consciousness.

At last he pushed into her, and she cried out, clinging to him with gratification as he began the first of the long easy strokes that intensified her enjoyment almost beyond endurance. The wild hunt was in full cry through her hot veins, and her flesh felt as if it were melting beneath him.

They reached the zenith at the same moment, their bodies shuddering together as they really became a single entity. Tears stung her eyes. "I love you, Brand, I love you, I love you, I love you . . ." she whispered.

"My love is yours too, my darling," he breathed in reply, his words muffled because his lips were against hers again.

Afterward they lay locked in each other's arms, luxuriating in the gently fading sensations that still undulated lazily through their bodies. She didn't want those moments to end, but end they must, as she knew only too well.

At last he pulled away and straightened his clothes, then he gazed down at her for a moment before tenderly pulling her skirts down to cover her again. He crouched beside her once more to retie her bodice, but as he took the little ribbons in his hands, he bent his head to kiss both her nipples in turn, before at last tying the ribbons. "You mean everything to me, Olivia," he said softly.

"Oh, Brand . . ." She began to link her arms around his neck again, but then paused as from out of the blue a dreadful thought struck her about Jeremy and Melinda. What was the one course any real fortune hunter would take to ensnare an heiress? Why, elopement, of course! She gave a sharp intake of breath. Confining Melinda to Bevincote and its grounds would do no good if all she had to do was ride to a secluded point on the estate boundary, where her lover was waiting with a carriage to whisk her away. And now Jeremy had just such a carriage!

Brand looked uneasily at her suddenly pale face. "Something's wrong, isn't it? Tell me what it is."

"It may not be anything, of course, but . . ."

"Tell me," he said again.

"What if Jeremy and Melinda plan to elope?" she whispered. "My carriage is supposed to be under repair at a Gloucester coachbuilder, but there's nothing wrong with it. Brand, I've let Jeremy have use of it."

He stared at her, then straightened. "You've what?"

"When he asked me, I didn't know about his liaison with Melinda, so it didn't occur to me. He said he wanted to return to Cirencester to try to help clear his name, but . . ." She looked wretchedly at him.

A new light cut into his eyes, and he breathed out with slow unease. "Damn it, you could be right," he murmured, sitting back on the opposite seat and running his hand through his hair. "What a fool I've been! After that business at Grillion's I should have *guessed*!"

"I may be wrong, so please don't fear the worst." But the more she thought about it, the more convinced she became that elopement was indeed the reason why Jeremy had wanted the carriage.

"No, Olivia, your guess is probably only too well-founded."

"Oh, Brand, if anything happens, it will all be my fault!"

"No, my darling, no blame attaches to you, for you weren't to know," he said gently, leaning forward to take her hand and raise the palm lovingly to his lips. "This makes no difference, I still love you, but for the moment I *must* return to Bevincote, you do understand, don't you?"

"Yes," she whispered. "You will let me know if—?"

"I'll send word whatever happens." He squeezed her fingers, then snatched up his gloves and flung open the carriage door to climb out. He retrieved his top hat from the carriage lamp, and a moment later he'd gone.

The coach house doors swung to behind him, and suddenly the carriage became so dark inside that she couldn't even see the seat opposite. Then she heard a click before another door closed somewhere, and she realized she was back in her bed at the beach apartment.

The click had been the recorder switching off, and the second door was that of the apartment across the landing, where the occupants had just returned noisily from a party.

Chapter Nineteen

Conflicting feelings ran endlessly through Summer the next morning. First there was joy because Brand loved her, then came conscience because she may have provided Jeremy with the means to abduct Melinda. As a result she was in a very restless, oddly talkative mood.

Andrew left early for his heavy day of appointments, so it was just Chrissie who sat at the breakfast table as Summer chattered nonstop and toyed with a knife so it kept clinking against her plate. At last Chrissie could stand no more. "What *is* the matter with you today?" she cried. "Your mouth hasn't taken a rest since you sat down, and if you rattle that darned knife once more, so help me I'll stick it into you!"

Summer put the knife down. "I'm sorry."

"I can't remember you *ever* going on and on at the table like this. Usually it's a case of dragging a word out of you!"

Summer shifted uncomfortably. "I know. It's just that I feel good today—I think," she added.

"You act like you're still high after spending a night of unbridled lust with Hollywood's biggest male star, big being the operative word!"

"Don't be vulgar," Summer murmured, but had to look quickly at her toast, for Chrissie's analogy wasn't all that far off the mark. She *did* feel high, and she *had* been with a man—one whom she loved beyond reason.

Chrissie studied her. "I haven't seen you like this since Jack."

"I haven't been like this since Jack."

"Someone's got your hormones going. Who is it? Did one

of the doctors at the hospital take your fancy? It has to be, unless of course you've met someone on one of your walks."

Summer looked at her, suddenly on the very brink of confessing what had been going on. The words hovered on her lips.

"Well, tell me, before I burst from the suspense," Chrissie implored.

"There *is* someone, but—"

The phone rang, and Chrissie reached over. "Yes? Oh, hi, honey." She put her hand over the mouthpiece. "It's Andrew," she whispered unnecessarily.

"I'd never have guessed," Summer murmured, sitting back a little weakly as Chrissie talked on the phone. She'd come within a heartbeat of blurting out the whole business. What a disaster that would have been, for she'd have had to confess about the recording. All thought of confession receded ashamedly into the wide blue yonder, and Summer wished she'd held her tongue completely.

Chrissie put the phone down and looked expectantly at her. "Right, you were about to tell me all about it."

"Well, there isn't really anything to say," Summer replied unconvincingly.

"What? Oh, come *on*!"

"No, it's truly something and nothing, Chrissie, so you're not missing anything juicy."

"Like hell I'm not. There's a guy involved, and I want to know all about him, so give, honey," Chrissie begged.

Summer sighed. "I know I was going to, Chrissie, but I've had second thoughts."

"You skunk! Getting me all wound up, then—"

"I know, I know, and I'm sorry." Summer held up her hands in submission.

Chrissie searched her face. "It's serious, isn't it?" she said suddenly.

Summer nodded. "I love him."

"But you won't tell me who he is?"

"Just that his name is Brand."

"So what's he like? What does he do?"

Summer didn't want to answer, but knew she couldn't wriggle out of it entirely. "Well, he's tall, blond, and far too handsome for my peace of mind," she murmured.

"That's you running true to form. You never could resist that type, could you? I'll bet you fantasize about being ravished by a Viking marauder."

Summer gave a weak smile. "Sure do, horned helmet and all."

Chrissie smiled. "So why haven't you mentioned him before? What's the big mystery? Is he married or something?"

"No, he's not married."

"Then what is it?"

Summer bit her lip and said nothing.

Chrissie got up and flung her napkin a little crossly on the table. "All right, keep it to yourself, I just wish you hadn't said anything at all rather than hint at it like it's some kind of state secret!"

Summer hurried tearfully around the table to hug her. "Please don't be angry with me, Chrissie, for I couldn't bear it! I love you, and I'm not holding out simply to be annoying, truly I'm not!"

Puzzled, Chrissie put her arms gently around her. "Okay, honey, okay, calm down," she murmured, resting her cheek against Summer's hair.

Summer blinked back tears, then searched in her robe pocket for a handkerchief. "I just want you to know that whatever happens, I love you and Andrew very much."

Chrissie was immediately anxious. "Whatever happens? What do you mean? Oh, Summer, is something wrong? Did they tell you something awful at the hospital?"

Summer seized her hands. "No, nothing's wrong," she said earnestly. "In fact, everything's right, as right as it could possibly be."

"Have you taken something you shouldn't?" Chrissie asked suspiciously.

"I'm not into that sort of thing, and you know it."

"There's a first time for everything."

"I'm clean, Officer Marchant."

Chrissie smiled. "So, you really love this Brand guy, mm?"

"Completely."

Chrissie shrugged and spread her hands. "Then I guess there's not a lot I can say, except I wish I knew more."

"All you need to know is that he makes me happier than I've ever been before, and that being with him is like . . . like . . . Oh, I don't know how to describe it."

"Good lord, you *have* got it bad," Chrissie said.

"Yes, I have. I'd like nothing more than to spend the rest of my life with him."

Chrissie's jaw dropped. "Really? Does he feel the same way?"

"Yes."

A thought struck Chrissie, and her eyes brightened. "He's English, right?"

"Yes."

"Then that means you'll stay over here? Oh, Summer, that will be great!" Chrissie glanced at the kitchen clock. "Gee, is that the time? I'd better get going. Are you quite sure you're all right to leave? I mean, you're not exactly normal this morning, and I'll gladly stay if you want me to."

Summer grimaced. "What, and be subjected to the third degree for hours on end? No, thank you. Go to your real estate, Chrissie; it's quite safe to leave me."

"Promise?"

"Promise." Summer smiled.

Chrissie hesitated. "Guess that'll have to do," she said, then kissed her on the cheek before hurrying out to fix her hair and makeup.

When Summer was alone, she went through into Andrew's study to search among the detailed maps of the United Kingdom he'd amassed on various vacations. She was sure he had one of the part of Gloucestershire she was interested in, and sure enough there it was. "Ordnance Survey, Outdoor Leisure Number Fourteen, you little beaut!" she declared, kissing the shiny yellow cover, but then she paused to look at the colored photograph on the front. There, set familiarly against the wild beauty of the Severn estuary, was the chapel!

She stared, for it was still exactly the same as it had been in 1807. Well, perhaps not *exactly* the same, for the ivy was more overgrown, and some of the stonework at the back had clearly collapsed. But it was still the chapel as she knew it. The scene was identified at the bottom right-hand corner: *Monastic Chapel, End of the World, Severn Estuary.*

Slowly, she returned to the living room to spread the map on the floor. Then she lay on her stomach with her chin on her hands to study it. All the names from the past leapt out at her. Berkeley, Bevincote, Oakhill House, the Severn estuary and embankment, and the End of the World. It was weird to know everything seemed to have changed very little over the years; and even more weird to realize that she—as her modern self—felt no urge to go take a look.

Puzzled about this, she sat up, crossing her legs and then leaning her chin on her hands again. Why didn't she want to go there? She stared at the map and suddenly knew the answer. Brand wouldn't be there now, nor would Caro and Uncle Merriam. Brand belonged in the past. "And so do you, Summer Stanway," she whispered to herself.

Slowly, she straightened. Yes, she *did* belong in the past. She'd meant every word when she told Chrissie there was nothing she'd like more than to spend the rest of her life with Brand! She closed her eyes. He was her destiny. Love was making her want to cross the Rubicon and return to him forever.

She opened her eyes again and stared across the room toward the wind-whipped sea, which today the sun had turned to the same deep blue as Brand's eyes. Was returning to him forever really such a wild fantasy for her? Because she was *extremely* susceptible to hypnosis, she had single-handedly been able to relive a past life, and not only relive it, but experience it with an intensity that surely went beyond mere memory. And because she was also diabetic, she had discovered that those experiences in the past were not interrupted by falling into a coma. After coming around in the hospital, she had felt almost certain that if Summer Stanway had died here in the future, she would still exist in the past as Olivia. Now, as she sat here alone, that feeling began to harden into an overwhelming desire to test the theory.

She scrambled uneasily to her feet, for until this moment that desire was something that had lurked on the edge of her thoughts and had never been allowed into the spotlight. The full glare was on it now, though. She went to the French windows and opened them. As she stepped to the balcony, the noise of the sea seemed to leap at her after the quiet of the double-glazed apartment.

It was a breezy September morning, sunny but with that edge of coldness that heralded autumn. Sailboarders skimmed the waves, and far out on the water she could see one of the large white ferries that sailed between Portsmouth and Brittany. What was it Andrew said they were called? Ro-ro ferries? Yes, that was it, because vehicles rolled onto them at one end at the start of a voyage, and rolled off at the other when it was over. Sailboards and ro-ro ferries. There weren't any of those back in 1807. In fact, there were a hell of a lot of things that didn't exist back in time, but one all-important thing *did* exist—Sir Brand Huntingford.

If she left this present life, whether to go to an idyllic previous life with him, or to end up six feet under because her hypothesis was harebrained after all, her only regret would be leaving Chrissie and Andrew. Oh, there were friends back in the States, good friends most of them, but Chrissie and Andrew were her only relatives. She would hurt them, but if she could somehow make them understand . . .

She put her hands on the balcony railing and watched the waves racing over the wet sand past the breakwaters. She could leave a letter or a cassette recording, explaining absolutely everything and begging them to understand why she'd taken such an irrevocable step, but all they'd see would be her lifeless body. Hallucinations followed by another diabetic coma, they'd think, only this time she hadn't been so lucky. It would break Chrissie's heart, unless of course the theory was correct, and that after the event the fact could be *proved*. But how? *How?*

Summer dwelt upon the problem for a long while, before

she suddenly felt cold and went back inside. The closing of the French windows eliminated the sound of the sea again, and silence descended. She sat down on the sofa, still trying to puzzle a way of letting Chrissie know if it was indeed possible for her to travel back in time forever. Gradually, her attention was drawn to the table where Andrew's precious piece of medieval pottery lay on some of his papers.

She leaned across to pick it up, then sat back to study it carefully. *I, Gerald of Salisbury do curse Thomas of Winchester. May he never profit from that which he stole from me, may he . . .* May he what, she wondered? Posterity would never know now, but posterity *did* know that the highly annoyed Gerald had put a curse on him. Just some words scratched into clay before firing, but they'd lasted over the centuries to be found in that modern plowed field. Gerald and Thomas were recorded forever.

A new light entered her eyes as she thought of the graffiti in the chapel. *S & S. Stephen and Susannah.* They too had carved themselves into immortality. She knew from the map cover that the chapel was still there, virtually as it had been in the past, and if she went there now as Summer Stanway to carve her own and Chrissie's name into the stone, it would look freshly done. But if, as *Olivia,* she were to carve those names in 1807, by now they would look old and weatherworn! Such a centuries-old message would *surely* prove she'd successfully gone back in time!

She replaced the pottery on the table, then got up to retrieve the map, which she carefully and painstakingly folded in order to leave the area south of Berkeley uppermost. Then she took a red pen and ringed the chapel as vividly as she possibly could, with a note that the same chapel was illustrated on the main cover.

After that she paused to inhale deeply, for she was trembling a little. The only thing that was needed now was the nerve to do what was necessary to bring about exactly the same conditions as before—a diabetic coma while she was in a trance—except this time she had to be beyond recovery. All it would take was a suitably large overdose of insulin.

She felt suddenly cold. There'd be no coming back if she did it. Summer Stanway would be no more within a very short time. Then she had another unsettling thought. What if Chrissie came home at midday, just to check up on her? That wouldn't do, for there mustn't be any chance of being rescued at the eleventh hour. This had to be done properly, or not at all.

Almost automatically she reached for the phone. "Hi, Chrissie, it's me. Yes, I'm fine, so fine I've called a cab to go to Chichester to shop till I drop. I'll leave the answering machine on in case someone tries to get in touch with Andrew, so don't panic if you call and I don't answer. Okay?"

The conversation was over almost before it began because someone came into the office to inquire about a seafront property and Chrissie had to ring off to attend to them.

Summer replaced the receiver slowly, then switched the answering machine on. She'd started it now. Coolly she went into Andrew's study, selected a blank cassette, and then began to dictate the full story of what she'd been doing over the past few days, and what she would have done by the time the recording was played. She also told them the words she would carve in the chapel—Chrissie and Summer—then she removed the cassette from the recorder and took it into the living room. She put it next to Andrew's piece of pottery and the deliberately folded map, together with a note she wrote in urgent red capital letters. "PLAY THIS RIGHT NOW, AND PLEASE TRY TO UNDERSTAND. SUMMER."

Tears pricked her eyes as she left the living room again. Her hands shook as she prepared the insulin. There was no careful measuring this time. She intended to finish the bottle; that way she'd be sure of speedy dispatch to the hereafter. Or rather, to the here*before* . . . Again her nerve almost failed her, but then she thought of Brand, and her courage returned tenfold.

It was easy to administer the dosage in the end, and she didn't feel any different when it was done, except perhaps unnaturally calm. She got the recorder out of the drawer and carefully wound the recording on past the commencing instructions and music, then wiped the rest of the cassette clean.

She didn't want to take any chance that Andrew's closing prompts might awaken her. When all was done, she rewound the cassette to the beginning, and resolutely pressed the button.

Lying back, she let Andrew's voice drift persuasively over her. She closed her eyes and breathed slowly in and out, in and out . . . Gradually the voice and the music faded gently away into oblivion, and there was just a long silence.

Chapter Twenty

She opened her eyes to find she was standing alone by the drawing room window at Oakhill House, watching the January sun beginning to sink beyond the distant Welsh hills. She was again wearing the cream woolen gown, and her thick dark hair was pinned up loosely on top of her head. Footsteps approached across the hall, and she knew they belonged to Brand because she'd just watched him urging his horse up the drive. She turned as the door opened and he entered. There was snow on his boots, his cheeks were ruddy from having ridden with all speed from Bevincote, and his golden hair was windswept.

It was the day after they'd been together in the carriage, and she now knew that their fears about an elopement had been realized. He and Francis had returned to Bevincote to find that Melinda had gone out for a ride. Men were immediately sent to search the grounds, and her horse was discovered by a little-used gate in the boundary wall. On the other side of the wall there were carriage tracks in the snow, which were followed south until they were lost on the main Bristol highway. Then it was found that her maid had disappeared with much of her young mistress's clothing and jewelry, so there could be no doubt what had happened.

Summer hurried anxiously toward him. "Is there any news?"

"Yes. She has been found in Bristol and brought back to Bevincote, thanks to an innkeeper who sent word to me."

"I'm so very sorry that I gave Jeremy the carriage, Brand. I would never have—"

He put a finger to her lips. "You do not need to say it again, my darling, for I swear I do not hold you to blame."

"I'll warrant Lord Lytherby does, though."

He caught her hand and pulled her into his arms. His lips were cold upon hers for a moment, then he looked down into her eyes. "Well, I have to say he did at first, but he has now been persuaded that Fenwick took you in. Besides, if you hadn't said what you did yesterday, no suspicion of elopement would have been aroused until much later, and my foolish runaway sister might have been beyond reach."

"You say an innkeeper sent word?"

"Yes, but he knows very little."

"Was Jeremy caught?"

"No, the felon escaped in your carriage, which, incidentally, I doubt you will ever see again." He looked intently into her eyes. "Olivia, will you ride back to Bevincote with me now?"

"Now?" Her glance flew toward the window, for it would soon be dark.

"Melinda needs a woman's company," he said quietly.

She stared at him. "Are you saying that Jeremy . . . ?"

"I don't know, because she won't speak to anyone, but I must fear the worst. They took a room at the inn as husband and wife, just as they did at Grillion's, only this time I didn't arrive to rescue her. She may already be Fenwick's wife for all I know. There's no wedding band, but that doesn't necessarily signify anything." He pressed his lips angrily together. "She's too distressed to say anything to me, but I think she might confide in a woman. You are a widow, and she will therefore know that you are familiar with the, er, finer points, shall we say? She also knows that I trust you, and in spite of everything that counts a great deal with her, for although it may not seem so at the moment, she and I are actually very close."

"Does she know yet that I was the one who caused the scene at the ball?" Summer asked uneasily, recalling all she'd said to him so publicly. Could any sister *forgive* a woman who called her beloved brother such terrible things, let alone *confide* in the same woman?

He smiled a little. "No, nor does Lord Lytherby, if that is

your next question. Neither Francis nor I have said anything at all, so your secret is safe."

"Maybe not as safe as I'd like, for she and I didn't exactly hit it off at the ball. You see, at that time I really did think she was hoping to steal him from Caro, and I was frosty with her as a result. She knows my voice because we spoke for several minutes, and although I was masked, she still saw my eyes and hair."

"To be truthful, Olivia, she seems to be in such a state of shock that I doubt very much if the ball is even vaguely in her thoughts right now. So will you come to Bevincote, or do you have pressing matters here concerning your uncle and cousin?"

"They've gone to Berkeley and will not return before dinner. Besides nothing could be more pressing than your request. I'll change into my riding habit straightaway."

He gave a rueful smile. "If anyone should feel guilty about carriages, it's me. What on earth was I thinking of *riding* here when it's almost dark, expecting you to ride back with me! If ever a carriage was called for . . ." He paused. "Perhaps Bradshaw would—?"

"I'd rather ride," she said quickly. "If you could have someone saddle a horse for me, I'll meet you outside the main door in a few minutes."

"Very well, but I'll bring you home in a carriage, you have my word on that."

She smiled, then caught up her skirts to hurry from the room.

Five minutes later, still adjusting the net veil of her little top hat, she hurried downstairs again in her riding habit and encountered George Bradshaw in the hall.

"You seem in a great hurry, Mrs. Courtenay," he observed, glancing in surprise at her attire.

"Would you please be so good as to inform my uncle and cousin when they return that Miss Huntingford has been found, and I have accompanied Sir Brand to Bevincote to be with her?"

"I will relay your message, Mrs. Courtenay."

"Thank you." She swept past him and out into the fading afternoon light, where Brand was waiting with two horses. He assisted her to mount, and within seconds they were riding at speed down through the park toward the gates.

She looked toward the End of the World and the estuary. The sun had almost vanished now, but the ruined chapel was visible in the gathering gloom. Would she soon be able to carve her message to Chrissie? She couldn't sense anything about what might be happening right now to her future self, but here in the past she felt perfectly well. Did that mean that her theory was going to be vindicated? She prayed so, oh, how she prayed so. For a moment tears stung her eyes as she thought of her sister. "Forgive me, Chrissie," she whispered, but the wind of the gallop snatched her words away.

The ride took half an hour, and night had fallen as they passed between the great gates of Bevincote. Summer heard the windbells she'd noticed on the night of the ball; gentle and melodious, their sweet tones drifted through the darkness like distant music.

At the house Brand leapt from the saddle and came quickly to assist her down as well, then they hurried into the red-and-gold entrance hall, with its Chinese river scenes and bright lotus lusters. The sweet scent of Oriental spices still drifted from the open potpourri jars in the hearths of the fireplaces, but there were no flowers now.

Lord Lytherby and Francis were waiting, the latter leaping to his feet from a sofa as they entered. His father stood with his back to one of the dragon-carved marble fireplaces, and was without the tight lacing he'd endured for the ball, with the result that beneath his dark blue coat and mustard brocade waistcoat, his rotund shape was only too evident. His wig was very slightly askew, and standing close to the fire had made his fair skin flush.

He seemed tired as he ran a finger around his collar before speaking. "Well, I trust at least *some* relevant information will result from dragging you all the way from Oakhill House, Mrs., er, Courtenay."

"I trust so too, my lord," Summer replied.

He held her gaze. "I had no idea that you and Sir Brand were so well acquainted," he said then. "Where did you meet?"

She prayed her face didn't color suspiciously, but before she could say anything, Brand spoke first. "We've encountered each other at various functions in London."

Lord Lytherby nodded. "Indeed? Well, that explains it."

Summer's guilty glance fled to Francis, to whom she'd told an entirely different story when she'd fled from the ball, but although there was a slightly quizzical glint in his eyes, he said nothing.

At that moment a gilded clock began to chime, and her thoughts darted to the future again. Surely by now Summer Stanway *must* have almost succumbed to the huge overdose of insulin? But Olivia Courtenay still felt nothing at all. . . .

As the chimes died away, she was filled with a superstitious fear that to even think of her future self now would be to ruin everything, so she turned quickly to Brand. "Perhaps you had better take me to Miss Huntingford," she said, deliberately keeping her back to the clock.

"Certainly. This way." Brand led her toward the staircase.

On the landing she caught a brief glimpse of the ballroom, before Brand led her along a lamplit passage that was lined on one side by Indian windows, and on the other by exotic statues of Hindu gods and goddesses. At the far end they entered an area where the floor was laid with the familiar blue carpet, and she knew she was in the private apartments again.

Brand halted by a door that was flanked by tall white porcelain vases. "This is Melinda's apartment, but before we go in . . ." He caught her hand and pulled her close.

"Yes?" She looked up into his eyes.

He smiled and put his lips softly to hers, then released her. "That was all, just one small kiss," he whispered before turning to knock at the door.

Chapter Twenty-one

After a moment the door was opened by a maid, who immediately stood aside for Brand and Summer to enter a small anteroom containing an Indian couch upholstered with silver silk and crimson tassels.

Brand turned to the maid, whom Summer noticed was very like Gwenny, perhaps even a relative. "How is my sister?" he asked quietly.

She lowered her eyes. "Miss Huntingford has not said anything to me, sir, but . . ."

"Yes?"

"Well, sir, she will not confide in me because I am not her usual maid." The girl, Martha, lowered her eyes, for Lord Lytherby had summarily dismissed Melinda's maid for assisting in the elopement.

Brand nodded. "Very well, you may go for the moment."

"Sir."

Martha hurried away, and Brand led Summer through another door into the candlelit apartment beyond.

The room where Melinda sat was decorated entirely in blue and white, with delicate bamboo chairs and tables and a golden birdcage containing a canary. Through some open sliding doors Summer could see a cream-and-gold bedroom that was dominated by a bed with a gold silk pagoda canopy. There was also a dressing room and a small chamber that seemed to contain a writing desk and bookcase.

The curtains were undrawn, and Melinda's slender figure was outlined against the window. She was seated on the deep sill, gazing steadily out at the darkness, and her unpinned honey-colored hair tumbled over the shoulders of her simple lavender woolen gown. Her face was very pale and strained, with tearstains on her cheeks. She didn't look around as they came over to her; indeed she was so withdrawn that she didn't even seem aware of their presence.

Brand put his hand gently to his sister's chin and turned her face toward him. "How are you now, Melinda?"

For a long moment she stared up at him with large sorrowful lilac eyes, then she pulled her chin from his fingers and looked out of the window again.

"Melinda, you *must* tell me what happened," Brand pleaded.

Summer put a warning hand on his sleeve and shook her head. "Go now, Brand," she said firmly.

"But—"

"Go. It's best."

For a moment she thought he would refuse, but then he nodded and went out, closing the door softly behind him.

Summer removed her top hat and placed it on a table, then sat at the other end of the window ledge. From here she could see Melinda's face much more clearly, and saw not only distress and anxiety, but that deep, deep dismay that comes from having one's illusions shattered beyond all redemption.

"Miss Huntingford—or may I call you Melinda?"

There was no response.

"Please try to speak to me, Melinda, for I want to help if I can," Summer said solicitously.

At last the lilac eyes moved toward her. "I know your voice, don't I? Didn't we speak at the ball?" Melinda said after a moment.

Summer gave a rueful smile. "We did. Not the best of beginnings, I fear."

"When Brand told me he was going to bring Miss Merriam's cousin to speak to me, I little thought . . ." Melinda gazed at her. "You were the woman who said all those things to him, weren't you?"

Summer nodded resignedly. "I cannot deny it."

Melinda searched her face. "Clearly, he hasn't taken umbrage," she murmured.

"I, er, hope you don't think I spend my time being rude to people." Summer shifted a little uncomfortably.

"I behaved very shabbily and deserved your wrath, but I do not know if Brand deserved it as well."

Summer drew a long breath. "Well, I thought he did at the time."

Melinda smoothed a fold of her skirt. It was an unhappy action that spoke volumes of the distress that engulfed her, and Summer leaned across to put her hand gently over those distracted fingers.

"I've come here to talk about you, Melinda, not me. Can you tell me what happened?"

Tears welled from Melinda's eyes, and she drew her hand away. "I don't want to speak of it."

"You must, Melinda, and maybe it will be easier to tell me than tell Sir Brand. You do know why he's so worried for you, don't you? He's afraid that Jeremy forced himself upon you."

Melinda's lips trembled, and suddenly she hid her face in her hands.

Summer got up quickly and went to put her arms around her. "What is it, Melinda? I want to understand and help, so please tell me."

Melinda took her hands away from her face to reveal eyes that were brimming with tears, and suddenly words spilled out passionately from her shaking lips. "No one can *possibly* understand how used, foolish, and ashamed I feel! I adored him and really thought he loved me, so we eloped because we knew we would *never* be permitted to m . . . marry." Melinda's fists clenched with stifled emotion. "He said we would be married in the morning, but that for one night we would have to pretend we already were, otherwise the innkeeper would turn us out."

Summer stroked Melinda's hair. "And *did* you spend the night as man and wife?" she asked gently.

The reply was uttered in such a tiny voice that Summer almost didn't hear. "No."

Summer took Melinda's hands. "Then what *did* you do?" she pressed carefully.

Melinda's lips shook, and she tried to turn away.

Summer wouldn't let go of her hands. "Please tell me, Melinda."

"Jeremy tried to persuade me. He was tender and loving, but I refused to sleep in the same room with him. I said it was wrong before we were married. He became angry and locked the door before trying to *force* me onto the bed. I struggled and fought him off, and managed to scream for help. He kept trying to make me do what he wanted, but I kept screaming. People in the next room broke the door down to see what was happening. Jeremy ran out and drove off in the carriage. I haven't seen him since."

Summer tightened her hold over Melinda's hands. "And that is all of it? There's nothing you're too afraid to mention?"

"Nothing."

"Do you swear it, Melinda?"

Melinda nodded tearfully. "Yes," she whispered.

"What happened after Jeremy left?"

"I told the innkeeper who I was, and he allowed me to stay the night. Then the next morning he sent a rider to Brand here at Bevincote."

Summer sat down again, still holding Melinda's hands. "Believe me, you've been fortunate, for no lasting harm has been done, except perhaps to your pride and your trust in men."

"I don't feel fortunate, I feel more wretched than you can ever know. Have you ever been taken in so completely by someone you loved?"

Summer thought of how devastated she'd felt when she'd watched Brand drive out of the Black Lion yard. "Well, I thought I had once, and for a time I felt as crushed as you do now, but Melinda, just think how very much worse it would be for you right now if you'd become Jeremy's wife. A man who could treat you so unspeakably *before* marriage in order to gain your fortune would have continued to treat you badly after, so no matter how dreadful your present feelings, you *have* been fortunate to escape from him."

Melinda clung to every comforting word. "Yes, yes, I suppose I have."

Adroitly, Summer turned the conversation to something pleasant and exciting. "Of course you have, and soon you'll have your first London Season. You'll be the center of attention, I promise, because you're a very beautiful young lady."

Melinda brightened a little. "I'll be assured of the Duke of Chandworth's interest."

"Really? Then you'll be the envy of every other woman in town, for he is without a doubt *the* catch."

Melinda had been smiling, but suddenly her face became sad again, and more tears welled from her eyes. "I don't deserve to be happy, not after the awful way I've behaved toward Francis and Miss Merriam. I can't believe I flirted so flagrantly with him, or that I was so cruel to Miss Merriam. How they must both despise me."

"Caro is too kind to bear a grudge, especially toward someone who has suffered such a dreadful ordeal; indeed when last I saw her, she was all anxiety for your safety. As for Mr. Lytherby, well, when I saw him a few minutes ago, he was anxious about you too and certainly did not look all daggers at the mention of your name."

"Do you really mean that?"

"Of course I do."

Melinda began to rally a little. "I'm glad Brand brought you to speak to me, Mrs. Courtenay."

"My name is Olivia. If I have taken the liberty of calling you by your first name, surely it is only fair that you should do the same to me?"

"Very well, Olivia." Melinda smiled at her, then drew a long breath. "Brand is right about the diamond necklace, isn't he? Jeremy *did* steal it from poor Lady Harvey?"

"I can think of no other explanation."

"And he stole from his fellow officers, as well as indulging in highway robbery?"

"That must also be so, I fear."

"I still find it hard to believe he is so villainous. When I first knew him, he was so perfect in every way . . ." Melinda swallowed. "Well, I don't know where the army money is, but I will see that the necklace is sent back to Lady Harvey."

"She will be overjoyed, for it is very special to her."

"I want to put *all* matters right, Olivia."

"What other matters are there?"

Melinda looked away. "Francis and Miss Merriam. Somehow I must make it up to them for my despicable conduct."

"They will not expect that of you."

"Maybe not, but *I* expect it of me."

Summer got up and tactfully changed the subject again. "Shall I bring Sir Brand now? He is so worried about you that it seems unkind to leave him pacing up and down outside, for that is what he has been doing, I'm sure."

But Melinda put out a quick hand. "If first names are the order, Olivia, I think you may refer to him simply as Brand, don't you? For it's clear even to me that you are more to him than a mere acquaintance, and I doubt very much if in private you call him *Sir*."

Summer colored a little. "No, I don't," she admitted, then hurried out to tell him that all was well. She found him in the anteroom with Francis, and he turned the instant the door opened.

"How is she?" he asked.

"I think everything is all right, Brand. She's ready to speak to you now."

"Did Fenwick—?"

"I'm sure not, and she will tell you all about it if you are gentle with her." Summer smiled. "Mention of the London Season is most remedial."

As he went in to his sister, Summer turned to Francis. "Miss Huntingford fears you will always be angry with her, so I promised her you wouldn't. I trust that it was not an ill-advised liberty?"

"Not at all."

"Good, for she feels very bad." She lowered her eyes. "Actually, so do I."

"You? But what have you to feel bad about?"

"Well, Brand and I have given conflicting stories about how we met, and you must be wondering—"

He laughingly interrupted her. "It's none of my business,

Mrs. Courtenay, and besides, conflicting stories make for interesting conjecture."

"I'm sure they do."

"More interesting by the moment," he murmured, observing the blush creeping over her cheeks. Then he exhaled slowly. "Mrs. Courtenay, may I presume upon your good nature and confide in you concerning a rather sensitive matter?"

"Sensitive?"

"It concerns Caro's father."

"Uncle Merriam? Why, certainly . . ." Unbidden, she recalled that moment at the ball when her uncle had clearly not wished to greet Francis. Was that what this was about now?

Francis smiled. "I'm grateful. Shall we walk a little in the corridor? I find it easier to talk if I do that."

"Of course." She took the arm he offered, and they left the anteroom to stroll slowly along the passage.

"Mrs. Courtenay, just before Melinda disappeared, my father informed me that he had reason to believe Mr. Merriam has become deeply opposed to my match with Caro."

She didn't know what to say.

Francis went on. "Apart from seeming a little odd toward me when he arrived at the ball the other night, Mr. Merriam hasn't given me any reason to think such a thing might be so. Although, on reflection, I fancy he was a little cool when Brand and I called at Oakhill House a day or so after that." He looked at her. "Is there anything I should know, Mrs. Courtenay?"

She abided by the decision she and Brand had made to say nothing until forced to, and so gave him a false smile. "There's nothing I am aware of," she said untruthfully.

Francis went on. "You have no idea how relieved that makes me."

Her conscience pricked, and she felt she had to say *something*. "To be frank, Mr. Lytherby, I would have thought any opposition more likely to come from Lord Lytherby."

"My father? Well, there is no doubt that like any father he would *prefer* me to snap up a great heiress, but he will always place my happiness first." He looked hastily at her. "Please don't tell Caro, for it gives the impression that my father does not care for her, and that isn't so; he's actually very fond of her."

Fond of her? That was why he referred to her as a nonentity, was it? Summer bit back the angry retort that blistered to her lips, for it was hardly Francis's fault that his father was so devious and unpleasant.

After a moment Francis smiled sheepishly. "I'm worrying unnecessarily, for my father has it wrong, does he not?"

Somehow she met the smile and was glad to retrace their steps because at that moment Brand and Melinda came out of the apartment.

Melinda was pathetically uncertain of how to speak to Francis. "I . . . I'm so sorry for behaving as I did, Francis. I can't think that you and Miss Merriam will ever be able to forgive me."

"It's over with, Melinda, so you must not think any more of it." He pulled her into his arms for a moment before drawing back to look into her tear-reddened eyes. "Come, we'll adjourn to the drawing room to broach a bottle of my father's best champagne to celebrate that all is well again."

Brand took Summer's hand and drew it over his sleeve, but as they all began to walk toward the drawing room, Summer's thoughts bore no relation whatsoever to the smile upon her lips. Celebrate that all was now well? How could she possibly do that when she knew all was still *far* from well!

Brand glanced at her. "I haven't forgotten my promise to convey you back to Oakhill House in a carriage," he said with a smile.

She nodded, then looked uneasily up at him. "We have to talk, Brand. Lord Lytherby has been saying things to Francis about my uncle having changed his mind about the match, and Francis asked me if I knew anything. I didn't like not telling him everything."

He searched her eyes. "It will seem churlish if we don't take champagne with them now, so we'll talk in the carriage on the way back to Oakhill House."

She nodded, and they followed the others to the drawing room, where Lord Lytherby soon joined them.

Summer found it hard to tolerate his frequently expressed relief regarding Melinda's timely escape from Jeremy, because she knew his only real concern was that his ward and her fortune were still available for his own purposes. As to the false warmth he also expressed toward Francis's match with Caro, that was beyond the pale, so she said very little as she sipped her champagne. But as she watched Lord Lytherby, she became aware of a subtle change in him, as if a little of his spirit had been dampened. He certainly wasn't the same man he'd been on the night of the ball.

When at last Brand led her out to the waiting carriage to take her back to Oakhill House, it wasn't of Lord Lytherby that she thought in the few moments before the vehicle drew away, but of the future, where surely it was now all over for her modern self? Oh, if only she could be certain, but she didn't dare rely upon anything. She almost wished she could become Summer Stanway again for a few moments, just to see. It was a very fleeting wish.

As the carriage drove away from Bevincote, Brand wrapped his cloak around them both. Her head rested on his shoulder, and as he stroked her cheek with ungloved fingertips, she gazed up at the starlit sky. Stars were timeless, but she prayed that from now on for her they would always gaze down on the nineteenth century.

Chapter Twenty-two

The snow-covered countryside was ghostly as the carriage swayed at a leisurely pace through the darkness. It was very cold outside, but before speaking of Francis, Summer and Brand used their minutes of privacy to steal kisses and embraces. They held each other close, making the most of the opportunity to whisper all the things that lovers whisper, and it wasn't until they were within half a mile of Oakhill House that she moved out of his embrace to tell him what Francis had said.

Then she looked at him in the shadows of the carriage. "Dare we still keep our own counsel on this, Brand?"

He leaned his head back against the upholstery and thought for a long moment. "On the other hand, dare we say anything?" he murmured. "I've already told you that Francis isn't aware of the true extent of his father's financial scrape, and look at how Lytherby behaved tonight. Nothing could have been more fond than the way he spoke of your cousin. Can we expect Francis to believe it was an act?"

"Lord Lytherby *loathes* poor Caro, and it was hypocrisy of the vilest kind for him to speak as he did."

"My darling, I beg to differ with your conviction that he *loathes* her, for it isn't true; what he loathes is her lack of fortune. His back is to the wall."

"You surely aren't *defending* him, are you?" she said incredulously, for that was indeed how it began to sound.

He studied her for a moment, and then suddenly got up to lower the window glass and call out to the coachman. "Pull up, if you please, Hoskins."

"Sir."

"Why do you wish to stop?" Summer asked as the carriage began to slow.

"Because I intend to scotch your obvious suspicion that I may after all be on Lord Lytherby's side in this," was the firm reply.

The carriage came to a standstill, and he alighted, his cloak swinging as he turned to assist her down as well. The night air seemed colder than ever, and the snow was freezing and crisp beneath her riding boots as she glanced around. They were at the junction with the little-used lane that led across the End of the World to the estuary, and even in the moonlight she could see the chapel ruins on the embankment.

Brand drew her hand over his sleeve and led her away from the carriage. She could feel the coachman's curious eyes upon them, but within a hundred yards the lane curved, and they passed out of his sight. They could hear water beneath the crust of ice in the ditches and the brittle rustle of a bitterly cold night breeze through a willow tree by a field gate.

Brand halted at the gate. "Now then, let us be in no doubt, Olivia. I do not defend Lytherby, although I do have some sympathy with his position."

"Sympathy?" She was indignant. "How can you possibly say that!"

"Because I too am a landowner, and so to some extent I understand his problems. I have a vast estate in Lincolnshire and can vouch that there are *always* expensive difficulties to be overcome. Olivia, given your own uncle's recent trials, I would have thought you would understand a little too. If there's one thing that can be said in Lytherby's favor, it's that he loves Bevincote. It's *everything* to him, and if Francis marries your cousin instead of a bride with a fortune, that estate is almost certainly forfeit."

"Through his lordship's financial incompetence," she observed uncharitably.

"Possibly, except that no incompetence would have been

evident if his cousin hadn't willed everything elsewhere," Brand said patiently.

"And that justified his vile plot to split Caro and Francis!"

"All I'm saying is that I can see *why* a man like Lytherby has resorted to the means he has. He's arrogant and manipulative and feels the cards are loaded against him. In such circumstances there isn't much room for playing according to Hoyle. The ace is my sister, but in order to play it, first he has to dispose of an undesirable card, to wit your unfortunate cousin. I don't think he relishes what he feels he has to do, but as I've already said, he believes marriage should be a matter of practicality, not mere love. However, since Melinda so ill-advisedly ran off with Fenwick, Lytherby has been faced with the unpalatable truth that it will take a miracle for the marriage he desired to *ever* take place. Personally, I doubt very much if he'll continue plotting now; indeed I already perceive a change in him. He said what he did to Francis *before* Melinda's elopement, and now I think he's resigned to the inevitable. I suspect that from now on his policy will be one of laissez-faire, which is why I don't think we should say anything to Francis."

"But what if his attitude toward Caro *hasn't* changed?" she asked.

"It's still better to wait and see than to stir up a hornet's nest."

She said nothing.

"Do you *still* believe I'm his lordship's secret henchman?"

She returned the smile a little sheepishly. "No, and I hope you'll forget I was so foolish as to accuse you of defending him. What I was thinking was that today I too noticed a change in Lord Lytherby, as if he'd, well, lost a little of his spirit."

Brand nodded. "Yes, that describes it exactly. He's defeated, and knows it."

"I pray you're right."

"For Francis and your cousin, yes, so do I, but I can't help a sneaking sympathy for Lytherby. He lavished everything on Bevincote and now stands to lose every brick."

Summer gave him a wry look. "You almost persuade me to forget his misdeeds sufficiently to admire him!"

"Ah, that is the power of my charm," he murmured, pulling her close and kissing her on the lips.

Her mouth softened beneath his, and she molded to him. He enclosed her with his cloak, then pressed her to the gate as the kiss became more urgent. Desire caught them up as it always did, but as his hand cupped gently over her breast and expectant quivers of pleasure ran through her, a long mournful howl drifted on the frozen air.

Her breath caught, and she drew back uneasily as memories of the Black Lion orchard returned.

Knowing what she was thinking, Brand pulled her close again. "*Les loups-garous* do not exist," he murmured, just as he had on Twelfth Night.

"No, but Jeremy Fenwick and his hound do," she whispered, glancing nervously around the dark, bleak countryside.

"I don't think he'll risk coming back here."

"Melinda's here," she reminded him.

"She's seen the light, and I fancy friend Fenwick knows it," he said soothingly.

Once again the howl wavered uncannily over the countryside, and Summer felt the hairs on the back of her neck stirring unpleasantly. "It's a terrible sound," she breathed.

"Probably an old hound with a bellyache."

A twig snapped nearby, and Summer started, her eyes wide with fear. "What was that?" she gasped, but then a fox dashed from the undergrowth and across the open field.

Realizing how unsettled she now was, Brand took her hand. "Do you want to go back to the carriage?"

"Yes," she said in a small voice.

He drew her fingers to his lips. "Come then," he said.

He ushered her protectively back along the lane, and it was with some relief that she soon saw the steady glow of the carriage lamps ahead. A minute or so later, the coachman stirred the team into action again.

Caro and her father emerged as the carriage at last drew up

at the door of Oakhill House, and Uncle Merriam was at pains to invite Brand into the house, but he declined.

"Thank you, sir, but I think I should return to my sister."

Caro was concerned. "How is Miss Huntingford, Sir Brand?"

"Shaken, but thankfully unharmed."

Summer looked at her. "And very anxious that although Francis has forgiven her, you will not be able to, Caro."

Caro smiled. "Of course I can forgive her."

Brand took her hand and brought it swiftly to his lips. "You are very gracious, Miss Merriam."

"Perhaps it would be in order for me to call upon her soon?"

"That would be more than just in order, Miss Merriam, it would be most acceptable."

Uncle Merriam cleared his throat. "Er, Sir Brand, would you be so kind as to convey a message to Mr. Lytherby for me?"

Brand's eyes slid momentarily to Summer, then back to her uncle. "Yes, of course, sir."

"Would you inform him that I would be most grateful if he could come here tomorrow? There are certain things I wish to discuss."

Summer's heart sank, but it was impossible to tell anything from her uncle's face.

Brand hesitated. "Certainly, Mr. Merriam. Is, er, is anything wrong?"

"Wrong? Oh, dear me, no!" Caro's father gave a dismissive laugh. "It's nothing of dire consequence, just a few loose ends he and I should tie."

Brand relaxed. "I'll inform him as soon as I return. No doubt he'll call in the morning, for I believe he has to go to Berkeley Castle in the afternoon, something about damage done to Bevincote land during the recent hunt."

Uncle Merriam nodded, then shivered. "Dear me, it's very cold out here. If you will excuse me, I think I'll go inside."

As he and Caro returned to the house, Brand turned to Summer. "No doubt I will see you again soon," he said softly, looking deep into her eyes.

She smiled. "I certainly trust so, sir," she whispered.

Ignoring the watching coachman, he kissed her before climbing swiftly into the carriage. The whip cracked, the team strained forward, and Summer watched the lamps dwindling away down through the park.

Chapter Twenty-three

Summer awoke the next morning to find herself still in the past, and still so alive and well that it was getting hard to believe how lackluster she'd felt as Summer Stanway. She hugged herself as she lay there in the warm bed, for surely she could now be certain that her theory was vindicated? The only thing she could think of that might yet prove her undoing was that Chrissie or Andrew had found her in time and rushed her to the hospital, where she was still in a very deep coma because of all the insulin she'd taken.

After breakfast she and Caro went out for a walk, then returned to find that Francis had called upon Uncle Merriam as requested. They were taking off their outdoor things in the entrance hall when they became aware of two raised male voices beyond the closed door of the library.

Summer glanced uneasily toward the muffled sound, for there was no mistaking that an angry altercation was in progress. Her heart began to sink as a sixth sense told her Lord Lytherby's plot was coming to fruition after all.

Caro's lips trembled as the argument became even more heated. "What has gone wrong?" she whispered to Summer, her eyes filling with swift tears. "I must go and see!"

She caught up her skirts in a flurry of white-spotted lime dimity to hurry toward the door, but Summer hastened after her, seizing her arm before she could go in. "No, don't!" she cried.

"But I *must*!"

"No," Summer said again.

To her relief Caro acquiesced, but they both remained outside the door, listening in increasing consternation as the bitter but indistinct exchanges continued. Caro became more and more distressed, but as Summer put her arms around her, she saw a nervous figure at the top of the staircase.

It was George Bradshaw. The lawyer drew furtively out of sight as he realized she'd noticed him.

Suddenly, the library door flew open and Francis strode out, so beside himself with fury that he didn't even appear to notice the two women. Caro tore herself from Summer's arms, her red-gold hair tumbling down from its pins because she was so overwrought. "Francis!" she cried hysterically. "What's wrong? Oh, Francis, *please* tell me!"

He turned, his brown eyes bright with bitterness. "It is over between us, Caro; I want nothing more to do with the name of Merriam!"

Caro ran to him. "For pity's sake, I love you, Francis!" she sobbed, trying to put her arms around his neck.

But he caught her wrists and held her away. "No, Caro, I cannot and will not suffer the unspeakable insults your father has just directed toward me." His bitter glance went to Summer. "Nor can I forgive you, Mrs. Courtenay, for allowing me to confide in you yesterday, when all the time you *must* have been well aware that something was very wrong. I will never forget that you were despicable enough to allow me to be sent for today without at least giving me some warning of the monstrous insults that awaited me!"

Guilt was written large and clear on Summer's face. Oh, how she wished she and Brand had decided to say something, for if he'd returned to Bevincote last night and told Francis all they knew, things might not have gone like this now. But it was too late, and the worst had happened. "Mr. Lytherby, I—"

"Spare your breath, madam!" he interrupted icily.

Caro looked at them both through a blur of uncomprehending tears. "What is going on? I don't understand, Francis, truly I don't! About what should Olivia have warned you? And what insults have been—"

"I will not lower myself to repeat anything! But one thing I *will* say—no one from this accursed house will ever set foot in Bevincote again, is that clear?" he cried, his voice catching on something close to a sob, although whether it was of anguish or rage, it was impossible to tell.

Caro was devastated. Her whole body shook with uncontrollable sobs as she hid her face in her hands and sank to her knees. "Oh, Francis, F . . . Francis . . ." she wept.

He continued to address Summer. "And if Brand imagines that my father or I will tolerate his continuing association with *you*, madam, he is sadly mistaken. Any contact with you will be deemed as disloyalty toward us, and that in turn will lead to his exclusion from all contact with Melinda until she comes of age, which is not for another year."

"You cannot mean that," Summer whispered in disbelief.

"Oh, I mean every word, madam!" He gave a harsh laugh that might almost have been his father's. "We will then very swiftly discover which lady he puts first, will we not? And I doubt if it will be you, madam!"

With that he strode to snatch up his hat and gloves from the entrance hall table. As he went out, the brightness of the snowy park was visible for a moment, then the front door swung violently closed behind him.

Summer caught up her primrose merino skirts to hurry to Caro, whose desolation was piteous to witness. Kneeling, she gathered her sobbing cousin into her arms. "It is all a terrible misunderstanding, you'll see," she said as soothingly as she could, but her anxious glance went to the library door. What on earth had Uncle Merriam said that could drive Francis into such a white-hot fury?

Caro's eyes swam with tears. "What did Francis mean, Olivia? About what should you have warned him?"

"I just knew that your father was anxious about something, that's all," Summer said inadequately, not certain what Brand would consider wise to say at this point.

"Father? But he hasn't said anything to me!" Caro looked away in confusion, more hot tears welling from her eyes. "Oh, Olivia, I wish I were dead, I wish I were dead . . ."

"No you don't, for you and Francis will still be married!" Summer declared firmly, turning toward a maid who was hovering uneasily at the other end of the hall. "Have Gwenny bring some sugared orange flower water immediately!" she ordered.

As the maid hastened away, Summer smoothed Caro's hair back from her hot forehead, then held her face in her hands. "Listen to me, Caro Merriam, I don't care *what* was said in the library just now, *or* what Francis said to us before he left; he still loves you, I *know* he does, so this will all be sorted out, I swear it will."

Caro shook her head. "No," she whispered. "It's all over."

"Don't talk like that! I won't let you!"

Startled by Summer's vehemence, Caro struggled to collect what she could of her self-control, but then recalled something else Francis had said. She looked up at Summer. "What is between Sir Brand and you, Olivia?"

"I love him, Caro."

"Does he love you?"

"Yes."

A fresh whimper slipped from Caro's lips. "Francis doesn't love me anymore, he hates me!" Her fingers dug pathetically through Summer's sleeves as the moment of calm came to an end in more hysterical sobs.

"That isn't true; Francis *does* love you," Summer insisted, looking up thankfully as Gwenny hurried toward them with the orange flower water.

"Cook says it's her own recipe, madam," the maid said, as if that ensured its efficacy.

Summer held the glass to Caro's lips. "Sip this, it will calm you."

For a moment or so Caro was still too overwrought to obey, but at last she put her shaking hands to the glass and drank a little.

Summer smoothed the disheveled red-gold hair again. "It *will* be all right, Caro, I cannot and will not believe otherwise. You and Francis were meant for each other, and nothing will change that."

Caro's tear-filled eyes shone with unutterable wretchedness. "I want to believe you, Olivia, but I cannot . . ."

Summer got up and gave the glass to Gwenny. "Take Miss

Merriam to her room, and see that she drinks all of this and then rests. Stay with her until I come."

"Yes, madam."

Summer assisted Caro to her feet. "Go with Gwenny now. I won't be long."

Still choking back sobs, Caro allowed the maid to lead her away toward the staircase, at the top of which there was now no sign at all of George Bradshaw.

Summer waited until Gwenny had ushered Caro out of sight on the next floor, then turned to the library door. She had to speak to Uncle Merriam, to try to find out what had been said. Taking a huge breath to prepare herself for what was bound to be a very awkward and sensitive conversation, she opened the door and went in.

Caro's father was seated at his desk, his head in his hands, and she saw that he too had tears on his cheeks. "Uncle Merriam?"

He rose swiftly to his feet. "Please leave me, Olivia," he said, searching his pockets for a handkerchief, then wiping his eyes as he strove to compose himself.

"I can't leave, Uncle, not without learning what happened."

"It isn't something I can speak of to you, my dear."

"Well, since Francis accuses me of callously allowing him to be lured here so that he could be unspeakably insulted, I think you owe me an explanation."

"Oh, my dear . . ."

"You told Sir Brand that all was well when it quite clearly wasn't."

"I had to, my dear, for Caro was within earshot, and I wished to protect her from worry. When Sir Brand brought you back last night, I made a spur-of-the-moment decision."

She faced him across the desk. "What happened, Uncle?" she asked again.

A nerve twitched at the side of her uncle's mouth, and he ran agitated fingers across the embossed leather surface of the desk. "I cannot speak to a woman of such shocking things, Olivia," he said again.

"What shocking things?"

He exhaled slowly. "I was obliged to speak to Francis concerning a matter of debauchery," he said then, being very careful to avoid her eyes.

"*Debauchery?* Uncle, I'm a widow, not a green girl," she reminded him.

"Nevertheless, that is all I am prepared to say."

She searched his face. What on earth had that devious toad of a lawyer been whispering? All manner of other wild possibilities coursed through her mind in those few seconds, but then one in particular stood out from all the rest. Of course. What was the single sexual circumstance that was bound to make a loving father like Henry Merriam feel he had to protect his daughter from marriage to a man she adored? A circumstance he would find too shocking to even discuss? "Uncle Merriam, has it been suggested to you that Francis has, er . . . How shall I put it . . . a less than suitable interest in his own sex?"

A horrid silence fell upon the room, and her uncle's eyes dropped unhappily to the desk. "You should not even be aware that such preferences exist, Olivia," he murmured.

Now she understood only too well why Francis had reacted as furiously as he had! "But I *am* aware, Uncle, just as I am also aware that Francis Lytherby is *not* of that inclination." She couldn't believe George Bradshaw had chosen this of *all* ways to carry out Lord Lytherby's wishes. Did the fool *really* imagine a man like Lytherby would approve of such a thing being said of his only son and heir?

Uncle Merriam looked sadly at her. "But I fear Francis Lytherby *is* of that persuasion, my dear," he insisted quietly.

"Who told you he was, Uncle?"

"I would prefer not to say."

"You don't have to, because I already know." She eyed him. "It was Mr. Bradshaw, wasn't it?"

He met her eyes, but remained stubbornly silent.

"Well, wasn't it?" she pressed. "Oh, Uncle Merriam, I warned you at the ball not to take his word for anything!"

He shifted uncomfortably. "I know you did, but how can a matter like this be verified other than by confrontation?

George told me that before leaving London he came upon some very unsavory rumors, and that after making inquiries he was dismayed to find they were well-founded. He came here knowing he couldn't shirk the disagreeable task of telling me. Olivia, his only thought was of Caro, and so he advised me to break off the match without saying anything of the true reason. He suggested I pretend to have decided that taking on the responsibility of Bevincote would be too much for her, and that is why he said what he did in the carriage on the way to the ball."

So that was how the lawyer hoped to get away with it, Summer thought.

Her uncle continued. "Once I had been apprised of these singularly unwelcome facts I knew I had to do something, so I went to the ball, intending to observe Francis, but found nothing untoward in his conduct. Then, when he and Sir Brand came here a day or so later, I was again left with the belief that the stories must after all be mischievous, but George *insisted* they were true, and his arguments finally convinced me to end the match on some invented ground or other. But when it came down to it, I knew I couldn't break off the betrothal unless I had a truly unassailable reason. I felt I owed it to Francis to be honest, just as I also owed it to Caro; nothing less than the truth would do. I said nothing to George of my decision, for it seemed disloyal to go so completely against his advice."

Summer recalled the lawyer's uneasy figure at the top of the stairs. What a shock he must have had when he realized his scheme had flown back in his face. No *wonder* he was nervous, for once news of this got back to Bevincote, he knew that he would bear the full brunt of Lord Lytherby's fury! At a stroke all hope of regaining his IOU's had been destroyed, and only ruin lay ahead.

She looked at Uncle Merriam. "He first told you in Berkeley on the day of the ball, didn't he?"

He nodded. "And I've been worrying about it ever since, so much so that when Sir Brand brought you back here last night, I suddenly felt the moment had come to take my courage in both hands. The rest you know."

"Yes, and I also know that Mr. Bradshaw invented the whole distressing story," she said bluntly.

"Oh, no, Olivia, I cannot permit you to say that. George was very upset indeed that he had to convey tidings that would break Caro's heart. She is his niece, and he loves her, so what *possible* reason could he have for inventing anything?"

"Every reason in the world. Send for him now, and I will prove it."

"Prove it?"

"Yes," she said with conviction.

For a moment he hesitated, then nodded. "As you wish." He picked up the little handbell on the desk and went out into the hall to ring it loudly. The maid who came was dispatched to find George Bradshaw.

Summer was nervous, but determined as she and her uncle waited in silence. In spite of the lawyer's undoubted state of panic right now, the mere fact that he was a lawyer meant it would be far from easy to extract a confession from him, but she had one trump card—she'd overheard every word in the billiard room at Bevincote.

George Bradshaw's steps sounded in the hall, then the door opened. "You wished to see me, Henry?"

"Yes, George. Please come in."

Chapter Twenty-four

The lawyer entered. "I could not help but hear you and Mr. Lytherby arguing, Henry. I confess I'm a little dismayed that you went against my advice," he said.

Summer almost wanted to laugh. A little dismayed? He was sick to the stomach! She studied him. He was pale, but controlled to the point of tenseness, she decided. This latter observation encouraged her, for it suggested he might not be as difficult to unsettle as she'd feared.

Suddenly, he noticed her. "Why, Mrs. Courtenay, I did not realize you were here."

"Sir." She inclined her head and went to sit on a chair by the window.

Her uncle gestured his brother-in-law to another chair. "Please be seated, George, for we may as well be comfortable."

The lawyer flicked his dark coattails as he sat down. "Before you commence, Henry, I regret I've received unexpected word from London and have to leave immediately. I've already ordered my carriage to be made ready. I do hope you accept my heartfelt apologies."

Summer's lips twitched, for the words were too transparent for belief.

"Of course I do, George," Uncle Merriam replied, but lowered his glance thoughtfully.

"So what is it you wish to say to me, Henry?"

"Well, it concerns this business with Francis Lytherby. I . . ." Caro's father glanced at Summer. "Perhaps you had better proceed, Olivia."

A new guardedness swept into George Bradshaw's small eyes. "I, er, fail to see how Mrs. Courtenay and I can have anything to say on such a delicate subject," he murmured.

She looked at him. "On the contrary, Mr. Bradshaw, I have a great deal to say. To begin with, not one word of your disgraceful charge against Francis Lytherby is true."

Affecting to be insulted, he leapt to his feet. "I will *not* be called a liar, madam!"

"But you *are* a liar, sir," she replied quietly.

Caro's father waved him to sit down again. "Please, Henry."

With an ill grace, the lawyer resumed his place. "As you wish, but I remain here under protest if Mrs. Courtenay intends to impugn my honor."

Uncle Merriam looked at her. "Proceed, my dear."

She nodded. "Mr. Bradshaw, you have invented this tale about Francis because in order to avoid debtor's jail you have to do what Lord Lytherby wishes."

Uncle Merriam's jaw dropped, and he stared at her. "Olivia, my dear, I trust you can back up such a shocking assertion?"

"Yes, Uncle, I can," she replied.

George Bradshaw leapt to his feet again and crashed his fist down upon Uncle Merriam's desk with such force that the inkstand rattled. "Oh, no, you *can't,* madam, for every word is grossly untrue!" he cried.

Meeting his eyes without a single flinch, she repeated verbatim the conversation she'd overheard.

His face went more and more pale, and when she finished, he tried to reply in a level tone. "This is the most preposterous and malicious invention I have ever heard. Lord Lytherby cannot hold IOU's that do not exist! No, this is just a mischievous female scheme to assist my poor niece to cling to a match upon which she has misguidedly set her heart! Have you no conscience? Does it not concern you that Caro will be made deeply unhappy if she becomes Francis Lytherby's wife?"

"There is nothing misguided about Caro's love for Francis, sir."

His eyes rested hatefully on her. "And since when have you

had any real thought for your cousin, Mrs. Courtenay?" he asked softly.

"What do you mean by that?" she demanded, but her heart tightened uneasily as she realized he'd guessed more than she hoped at the Black Lion.

"Oh, I think you know, Mrs. Courtenay. I refer to the questionable scene I happened upon in yard of the Black Lion in Tetbury? Was Sir Brand departing without paying for services rendered?"

Uncle Merriam got up hastily from his seat. "George!"

The lawyer turned to him. "Don't be fooled by this young woman, Henry, for she is not the lady she pretends to be; far from it, in fact. I arrived at the Black Lion to find her running after Sir Brand Huntingford in a most undignified and shocking manner, so I made one or two inquiries at the inn. Inn servants are very observant, my dear, and most communicative if their palms are crossed with a coin or two. I learned that Mrs. Courtenay had spent the previous night in her room with Sir Brand Huntingford, whom she had met only a few hours before! They were witnessed kissing tenderly as they parted on the gallery at dawn."

Uncle Merriam looked at Summer, who was now at such a disadvantage that humiliated color flooded into her cheeks. The situation she'd dreaded since the Black Lion had now come about, and she was so stricken she almost lost her nerve, but from nowhere her courage suddenly flooded back, and she raised her chin haughtily. "If you knew this, Mr. Bradshaw, why did you not tell Lord Lytherby? After all, I'm sure he would prefer the match to be ended due to the scandalous behavior of a member of the unwanted bride's family, than because of a monstrous calumny against his son!" she cried, silently giving thanks that the lawyer hadn't also found out about her dinner assignation with Jeremy.

He met her eyes without replying.

His silence made her mind race, for it suggested she had always had a safety net she still couldn't perceive. What was it? *Why* hadn't he used his knowledge? Suddenly, it came to her, and she gave a cry of triumph.

"Of *course*! You couldn't say anything because you knew that Sir Brand, being a true gentleman, would promptly protect my reputation by denying every word." The irony of it made her almost want to laugh, for the lawyer had realized the one thing she herself had not—that Brand was a man of honor!

Fury quivered visibly through him. "Oh, how very sure of yourself you are, madam, but I fear your smug confidence is a little premature. Maybe I could not employ my knowledge where Lord Lytherby was concerned, and maybe Sir Brand would indeed shield your reputation, but after your despicable charges against me today, can you suggest a reason why I should not secretly acquaint *London society* with every wanton detail? There are many newspapers eager to fill their columns with *on dits*. I'm sure the beau monde would be immensely titillated to learn how lewdly Major Courtenay's apparently upstanding widow conducts herself when she stays at country inns! *I* have nothing to lose; *you* most certainly do!"

She didn't flinch. "Do that and you'd have to face Sir Brand," she declared with confidence, then added. "He always carries a pistol, you know."

His eyes wavered.

She pressed her advantage finally home. "As soon as Francis returns to Bevincote and informs his father what happened here today, you can be sure that jail awaits you. Ending the match with Caro may have been Lord Lytherby's aim, but certainly not at the expense of his son's reputation! He'll be furious enough to carry out his threat—what was it? That he'd tear your heart out with his bare hands?"

The lawyer was completely silent.

Caro's father, who was shaken to discover what had been going on, rose slowly from his chair. "Your silence speaks volumes, George. Clearly Olivia is the one telling the truth, sir," he said coldly.

The other capitulated suddenly. "I *had* to do it, Henry! Lytherby *does* hold my IOU's, and forced me to assist him to destroy the match if I wished to redeem them! I could think of no more certain way to end it than to cast doubt upon the groom's suitability! And if you'd only held your lunatic tongue, all would have been well!"

Uncle Merriam looked at him with utter dislike. "For you maybe, but certainly not for Caro. Get out of this house, George," he said quietly.

"Henry, I—"

"Get out! I never want to see your miserable face again!"

The lawyer turned on his heel and hurried away.

As his footsteps died away up the staircase, Uncle Merriam turned to Olivia. "So *that* is how you and Sir Brand became acquainted," he murmured.

Her cheeks flamed again. "I've never behaved like that before, Uncle Merriam, truly I haven't, but when I met Brand, I mean Sir Brand, I . . ." Her voice limped to a halt, and she bit her lip before looking at him again. "I just couldn't help myself; I love him with all my heart."

"And so you spent the night with him?"

"Yes."

He drew a long breath. "Well, as it happens your conduct—or rather misconduct—hasn't made the slightest difference to the situation, for *I* am the one who has in the end brought Caro's life tumbling about her ears." He sat down unhappily. "Oh, Olivia, how am I going to right the terrible wrong I've done to Francis, and how am I going to repair the damage I've done to Caro's happiness?"

"Uncle, it was George Bradshaw's doing on Lord Lytherby's behalf; you were merely the unwitting tool," she said gently, her heart almost breaking for him because she and Brand suspected Lord Lytherby's opposition had become a thing of the past anyway.

He sighed. "Ah, yes, Lord Lytherby. Well, if he is now so set against the match that he is prepared to stoop to such vile methods, I cannot see there is any point in my attempting to put matters right with Francis. What happiness will there be for poor Caro if Lytherby despises and resents her?"

"But there has to be a way of undoing all this damage. Uncle, you may as well know that last night Brand convinced me that Lord Lytherby had given up all thought of opposing the match with Caro. Maybe the things that were said here today were heinous, but they can be retracted, can't they?"

"I would willingly retract them, my dear, but right now I cannot imagine that even if I were to write a letter to Francis, its fate would be anything other than to be ripped up and burned."

"Brand will help us, Uncle, I *know* he will."

"And put his friendship with Francis at risk?"

"Brand and I are allies in this, so I must get word to him without further delay, for the sooner he learns that you now know the whole truth and wish to right the wrong, the better."

A scheme was already beginning to form in her mind, and she caught up her skirts to hurry up to Caro's apartment.

Her uncle gazed perplexedly after her. "What are you going to do, Olivia?" he called, but she didn't even glance back.

Caro was lying on the bed, her face hidden in her pillows, and her red-gold hair was a tangle that would take an age to comb. She still sobbed a little, but was much more quiet now. Gwenny was standing next to her and turned relievedly as Summer entered. "Oh, there you are, madam. I think the orange flower water has worked a little," she said.

"I'm sure it has, Gwenny," Summer said reassuringly.

"Shall I go now, madam?"

"No, for it's you I wish to speak to." Summer drew the puzzled maid over to the window and lowered her voice to a whisper. "Gwenny, is Miss Huntingford's maid a relative of yours?"

Gwenny nodded. "Why, yes, madam, Martha's my cousin."

"I thought so, she looks so like you."

"Oh, we're almost like peas in a pod," Gwenny smiled.

Summer paused as she noticed George Bradshaw's carriage driving out through the gates, then come up to breakneck speed toward Berkeley, hurtling along the lane as if the Gabriel hounds were in pursuit. Or Lord Lytherby. She felt no compassion. Let him face the consequences, she thought, then turned to Gwenny again. "Apart from Martha, does anyone at Bevincote know you work here?"

Puzzled, Gwenny shook her head. "No, madam."

"Good, because I want you to do something for me. I'm going to write a letter to Sir Brand Huntingford, and I want you to take it immediately to Bevincote in the pony trap. You are to give Martha the letter and tell her to give it secretly and without delay to Sir Brand."

The maid's eyes widened. "Secretly, madam?"

"It's vital, Gwenny. No one else is to know about it, no one at all. Do you understand?"

"Yes, madam."

"Please get ready to leave, and I'll write the letter now."

"Yes, madam."

Chapter Twenty-five

Gwenny returned from Bevincote with a hastily written but long reply from Brand, and Summer adjourned to the privacy of her own room to read it.

My darling Olivia,

Lytherby is both livid and distressed about the unbelievably foolish way Bradshaw went about things, but is persuaded that to call in the fellow's IOU's would be to risk spreading far and wide the unwelcome allegations about Francis, with the consequence of some mud sticking. So, for the time being at least, Bradshaw lives to fight another day, although I shall take it upon myself to advise him to leave the country if he wishes to see old age.

Lytherby is also resigned to losing Bevincote. Last night he intimated in a most genuine and believable manner that he was happy to welcome Caro as his daughter-in-law as she is undoubtedly a most delightful young woman and Francis clearly loves her to distraction. I intended to communicate these welcome tidings to you this afternoon, but your letter arrived first, and, of course, there was the bombshell to Francis in the interim.

I tell you all this about his lordship in order to explain my desire to try to leave his name out of what has happened. While I know he doesn't deserve protection, we must consider the future. Why destroy Francis's love for him? Why ensure that Caro always resents him? Why estrange him from any grandchildren he may have? He is to lose Bevincote, and that, I feel, is punishment enough. I note from your letter that while Mr. Merriam is now in full possession of the facts, Caro as yet knows nothing. For the sake of the plan, I have in mind to bring Francis and Caro together again; this is how the situation must remain, so I hope you will be able to persuade your uncle to say nothing. Trust me in this, my darling.

Unfortunately, there is one rather signal obstacle to any reconciliation, namely Francis himself. He will not even speak the name Merriam, and given the nature of the slur that has been cast upon his character, I suppose I cannot blame him. On top of that he is not disposed to listen to me because he believes I am too infatuated with you to be impartial. I therefore see no alternative than to *force* him to be sensible.

To this end, tomorrow morning at about eleven I will bring him to the ruined chapel on the embankment and hope you will be able to do the same with Caro. I suggest that you get there early and keep your horses out of sight, for in his present mood he is only too likely to ride off again in high dudgeon. Once we have them together, leave the talking to me. All will soon become clear, and you will be able to follow my lead. Don't be apprehensive at all, my darling, for I am *certain* I can bring this whole thing to a fitting conclusion.

À bientôt, ma chère, and have faith that love will conquer all, not just for our star-crossed friends, for Francis is right—I *am* infatuated with you, besotted beyond all redemption, in fact.

Brand

Folding the letter again, she smiled. She would do everything he asked, beginning with persuading Uncle Merriam to go along with it.

After hiding the letter in her reticule, she went to find her uncle. Half an hour after that she had his consent. All that remained was to persuade Caro to go for a ride the next day.

Caro proved very difficult, for the last thing she wished to do was emerge from the haven of her apartment, but eventually she agreed, and the following morning the cousins set off beneath the frozen brilliance of the January sun. The countryside was still covered with snow, and except for the screams of seagulls high above, everything was very quiet as they rode along the lane into the End of the World.

Summer wore her usual rose woolen riding habit, and a tasseled military-style hat borrowed from Caro. Her mount was the same bay hunter she'd ridden before. Caro wore a bottle green riding habit and Summer's top hat because its veil concealed how pale and tear-stained her little face was. She rode a chestnut mare and showed no interest in anything as she stared at her mount's plaited mane.

The ride was taking a little longer than anticipated, and it was nearly eleven as they at last neared the embankment and urged their horses up the slope. "Come on, just to the chapel and back," Summer said, kicking her heels to bring her mount up to a canter along the path at the top, and as she glanced over her shoulder, she was relieved to see Caro following.

She was further relieved to see no sign of anyone at the chapel, and as she and Caro maneuvered their mounts into the lee of the ruins out of the icy air that swept off the estuary, she could only hope that Brand had managed to persuade Francis to come out.

As she began to dismount, Caro's face fell still further. "It's too cold to stop, Olivia; can't we ride back immediately?

"We have to rest the horses," Summer replied.

"But—"

"We won't be long."

With a sigh Caro slid down from the saddle. "Very well, if you insist."

They tethered their mounts to the ivy overgrowing the walls, and then Summer caught Caro's hand. "Come on, it won't be so drafty inside."

As they hurried around the front of the chapel, Summer saw Brand and Francis emerging from the fox covert farther on, so she quickly ushered Caro through the doorway.

Once inside, Caro looked around uneasily. "What a horrid place," she said.

"Oh?" But even as Summer replied, she was aware of the whispering she'd heard before. *I, Stephen, adore thee, Susannah . . .*

She glanced at her cousin, wondering if she heard it too, but Caro raised her veil over her hat and stood in the doorway to stare across the estuary toward the Welsh coastline with eyes that were full of shadows.

A trick of the breeze carried the sound of jingling harness, and Summer decided it was time for honesty. "Caro, I haven't been entirely truthful with you about the ride. You see, Brand is bringing Francis, although I fear the latter is as unaware of the situation as you."

Caro's green eyes widened accusingly. "Oh, Olivia, how *could* you!"

"You and Francis are going to speak to each other again if it's the last thing Brand and I do."

"At the very least you could have confided in me!"

"Would you have come if I had?"

Caro looked away. "I don't know," she admitted.

"Well, you're here now, and there's no escape, so it's up to you, Caro."

The two men had drawn close enough for the breeze to carry a snatch of their voices, and Summer looked intently at Caro. "Well? Are you going to do the sensible thing and speak to him?"

After a moment Caro nodded, and Summer smiled. "Good, for I would put my hands around your obstinate throat if you'd said anything else."

Caro lowered her eyes. "Summer, what does it matter what *I* say if Francis no longer loves me?" she said quietly.

Summer said nothing more as she leaned cautiously out to watch the approaching riders. Francis was pale and strained, clearly in no mood to enjoy either the scenery or Brand's conversation. His handsome face was unsmiling, and suddenly he reined in impatiently.

"For God's sake, Brand, will you *please* stop trying to *rea-*

son me into changing my mind about the Merriams! Can't you get it into your head that I don't want to hear any of it? Besides, your motives are patently selfish, for your sole concern is Mrs. Courtenay."

Brand glanced toward the chapel doorway and saw Summer peeping out. He raised his eyebrows, clearly wanting confirmation that she had Caro with her. She nodded, and with a faint smile he dismounted and came around the horses to drag his startled friend from the saddle.

"Eh? What the devil—!" Francis cried, beginning to struggle as soon as he'd recovered from the shock.

But being the taller and stronger by far, Brand took no notice. He hauled his captive to the chapel doorway, and Summer and Caro drew back among the shadows as Francis was unceremoniously bundled inside.

Shaken by such high-handed treatment, Francis staggered backward, but then his bewilderment turned to dark fury as his eyes grew accustomed to the shadows and he saw the two women. He immediately began to stride toward the doorway again, but Brand's imposing figure darkened it.

"No, Francis, you've been tiresomely obdurate, so matters are being taken out of your hands."

"Damn you, Huntingford!" Francis breathed.

"So it's *Huntingford* now, is it?" Brand gave a faint smile. "Shall we see if it's still that in half an hour's time when you and Miss Merriam are in each other's arms again?"

Francis raised his chin. "I have no intention of even *speaking* to her," he replied.

"Then you are ill-mannered as well as a fool," Brand replied bluntly. "Olivia, come here." He held out his hand to her, and she went to him. His fingers closed reassuringly over hers. "I trust your cousin has been more reasonable?" he murmured.

"Only just," Summer replied.

Brand looked at Francis again. "Francis, there isn't a soul at Oakhill House who still believes the vile things that George Bradshaw suggested of you. Indeed the only reason Mr. Merriam mentioned them at all is that he is so very fond of you that he felt he *had* to be honest. Put yourself in his place, would *you* have said nothing?"

Francis lowered his eyes.

Caro looked at him, then at Brand. "What did my father say? Please tell me, Sir Brand, for I have no idea at all, and I do so need to understand. I know that it must be very terrible, for my uncle has been thrown out of Oakhill House and told never to return, but no one will tell me what was said."

"Francis will tell you in due course," Brand replied quietly.

Francis stiffened. "Never!"

"Oh, yes, you will, my friend, for it is only right that she should know the terrible lies that were invented in order to part her from you."

"They were invented, that's true enough, but *why*?" Francis cried then. "What possible reason could Bradshaw have had for—"

"To ingratiate himself with your father, who holds his IOU's and could ruin him by calling them in," Brand interrupted quietly.

Francis looked blankly at him. "That makes no sense. How can lying about me achieve my father's favor?"

"Bradshaw believed your father had come to deeply regret the Merriam contract because Miss Merriam brings no fortune with her, and thought that by being instrumental in ending the match he'd be able to retrieve the IOU's. But the truth is that your father has *never* regretted the match; indeed he has told me most honestly how very glad he is that Miss Merriam is to be his daughter-in-law."

Caro's lips parted. "Forgive me, but I find that hard to believe, Sir Brand. Lord Lytherby has clearly changed toward me of late, and—"

Brand interrupted her. "No, Miss Merriam, he has simply had a great deal on his mind. His finances are somewhat precarious, to say the least, and losing Bevincote seems the inevitable outcome."

Francis straightened. "Losing Bevincote?" he repeated incredulously. "Why haven't I been told?"

"Because your father feared you might regard it as pressure

to marry Melinda, who was rather reprehensibly pretending to be in love with you. Your happiness is what matters, Francis, and that happiness depends upon Miss Merriam."

Brand's eyes met Summer's for a moment, for the statement was half truth, half very definitely lie! She smiled a little, then looked away. Lord Lytherby certainly *didn't* deserve exoneration, but that was exactly what he was getting with every clever word.

Brand went on. "As I said, Bradshaw thought your father opposed the match and knew the one slur on your character that would horrify Mr. Merriam, so planned accordingly. Anyway Bradshaw has been ejected from Oakhill House and will never be accepted there again. This is because contrary to your belief, Olivia spoke up so strongly on your behalf that she tricked Bradshaw into admitting his scheme in front of Mr. Merriam. So be sensible, Francis, put this sad business behind you, admit that you're in love with Caro, and look to the future!"

Francis drew a long breath and hesitated as if about to concede the point, but then he shook his head again. "No, I cannot and will not forgive!"

Brand wasn't prepared to tolerate any more stubbornness. Slowly, he slipped a hand into his coat and drew out his pistol, which he cocked and leveled at Francis. "With this undoubtedly unfair move, I've put you in check, my friend, so before I lose my temper completely, I suggest you reconsider."

Caro's eyes became saucers, and she flung herself in front of Francis. "We'll talk, truly we will, Sir Brand!" she cried, then turned imploring tear-filled eyes upon Francis. "Please, my dearest love, for I cannot bear to be without you!" she begged, her voice catching because she was trying so hard not to cry.

Perhaps it was the heartbreak in her voice, the perfume of her hair, or just the unhappy trembling of her body against his, whatever it was, the hardness in his heart softened and suddenly he pulled her close. "Oh, Caro, my darling, my darling," he whispered, and she sank into his embrace as he kissed her.

Brand replaced the pistol in his coat, then smiled at Summer. "Checkmate," he murmured.

"Oh, I pray so," she whispered.

He pulled her out of the chapel into the sunshine, where he took her face in his hands and brushed his lips softly to hers. "I think we may permit ourselves to be well pleased, don't you?"

"Yes, I do, and I think your explanation was masterly, sir."

"Masterly? It was a shameful distortion, the truth honed to a shadow of its former self. Perhaps it's a little unfair to heap the blame entirely upon Bradshaw, but the fellow has escaped his debts, though not my revenge if I ever come upon him," he murmured wryly. "My only regret now is that Fenwick has also escaped, for if anyone deserves to suffer the consequences of his actions, he does."

Summer nodded. "Yes, he does, but perhaps it's as well he's gone, because the last thing I want is for your anger to get the better of you should you confront him."

He was about to respond, when something caught his attention along the embankment toward the fox covert. "What in God's name . . . ?" he breathed.

She turned and saw Melinda riding toward them, accompanied at a discreet distance by one of the Bevincote footmen. She wore a sapphire blue riding habit and a little beaver hat, and long honey-colored ringlets bounced on her shoulders as she urged her roan mare into a canter.

As soon as she reached them, Brand seized her horse's bridle. "What are *you* doing here?" he demanded.

Melinda smiled. "Lord Lytherby has permitted me to come out because I'm no longer in disgrace. I've been following you and Francis and lost you for a while in the covert, but then saw as you halted by the chapel. It was most enlightening to see how brutish you can be, Brand. I felt quite sorry for poor Francis when you manhandled him like that." She reached down, and he caught her as she slid from the saddle.

Brand looked into her lilac eyes. "You had no business following us, miss."

"I'm quite safe," she replied, indicating the burly footman.

"Besides, I had every business in the world." She turned brightly to Summer. "Hello, Olivia."

"Hello," Summer replied, thinking how good it was to see Brand's sister smiling so happily.

Melinda glanced toward the chapel. "I waited in the covert until you two came out and I could be sure Francis and Miss Merriam must be making up. They *are* making up, aren't they?" she added quickly.

"At the last glance, yes," Brand replied, eyeing her. "You have a conspiratorial look about you, miss."

"Do I? Perhaps that's because I've been up to no good again."

His face changed. "You've what?"

She laughed. "Oh, how easily you rise to the bait."

Summer had to hide a slight smile, for Melinda clearly knew exactly how to tease him.

Brand raised an eyebrow. "You're a minx, Miss Huntingford."

"Maybe, but I'm here with some news that I'm sure will please everyone here as much as it has already pleased Lord Lytherby."

"Oh?" Brand's reply was guarded.

"Before I tell you, there is a condition."

"Go on."

"Well, I am to have my first London Season this summer, and Lord Lytherby wished to foist me upon some odious dowager or other, but I want Olivia to chaperone me."

Summer was startled. "Me? But—"

"You must agree, Olivia, or I will withdraw my promises to Lord Lytherby," Melinda warned.

"But I haven't a say in the matter of your Season, Melinda. Lord Lytherby is—"

"Lord Lytherby has already given his permission; in fact he was delighted to do so," Melinda interrupted.

"Delighted?" Summer repeated in astonishment.

Brand was baffled too. "Melinda, exactly what is all this about?"

Melinda looked at Olivia. "Will you chaperone me this summer?" she pressed.

"Well, yes, of course, if it really is in order with everyone else . . ." Summer glanced at Brand.

He shrugged and nodded. "I have no objections; indeed it would please me immeasurably, for it would give me every excuse in the world to call upon you—and keep an eye on *you*," he added, fixing his sister with a look.

Melinda smiled. "Keep as many eyes upon me as you wish, sir. Very well, my plan is all as good as settled." She breathed in, clearly very pleased with herself. "Brand, I am going to give Lord Lytherby the money he needs to save Bevincote."

He stared at her. "You're what?" he said faintly.

"I can more than afford it, as you well know."

"Possibly, but what I don't know is how you have become party to financial problems that were being kept from Francis."

"I listened at the door when you and his lordship were talking."

"Did you, be damned!"

"I'm afraid so. Anyway, I'm not doing this for Lord Lytherby, but for Francis and Miss Merriam. I still feel bad about how I behaved, and this is my way of making it up to them. Francis loves Bevincote as much as his father does, and it isn't fair that he shouldn't inherit it one day." Melinda looked at Summer suddenly. "When I told you at the ball that I loved Bevincote, I really meant it, Olivia. This way it stays in the family where it belongs."

Brand sighed. "Melinda, do you really understand how much money may be at stake here?"

She nodded airily. "Oh, yes. When you and Francis were playing billiards late last night, Lord Lytherby and I went over all his accounts." She smiled. "I'm not always a silly creature, Brand, and although I made a horrid mistake with Jeremy Fenwick, I'm not making a mistake now. So, you see, all is going to be well in the end."

"Well, it would seem you've considered every aspect."

"Oh, I have." Melinda's smile became feline. "And when I

go to London, with Olivia's help I intend to snap up the Duke of Chandworth."

Summer's lips parted. "With my help?" she said warily.

"Well, you've snapped up my brother, who is *much* more difficult than the duke, so I'm sure your advice will be all that's necessary."

Brand gave an incredulous laugh. "You saucy baggage!"

Melinda smiled.

He sighed. "So you intend to snap up Chandworth, do you? It may interest you to know that half the women in London have been endeavoring to do the same for the past four years, ever since he showed his handsome hide in town, in fact."

"I will have him from under their noses," Melinda replied confidently.

Brand rolled his eyes heavenward. "Ye gods, how mercurial is the female of the species. One moment in an agony of despair over a ne'er-do-well like Fenwick, the next setting her scheming cap for a peer of the realm!"

"No more mercurial than the male," Melinda said immediately. "Take you, for example. Only a few days ago you'd never even heard of Olivia; now you are quite clearly head over heels in love with her."

Brand turned to Summer and smiled into her eyes. "Yes, I am," he said softly.

Chapter Twenty-six

The chapel was deserted the next day when Summer returned alone. A thaw had commenced overnight, and the air was noticeably milder as she dismounted and made the reins fast to the ivy. As she looked back toward Oakhill House, and Bevincote beyond, she could see how the snow was melting, for although in the hollows it was still dense and white, on more open areas the grass and undergrowth was beginning to peep through.

To say she felt a hint of spring in the air was perhaps going a little far, but there was a definite change. The sunlight was different too, seeming softer and more benevolent than it had only the day before. She smiled to herself, for such thoughts were clearly fanciful—the change came from within herself.

She was now certain that she was Olivia forever, for too much time had elapsed for there to be any chance of her returning to the future to become Summer Stanway once more. It was an awe-inspiring thought. Andrew had always insisted that there wasn't any actual traveling in time, just a certain type of hypnotic trance that aroused deep-seated memories of past existences. Well, if this was just a memory, how could she possibly be feeling it all so *fully*? The smell of the sea was real, as was the taste of salt on her lips and the flutter of her veil against her face, and when she was with Brand, the passion and love transcended everything.

The fact was now irrefutable. She had achieved the impossible and traveled permanently through time to a past life where she could enjoy again the health and happiness her future self had lost. All that remained was to try to let Chrissie and Andrew know about that health and happiness.

From the saddlebag she took out the small hammer and chisel she had brought with her from the gardeners' storeroom at Oakhill House, then she gathered the rose woolen skirt of her riding habit and made her way around to the front of the chapel. She paused, raising her veil over her hat to look more clearly at the estuary. How wide and open it was here; just to look at it today made her want to fill her lungs with the sea-fresh air.

As she went into the chapel, she listened for a moment in the hope of again hearing Stephen's whisper to Susannah, but although this time there was only silence, she could still sense the words buried deep in the ruins. Could a message of her own be trapped in the stone as well? She would never know, but maybe Chrissie and Andrew would when they came here in the future.

"Chrissie, it's me, Summer, I really am here in the past, and I'm happy," she whispered, and then smiled as it seemed the chapel absorbed her voice.

Raising the hammer and chisel, she began to chip "Chrissie and Summer" into the stone, just beneath Stephen and Susannah's initials and date.

It took a long time, especially the letters with curves, but at last she finished and stood back to admire her rough but legible work. Not bad, she thought. Maybe not stonemason quality, but not bad. Her three words would still be here when Chrissie and Andrew came, as come they would, she had no doubt of that.

A shadow suddenly darkened the doorway, and a sinister male voice spoke coolly to her. "Ill met by sunlight, proud Olivia."

Jeremy! She gasped, and the hammer and chisel fell with a loud clatter as she whirled about to see him standing there.

He wore the same clothes he'd had on the last time she saw him and hadn't shaved for a day or so. "I've been waiting to get you alone, and when I saw your horse, I could not believe my good fortune." There was no trace now of his former easy charm as his glance moved slowly over her and then to the message she'd carved. Curiosity lightened his eyes. "What's this?"

"Nothing."

"Nothing? Oh, come now, Olivia, you've clearly spent some time laboring over it."

"It's nothing, truly. What do you want of me, Jeremy?"

His eyes darkened again as they returned to her face. "You betrayed me, Olivia, and now I've come for my revenge."

She stared at him. "Betrayed you?" she whispered.

"By setting Huntingford on my trail."

"I didn't; it was the innkeeper who sent word to Bevincote."

"Oh, that's as may be, but the chase was on well before then. I left Melinda and the carriage at a livery stable on the Bristol road and hired a horse to ride back to see if anything was afoot. I saw the alarm being raised and the search commenced. You gave the game away, didn't you? And you did it because you suddenly realized why I wanted your carriage."

She pressed back against the chapel wall and didn't reply.

He gave a thin smile and came a little closer, putting a hand almost tenderly to her throat. "After all I did for you when Roderick died, you've been a Judas to me, Olivia."

She was terrified. Her heart was thundering, her mouth was dry, and the sunlight outside seemed a million miles away, but defiance shone in her scornful eyes. "And what of you, Jeremy? You've resorted to lying, stealing, highway robbery, and even attempted to force an innocent young woman to submit to your vile advances! Those are the acts of a criminal, not the man I once liked and respected."

His fingers moved sensuously against her skin. "I couldn't care less whether you like and respect me, my lovely, for it's retribution time. I've always had an itch to sample your charms, and now see no reason why I should not enjoy them to the full."

He began to put his lips to her unwilling mouth, but as she tried to wrench free, to her unutterable relief she heard Brand's voice a few feet away.

"Take your foul hands off her, Fenwick, or so help me I'll squeeze this trigger!"

Jeremy froze, then released her and began to move away. As he did so, she saw Brand right behind him. He wore a sky blue coat and cream corduroy breeches, and his untidy golden hair moved slightly in the draft from outside. He'd edged sideways through the doorway in order not to cast a warning shadow, and now had his pistol pressed to the back of Jeremy's head.

Brand jabbed the weapon a little. "Faster, you mongrel, for I'm looking for a justifiable excuse to exterminate you. Get away from her!"

Jeremy's tongue passed nervously over his lips. "I didn't mean her any harm, Huntingford!"

"You meant her *every* harm, just as you meant my sister harm," Brand said softly.

"No! I swear it! Don't shoot me, I beg of you!" Jeremy sank to his knees in terror.

"What a contemptible coward you are," Brand breathed witheringly. "Well, much as I'd like to do the honors, I have to bow to the rule of law. Now, get up and come outside."

Slowly, Jeremy obeyed, moving step by step through the doorway into the sunshine, with Brand's pistol still pressed to his head. Then Brand glanced along the embankment and waved an arm.

Summer heard hoofbeats and ventured to look out. She saw a detachment of red-uniformed soldiers riding toward the chapel. Brand kept Jeremy in his sights until Jeremy's hands were tied behind his back and he was bundled unceremoniously onto his horse to be taken back to Cirencester to face a court-martial.

As the small column of soldiers rode away, Brand took Summer's hand. "Are you all right, my darling?"

She held him tightly. "I was terrified."

"I came as soon as I realized your horse was here. Fenwick had been seen in Berkeley yesterday, and I notified the barracks in Cirencester. We'd just begun to investigate a report that someone answering his description had been sighted in the fox covert, when some sixth sense told me you were in danger here." He cupped her face in his hands. "If he'd harmed so much as a hair of your head . . ."

"He didn't, you came in time," she whispered, shivering as much from shock as the cold estuary air.

Brand drew her back into the chapel, where he pulled her close. He didn't see the tools she'd dropped earlier, the fragments of freshly chipped stone, or the words she'd carved. "I could not have endured if anything had happened to you," he said softly.

"I'm safe, my darling, I'm safe," she answered.

He drew back slightly, reaching up to remove her hat, and let it fall to the floor. Then he took out some of her hairpins, so that her thick black curls cascaded over her shoulders. "I intended to come to you today anyway, for I have come to realize that I want you with me all the time. I cannot bear to be apart from you, not even for an hour."

"I feel the same. Each moment away from you is torture."

"There is only one solution, and it's what I intended to ask when I called upon you." His eyes were dark as they looked down into hers. "Marry me, Olivia."

Her heart turned over, and she stared up at him. "Do . . . do you really mean that, Brand?"

"Can you doubt it for a moment? Can you doubt that the love and passion we share can be honored any other way? I don't want you for my mistress, I want you for my wife." He took her left hand and drew the fourth finger to his lips.

Happy tears shone in her eyes. "Nothing would make me more happy than to marry you, Brand," she whispered.

His arm slid around her waist, and he pulled her against him. "The new Lady Huntingford will be the most desirable woman of *ton* in London."

"She will want to be desired only by her husband, sir," Summer replied.

"Oh, he will desire her, she may be certain of that. Desire fills him right now." He pressed his hips closer so that she could feel the swelling at his loins.

"Then let your bride be your mistress for a little longer," she murmured, closing her eyes as little waves of pleasure washed excitingly through her.

"Where is your shame, Mrs. Courtenay?"

She moved against him. "I have none, Sir Brand."

"Then let us be shameless together," he breathed, beginning to undo the buttons of her jacket.

The October afternoon was drawing in as the car pulled up at the foot of the embankment. Chrissie and Andrew got out, and Chrissie looked around a little uncertainly. "Are you sure this is the place?"

"According to the map," he replied, waving the crumpled copy of Ordnance Survey, Outdoor Leisure Number Fourteen. "The End of the World. Aptly named, eh?"

"You're right there," she murmured, turning up her jacket collar to gaze at the lonely landscape of autumn-tinted orchards, ditches, and scattered farms. She was pale and drawn, and there were shadows under her eyes. Her glance moved to the rising land about half a mile inland, where a beautiful old manor house stood next to a church. Then her lips parted as through the misty gloom of the dying day she caught a glimpse of Oriental domes and turrets just over the hill. "Hey, look at that!" she pointed.

Andrew followed her finger and nodded. "Bevincote," he said. "Some people say it outdoes the Brighton Pavilion."

"Maybe we can take a look at it before we go back. Is it open to the public?"

"I think so. In fact, I'm sure so. It's one of the well-known stately homes."

A dog howled on one of the farms, and Chrissie turned sharply toward the sound. Then she gave a nervous laugh. "Thank God I don't believe in werewolves," she murmured.

"*Werewolves?* What on earth made you think of that! It's only a farm dog," Andrew replied.

She shrugged. "I don't know why I thought of it. It just seemed appropriate, that's all."

"Look, werewolves are the last thing I want to think about when it's getting dark and I'm in the middle of nowhere like this! It makes me think of that movie. What was it called? *An American Werewolf in London?* Or was it *in England?* Whatever its name, there's that scene on the moors when the two guys hear howling and start to run back to the village. That's what I feel like doing now."

"I'll bet when you were a kid you used to hide behind the sofa when the spooky bits came on TV," Chrissie said with a faint smile.

"I'll let you into a secret, I still do when you're not around to hold my hand." Andrew grinned at her, then turned to search along the embankment until he saw the ruined chapel. "Well, are you ready?" he asked gently.

Chrissie hesitated. "I guess so," she said after a moment.

"We don't have to go," he ventured, for he was desperately afraid she was pinning her hopes upon the impossible. They'd listened to the recording Summer had left; God, how they'd listened! And since the funeral they'd still been sitting up nights, getting emotional on too much brandy, and playing the wretched thing over and over again until by rights it should have been worn out. Now, at last, they'd plucked up the courage to put Summer's story to the test.

He came around the car to take Chrissie's cold hand. "I want you to be absolutely certain before we go one step farther," he said.

"Summer said she'd leave our names, Andrew, and I believe her."

"And I'm equally sure *she* believed it when she made that recording and left the note, but the mind is a complex thing, and—"

"I'm not interested in what science has to say, Andrew. If my kid sister said she experienced all those things, then she did."

"What if there aren't any names?" he said, looking concernedly into her eyes.

"There will be."

He didn't say anything more, but he hoped to God she was right, for if those three damned words weren't anywhere to be found, the only conclusion to be drawn would be that Summer killed herself for nothing.

Holding hands, they went up the steps that had been cut into the embankment, and at the top they both hunched deeper into their jackets because the wind off the estuary was raw. Chrissie paused for a moment. "She *was* here, I can just feel it," she said.

"All I feel is bloody cold," Andrew replied, looking at the desolate expanse of channels, rocks, sandbanks, and pools. Navigation lights were beginning to twinkle in the haze, and on the far side of the water a brightly lit train ran along the main track, its metallic rattle carrying clearly on the breeze. Downstream he could make out the motorway suspension bridge that crossed the river, but the second motorway crossing farther downstream beyond it was lost in the gathering gloom of the autumn evening.

They hurried on toward the chapel and stepped thankfully inside out of the cold. The musty smell of old stone was strong as Chrissie immediately began to glance around, but it was too dark. She turned anxiously to Andrew. "Did you bring the flashlight? Oh, God, please don't tell me you forgot!"

"It's here." He took it out and switched it on. The beam of bright light swung wildly over the walls until he held it steady. "Right, let's be methodical about this. We'll start over here by the door, and work our way around."

"Okay."

He did as he said, but began at the other side of the door from the place Summer had carved her message. Slowly, the light moved to and fro over the old stones, but as the seconds ticked fruitlessly by, Chrissie's spirits began to drop. She crossed her fingers behind her back and whispered to herself. "Don't let me down, Summer Stanway, don't let me down."

"Chrissie, it's me, Summer, I really am here in the past, and I'm happy."

The faint whisper made Chrissie freeze. Then she heard it again.

"Chrissie, it's me, Summer, I really am here in the past, and I'm happy."

Chrissie caught Andrew's arm. "Did you hear that?"

"Hear what?"

"Summer's voice."

He looked uneasily at her. "Look, sweetheart, I'm going along with this, but if you're going to start hearing things . . ."

Chrissie hardly heard him. "It's almost as if the stone itself has recorded her," she murmured, beginning to smile.

"Which is more than it's done with any visual message," he declared, still shining the flashlight methodically over the wall.

"It's here somewhere," Chrissie replied, suddenly confident that all was going to be well.

Andrew's search had almost returned to the door, and just as he became sure Chrissie was going to be deeply disappointed, suddenly the three words seemed to leap into the beam of light. He stared at them. "It's here, Chrissie!" he cried incredulously. "Dear God above, it's actually here!"

Tears sprang to Chrissie's eyes as she stared at the carving caught in the beam of light. "Look at it, Andrew, it's old, it can't *possibly* have been done recently."

"I can't argue," he replied.

"My sister, who was laid to rest only a week or so ago, was alive here in 1807, just as she promised she would be! She went back to be with Brand! Oh, Andrew!"

Laughing and crying at the same time, Chrissie flung her arms so happily around Andrew that he dropped the flashlight. It struck the uneven floor and went out, leaving only the gathering shadows of the October day.

Far beyond Chrissie's present-day gladness, Summer's whisper still echoed through the ancient stonework. *"Chrissie, it's me, Summer, I really am here in the past, and I'm happy, happy, happy . . .*